Six Weeks of Love & Larceny

REBECCA GOULD BAEURLE

Published by Zolly House Press.
Boulder, CO 80544
zollyhouse.com

Zolly House Press is an imprint of Nymblesmith.
zollyhouse.com

This is a work of fiction. Names, characters, businesses, places, events, and incidents are either the products of the author's imagination or used in a fictitious manner. Any resemblance to actual persons, living or dead, or actual events is purely coincidental.

Book & cover design by Zolly House.

Library of Congress Control Number: 2025919987
Identifiers: ISBN (hardcover): 979-8-9892659-5-4 | ISBN (paperback): 979-8-9930546-3-6 | ISBN (paperback) 979-8-9930546-6-7 | ISBN (ebook): 979-8-9930546-4-3

Coming soon from Rebecca Gould Baeurle...

Twelve Weeks of Love & Loss

Dedication

This book is dedicated to my children − Kate and Alex, and my husband Mike. Go Birds!

THE CHARACTERS

For those who need reminding...

***Nikki** – Drexel student, younger of two sisters

***Lauren** – Writer for *The Philadelphia Inquirer*, older

      of two sisters

Chris – Temple student, Nikki's love interest

John and Tony – Chris's roommates

Michelle – John's love interest

Drew – Lauren's boss

Amanda – Lauren's intern, Penn student

Caroline (John's cousin) and **Maggie** – Amanda's roommates

Rocco – Drug dealer

Mike Rameriz and **Tim Batiste** – DEA cops

Officer Gaines and **Officer Burns** – Philly beat cops

Clyde, **Jerry** and **Lucy** – Café staff

Nikki

The wail of the siren only intensifies my anxiety. I'm holding him in my arms pressing a dish towel on his wound attempting to control the bleeding. "Shhhhh, we're getting you help," I whisper in his ear and kiss his head. The police car makes a sharp right turn, and we are jostled in the back seat. He whimpers in pain from the sudden movement, and I try to console him again. I stroke his hair gently, "Everything is going to be okay." But will it? How is any of this going to be okay?

"I'll need your account of what happened once we get him inside," the officer says from the front seat. "We're almost there." I can see the hospital in the distance. The blood is seeping through the towel and puddling in my palm. I have to look away to gather my thoughts.

The officer pulls into the parking lot and before I'm even aware of what's happening, arms are lifting him out of my lap onto a gurney. "We'll take it from here ma'am," someone says. I look down at my lap. All that remains is a blood-soaked dish towel, worry and confusion.

WEEK ONE

Five Weeks Earlier
Monday, Week 1 – November in Philadelphia

Nikki

I'm just about to hang up my apron and clock out when the bell above the café door jingles. I look up to see three handsome young guys walk in and sit down in my section. Okay, I guess I can stay for one more table…

I re-tie my apron and approach their booth. "Hey guys. You're the last lucky customers of my shift today so let's make it matter."

The one with dark wavy hair and deep brown eyes raises an eyebrow and tilts his head. "Make it matter?"

"Yeah," I say with confident authority, shifting my weight onto one hip. "Easy order, quick turn-around, good tip. You do your part, I'll do mine. So, what can I getcha?"

Dark-hair smirks. "Okay, I'll have the supreme western omelet with a side of bacon and a double shot of espresso."

"That sounds good," says the sandy-blonde guy across from him.

"Make it three," mutters the third guy, who's wearing a skull cap and sunglasses indoors like he's trying not to be recognized.

I tuck my pad and pencil back into my apron and brush a strand of hair behind my ear. "Okay, so scrambled eggs and black coffee all around."

The dark-haired guy looks up at me with a mischievous grin. "Um, the good tip part of this arrangement might not be headed in the right direction." His tone is playful and a little fresh.

I smile back meeting his flirtation with my eyes and then up the ante. "Well neither is the easy order, quick turn-around part I mentioned. I've already cleaned the espresso machine and we're two minutes away from switching to the lunch menu, so I'll be right back with your coffee." As I turn to leave, I do this sassy little hair flip thing and immediately feel ridiculous. What am I doing?

The door opens again and the cold air rushes in. Two guys probably in their mid-thirties walk in and sit at the table next to my other three customers. "Sorry guys, my section is closed. Can I move you over there?" I ask, pointing across the room.

Lucy, who is just starting her shift, surfaces from behind the counter, "I've got you guys right over here," she says and shows them to another table.

The café is rather eclectic. It used to be a diner so there are booths lining both walls with old school mini jukeboxes in each, but when it was repurposed as a café both round and square reclaimed wood tables were added to the center of the room coupled with multicolored metal chairs in an attempt to make it look more current. The original tile flooring is still in place and the counter at the front of the room that used to hold pies, cakes and other desserts now has muffins, croissants, various egg wraps and a cash register for take-out orders (really jumping headfirst into the 21st century). The wall that separates the front of house from the kitchen is exposed brick and the ceiling is industrial. There's artwork for sale hanging on the walls, but I don't think a single piece has sold since I started. There is no common theme to them either. Some are stills, some are photography and others are abstract. The café is the definition of the expression, "A camel is a horse created by a committee."

I bring the guys their coffee, carefully balancing the steaming mugs in my hands. Dark-hair looks up with those doe eyes and that grin again as I pass them out. "Are we allowed to have cream and sugar?" he asks, his voice low and teasing and starting to feel a little daring.

"Sure," I volley back, "that qualifies both under the easy order rule and the quick turn-around criteria."

"Okay." There's a satisfied confidence about him as he continues, "we don't need them anyway. Just trying to figure out your rules." He pauses for dramatic effect, knowing that as the customer he's controlling the pace of the conversation, my sass aside. "But we'll definitely need ketchup when the eggs come out."

I place a hand on my hip and give him the once-over with my eyes, determined to regain the upper hand in this banter. "Ketchup, huh? I had you pegged as a hot sauce guy."

He locks his eyes on mine and holds them there while he responds, the corners of his mouth fighting off a smile. "Oh, I like it hot alright. We're just easing into the day today. Rough night last night, fun but rough."

"In that case, I'll put on another pot of coffee." I turn to leave, this time making sure not to touch my hair. I have to force myself not to look back but can feel his gaze on me the whole way, so I add a little extra swagger to my step.

A few minutes later, I return with three plates of scrambled eggs, ketchup on the side and a bottle of siracha just in case. The incognito guy looks genuinely pissed-off that they're not supreme western omelets and barks, "Jesus, you weren't kidding about the scrambled eggs – what the hell?"

Before I can even get a word in, the flirty guy snatches one of the plates from my hand and, without a second thought, half-throws it at his friend. "Shut up shithead. You're lucky to be getting breakfast during the lunch shift at all." He turns back to me and smoothly takes another plate from my hands, his fingers brushing against mine and flashes me a full-wattage smile, "I see you remembered the ketchup. And the siracha was a good call."

"I aim to please," I say, feeling the electricity between us. I place the last plate in front of him, my eyes meeting his for just a moment longer than necessary. "Can I get you anything else?"

"No, we're good," he says, leaning back in the booth like he owns the place. "Just the check when you get a chance. We're kinda in a hurry," he adds, but I get the sense he wishes he wasn't.

I can't resist going with my hunch. "You sure? I could bring you a side of something from the lunch menu to go with that attitude."

He gives me a look that says he's not finished with me just yet. "Tempting, but I think we'll stick with the check. *For now*."

"No problem." I pull the billfold out of my apron and place the check on the table. He doesn't even glance at it, just hands me his card while the other two dig into their plates with no intention of pitching in for the bill.

After running the card, I bring back the receipt for him to sign. "Here you go. Stop in again sometime."

"You can count on it," he says with a devilish grin. And can brown eyes actually sparkle?

Before clocking out, I swing by the booth to pick up the signed receipt. When I open the billfold, there's no tip − just a number written on the line: *215-555-3833*. I flip the slip over and read:

Text me your Venmo name for your tip
Round One goes to Chris
thats me by the way
Round Two is in your court

Hmmm. Maybe the hair flip wasn't so foolish after all. But do I really want to make the next move? Something in my gut warns me to be cautious. I can hear my sister Lauren's voice in my head, *"Don't be stupid Nikki, you don't give your number to a total stranger just because you think he's cute. I know you need the money, but really?"*

She's right and I know it. He knows where I work, so if he's serious, he can come back in. Plus, I'm equally impressed by his move and annoyed that he's holding my tip hostage.

Lucy's voice snaps me out of my thoughts. "Well, that was a bust. I thought I might get a decent tip from those two guys who came in after your last table, but they only ordered coffee and left right after your guys."

"Sorry, what?"

"Never mind. I just hope lunch is better."

"Yeah, good luck," I say, grabbing my things. "I've gotta run. Staying to wait on those good-looking guys is making me late for class. I'm off for the next two days but I'll see you Thursday. Ciao!"

Earlier that Day

Breakfast Round II

"After last night I gotta get some caffeine and greasy food before we meet this guy." John and Tony nodded in agreement and followed Chris out the door. They walked down the street toward the subway station zipping their coats against the cold.

"Fuck, its freezing out here," Tony complained, rubbing his hands together and pulling his hat farther down on his forehead.

"Buck up, buttercup," John grumbled, not in the mood to hear Tony's whining when he was living the same misery.

They trudged along in silence, all nursing hangovers. They got off the subway one stop early to hit Mocha Loco for some breakfast before the meet-up. Desperate for warmth, they rushed inside and snagged the booth farthest from the door. The comforting smell of bacon and coffee filled the air – it was just what they needed to jumpstart their day (even though it was almost noon). As the waitress approached, Chris's eyes lit up. She had red shoulder-length hair, silky and straight, penetrating green eyes and porcelain skin. A tiny diamond stud sparkled in her nose. Suddenly he couldn't have cared less about his hangover, the meet-up or his friends; his attention was all on her.

"Hey guys. You're the last lucky customers of my shift today so let's make it matter," she said with a smile, revealing perfectly white teeth. *Oh, this is gonna be fun*, Chris thought, jumping right into a playful banter with her before she left to grab their coffee.

John ignored Chris's distraction with the waitress and got down to business. "So how are we gonna know this guy's legit?"

"Uh, probably because he'll have the drugs," Chris rolled his eyes and shook his head like it was the stupidest question he'd ever heard.

"No," John kicked Chris under the table annoyed that he wasn't taking him seriously, "I mean like where he's getting it and if it's any good."

"Well Tony, isn't that your department – all things underworld and unsavory?" Chris asked, half joking – half serious.

Tony didn't even look up from his phone. "Yeah, I know a guy," he muttered, his voice distant.

The waitress returned with their coffee, and Chris flirted with her some more before she was off again. "We've gotta make this quick," he said, checking the time. "We're meeting this guy in fifteen."

"Well, I'm starving," John grumbled. "So quick it is."

Tony didn't respond, still glued to his phone. Chris couldn't help but wonder how the hell he was reading it with sunglasses on, but he kept that to himself. A few minutes later, the waitress returned with their food, and Tony finally dragged himself away from the screen long enough to be a dick to her. Chris put him in his place and helped the waitress distribute the plates. *Honestly, sometimes I don't even know why I am friends with this guy...* he thought, before digging into his eggs.

John's phone buzzed. He glanced at it and then back at his friends. "You guys want to take my cousin and her roommates out Friday night?"

Tony perked up for the first time all morning. "Isn't she the hot one who goes to Penn?"

John shot him a warning glare. "Yeah. But she's off-limits Tony – she's my cousin. You can focus on her friends."

Tony ignored John's attempt at setting the ground rules, shoveled a fork-full of eggs in his mouth and mumbled, "Hot girls always have hot friends. I'm in."

"Yeah. Me too," Chris echoed.

They scarfed down their food and left in a hurry. Chris wished he had more time to linger with the waitress but wasn't going to be denied a good opportunity, so he left her a challenge on his credit card slip that he was pretty sure she was spunky enough to accept. *She'll either love it or hate it, but it's a risk I'm willing to take. Shooter's gotta shoot.*

They walked several blocks before spotting the car they were looking for parked exactly where they were told. Chris was the least hungover of the three of them and newly invigorated by his interaction with the waitress, so he took it upon himself to take the lead. He made his way toward the driver's side window, the others lagging behind, and tapped on the tinted glass. It cracked open just a smidge.

"You Tony?" the guy behind the wheel grunted.

"No. I'm Chris. This is Tony," he said and motioned behind him. "You Rocco?"

"Yeah. Get in."

Chris walked around to the passenger side and the other two slid into the back. Rocco looked like he hadn't slept in days and couldn't have been dressed more like a drug dealer if he was auditioning for a part. Baggy jeans, a pulled up dark hoodie and tattoos creeping up his neck like a warning. If the dude wasn't so scary looking, Chris would've laughed.

"Here's how this goes," Rocco started. "We start you slow. If you move the pack without getting caught, we give you more. I contact you. You don't contact me. We never meet in the same place twice. This is how I reach you," he handed Chris a burner phone. "Any questions?"

Chris glanced at the phone for a beat and then locked eyes with Rocco. "Pretty clear to me." His tone was deliberately low and confident to let Rocco know he wasn't intimidated.

Tony leaned forward, clearly itching to jump in, but Rocco was already handing Chris a plastic bag with pills and small vials, cutting off any chance for more conversation. "I'll be in touch," Rocco said, flat and final, like an order.

Chris tucked the bag into his jacket and Tony read the cues – it was time to get out of the car. They walked back to the subway in silence. As they reached the platform, John broke the quiet with a nervous laugh. "Well, that wasn't shady at all," he said, a trace of sarcasm or possibly apprehension in his voice. "Did you guys notice he was packing?"

"If you don't want in, you can always back out," Chris told him. "But I think it'll be easy money. Selling weed is a joke now that all you need is a medical card."

John wasn't letting it go. "Rocco doesn't seem like a small-time operator, though. Tony, how'd you hook up with this guy anyway?"

"I told you," Tony grumbled, "a guy from my neighborhood in the Bronx is making a killing with the dude." Then he turned to Chris, clearly pissed, and added, "And thanks for hijacking the meeting, Shepp. This was supposed to be my gig!"

Chris's last name is Sheppard, so he gets Shepp, Big Dog, K9 and other stupid nicknames. "Next time try not to be too hungover to function and you can be in charge," he snapped back. "What ever happened to my tailgate sous chef and champion flip-cup partner? I miss that guy. You seem pissed-off all the time lately."

Tony shot Chris a look. "You'd be pissed-off too if you *actually* needed the money when you spoiled assholes are just doing this for shits and giggles," he barked. "I want that burner and the bag when we get home!"

"Fine. I don't want to deal with this guy anyway. I just want the extra cash." Chris tossed the burner over to him without a second thought, "Here you go Scarface."

The Po-Po

Mike Rameriz and Tim Batiste sat in a car across the street and back a block from where Rocco was parked. Mike looked through binoculars and Tim said, "Tell me what we know about this guy."

"He goes by 'Rocco' and is running drugs from NY to DC. Philly is a convenient mid-way point to increase business. We think he's working for a bigger operation out of New York. We're collaborating with our agents there but need solid evidence against him for leverage in catching the bigger fish," Mike answered. "Wait, wait, look there. Three kids are approaching the car." Tim grabbed the binoculars and watched the three get in the car. A few minutes passed and they got out and began to walk away. "Batz, get out and follow those kids," Mike shouted, "I'll follow the car."

Same Day

Lauren

Blnnnnnnn!!! Blnnnnnnn!!! Blnnnnnn! My arm flies reflexively across my body, hand landing squarely on the snooze button on my phone. Could there be a more annoying sound? Note to self: Change alarm tone to something a little less "alarming." Aren't I supposed to be getting rid of things that don't bring me joy? Or does that only apply to cleaning out closets?

Leaving the window open in the cold weather is a great way to get a good night sleep, but it makes the transition into morning especially torturous. One, two, three… I throw the covers off and lunge toward the window, pushing it shut as fast as I can before scrambling to the trunk at the foot of my bed where I left my robe and slippers the night before. Ahhh, that's better. Wrapped up tight, I start the coffee and wait the annoying few minutes it takes to perk.

Most mornings I go for a jog after coffee, but today I have to get into the office early, so I pack a bag with running clothes in case there's time to go after work. I write a weekly segment for *The Philadelphia Inquirer* called 'Philly's Top 10.' Each week features a different list of recommendations: Top 10 Sandwiches in Philly, Top 10 Fashion Finds, Top 10 Must-Have Household Items for Under

$20... You get the idea. My research for the column takes me all around the city, experiencing new things and meeting all kinds of different people. It's interesting and fun but doesn't pay enough for me to join the gym in my neighborhood, so for now I get my exercise by jogging through the streets of Philadelphia Rocky Balboa style.

The Inquirer has a mentor partnership with several area universities. This gives college students something to put on their resumes and gives *The Inquirer* some cheap extra help. Since none of the people at the paper who are actually in a position to impart valuable wisdom on these students have the time or the inclination to do it, the program has been handed off to the young up-and-comers like me. I don't mind though because I always pass off maintaining 'Philly's Top 10' social media presence to the interns – I hate keeping up with that. This morning I'll be meeting with my new intern, Amanda Shields.

After the coffee warms my body, comes the dreaded "getting ready" ritual. I hate picking out what to wear. I was spoiled growing up with a younger sister who was a fashionista since birth. Nikki always styled me, so I never had to worry about keeping up with trends or choosing outfits. I didn't realize what a luxury that was until I started packing to go off to college. Most of the clothes Nikki would normally choose for me were actually her own, so she was horrified when she saw what I was putting in the suitcase.

"Oh my God Lauren! Do you want to show up at school looking like an advertisement for the Geek Squad? We're going shopping now!" she insisted. "You need a capsule wardrobe that you can mix and match." I didn't even know what a capsule wardrobe was, but I trusted her because she was always winning "best dressed" in the class superlatives. She introduced me to clothing rental services like Nuuly and Rent the Runway, got me a subscription to her favorite fashion magazine as a going away present and hoped for the best. Paying more attention to my wardrobe has given me a keener appreciation for what others wear and what it says about them, but I still hate the morning routine. I much prefer picking out household décor. You only have to get that right once, not every damn day.

I slip in my AirPods, queue up my jam of the week, and head out for the eight-block walk to the office. I arrive with plenty of time to spare, giving me a chance to get things set up upstairs before meeting Amanda in the lobby at eight thirty. As I make my way down the hall to start the coffee brewing in the conference room, I notice a light coming from Drew Davis's office. Drew is the Senior Editor at the paper who has to approve all my columns. This, coupled with the fact that he's incredibly good looking, makes me nervous around him. In my defense, he has a similar effect on most of the women in the office. He's a bit of an enigma. No one seems to know much about him other than he's always impeccably dressed and appears to be busy doing important things – though no one is quite sure what they are. He's also always in the right place at the right time. With so much shift to online news there's been multiple layoffs in recent years, but Drew has somehow benefitted from it, rising quickly to his position. Around the breakroom he's affectionately referred to as "Mr. Drew-tiful," man of mystery.

As I walk by his office, he peers over the top of his wire-rimmed glasses and gives me an approving nod. I almost trip as I smile back at him and have to make a quick recovery, one I hope he doesn't notice. Pull it together Lauren.

Amanda arrives right on time – one point for the intern. She has short stylish red hair that reminds me of the color of Nikki's. She's wearing large tortoiseshell glasses, hoop earrings and carrying a leather messenger-computer bag that I think is tripling as a purse. She has on a fitted white t-shirt under a dark blazer and flowy wide-leg pants paired with leather lace-up witch boots that were popular in the 80s. None of these pieces really seem to go together, but as an overall look, she's more than pulling it off. Hmmm, she's going to lend a unique perspective to 'Philly's Top 10.'

"Hi, I'm Amanda Shields," she says, walking toward me with a confident smile and extending her hand.

I return the greeting, "Pleased to meet you. I'm Lauren Taylor."

"Oh, I know who you are, Ms. Taylor," she says, her voice full of enthusiasm. "'Philly's Top 10' is bible around campus. It's our go-to guide for navigating the city, and nine times out of ten, your recommendations are spot on. I'm really excited about this opportunity."

I laugh as I release her hand. "Please, call me Lauren. And maybe you can help me make that tenth recommendation a winner. Let's head upstairs. We can meet in the conference room. There's coffee in there and we'll have room to spread out. Then I'll show you around the office."

"Sounds great." She follows me toward the elevator practically bouncing as she walks. We reach the corridor and head down the hall toward the conference room. "Good morning!" Amanda says cheerfully as we pass Drew Davis's office.

He looks up from his desk, tips an imaginary hat in our direction and says, "Mornin' ladies," with an exaggerated drawl before mimicking a straw in his mouth.

Really? That was the most casual interaction I've ever had with that man, and it was initiated by a clueless college student who doesn't know enough to be intimidated by him.

Amanda turns to me as we continue down the hall, "He seems nice." I just nod and stifle the laugh in my throat.

"Why don't we start by getting to know each other a little better?" I suggest, reaching into the cabinet for coffee mugs and handing one to Amanda.

"Terrific." She pours herself a cup, takes out her tablet, and jumps right in. "I'd love to hear how you got into journalism."

I blow on my coffee before taking a sip. I've suffered the consequences of not doing that in the past. "My mom wrote for the local paper when I was growing up, and later became an English teacher after she and my dad divorced. She'd practice her lesson plans on my younger sister and me, and since ending a sentence with a preposition was a punishable offense in our house, I kinda came by it naturally."

I'm about to ask her about herself when she beats me to it with another question. "How did you land the job here?"

I lean back in my chair, taking a moment before answering. "I was a Communications and English major at the University of Delaware and wrote for the school paper, *The Review*. When I graduated, my sister Nikki was looking at schools in Philly, so I decided to look for a job here, too. My writing samples from *The Review* helped me get the interview." I pause, then grin. "I feel like I'm doing all the talking. What about you? What got you interested in journalism?"

Amanda blushes a little, looking sheepish. "Sorry, I've been asking a lot of questions. I'm just really excited to meet you." She shakes her head and sighs. "Honestly, I picked journalism because it required the fewest math credits. I know that sounds terrible, but surprise, I actually really enjoy it, and I think I'm becoming a decent writer."

I chuckle at her honesty. "I get it. I have to use the calculator in my phone just to figure out tips. And lucky you that you stumbled upon something you like. Tell me, what kind of writing have you been doing in your classes – more creative or more research-based?"

She adjusts her glasses before answering. "It's a mix, depending on the assignment. A lot of it's about choosing a compelling topic and then researching to make sure the facts are right. Can I ask one more thing?"

"Of course."

"How do you come up with content for 'Philly's Top 10?'" She rests her chin in her hands and anxiously awaits my response.

"I run a lot," I answer, taking another sip of coffee. "It's a great way to explore different parts of the city and get inspiration. That's how I came up with topics like Top 10 Street Vendors, Top 10 Best Cups of Coffee and Top 10 Food Trucks. I also keep lists in my phone – just a constant stream of ideas. It's one big, never-ending brain dump." As I'm talking, I notice Amanda hasn't typed a single thing on her laptop. She's listening intently and taking it all in. It's as if someone told her she should have a tablet in front of her for a meeting like this, but she doesn't need it. I like this girl. I continue, speaking over my thoughts, "My sister Nikki is a huge help, too. She's a fashion major at Drexel, so she gives me tips in her area. She's also a waitress, so I get her to poll her customers when I need to round out a list. Oh, and she walks dogs for Uber Leash, so she's always in different neighborhoods, discovering new places I might have missed."

"That sounds amazing! I'd love to help out with your column like that!" Amanda's enthusiasm is contagious, and I find myself wanting her to enjoy the internship.

"Well, that's why you're here." I smile and put my mug down on the table. "I'm looking for a fresh perspective, so I'm glad you pursued the internship program. I was really impressed with your credentials. Penn's no joke."

"Thanks! I'm really enjoying it," Amanda says. "I've met some great people – like *my* people, and so far, I've been able to keep up with the workload. Plus, Philly's great." Eager to learn more about her assignment, she switches direction without bothering to segway, "How do you think I can help with your column?"

An idea pops into my head that I'm sure she'll jump at (sorry mom… for ending a thought with a preposition, but I didn't say it out loud). "How about this for your first assignment," I pause for a silent drum roll. "Research the Top 10 College Hot Spots in Philly. Talk to your friends, read reviews, interview students at other universities, and visit the places that get mentioned the most. Then come back to me with a list and a solid justification for each spot. I'll need you to sell me on it before it gets published, so make sure your research is rock solid."

Amanda's eyes light up. "You're on!"

The rest of the morning flies by as I show her around the office and introduce her to people in nearby cubicles. We create a makeshift workspace for her with some mismatched forgotten furniture that reminds me of "The Land of Misfit Toys," but it'll do.

I suggest she start researching in her free time during the week and check in next Monday to update me on her progress. We agree, and she leaves for the day, seemingly excited about the assignment. I mean, what college student wouldn't be? After all she's getting paid to bar hop! I wish I had a boss like me rather than one who makes me feel like I've had *way* too much coffee every time I'm in his presence.

Still Monday

The Assignment

Wow – this is going to be great! I should have thought of interning sooner, Amanda thought as she hustled her way across town to get to Spanish class. She rushed into the lecture hall just in time and found her roommate Caroline saving the seat next to her. "Hola," she said playfully. Caroline rolled her eyes and moved her backpack off the seat next to her, "Sientate."

"Wait 'til you hear about my morning. I've got a great new assignment that you and Maggie are definitely going to want to help me with. Lauren Taylor is giving me a shot at ghost writing for 'Philly's Top 10' and the topic is... wait for it... 'Top 10 College Hot Spots in Philly!' Isn't that amazing? I want to get started right away. I already know the places that would make our group's Top 10 like Cav's and City Tap House, but I want to talk to some students at Drexel, Temple, La Salle and St. Joe's to see if there are places we haven't discovered. Then we can go check them out. Doesn't your cousin go to Temple?"

"Jeeze. Take a breath," Caroline said and nodded in response to the question. "Yeah, John goes to Temple, and I think he has some good-looking friends too. We haven't had a chance to meet up yet this semester, so this'll be the perfect excuse. Are you getting paid for this?" she asked. "This could get expensive."

"Yeah. It's not much, but I plan to make one of the ranking criteria 'best happy hours and drink specials' to keep the cost down. Plus, if we play our cards right with your cousin's friends, maybe they'll be the ones financing our research," she said, nudging Caroline with her elbow.

Caroline feigned disgust. "That's not a very modern-day woman thing to say."

"Oh please, who are you kidding? Like you've never let a guy buy you a drink? Besides, if we're going to be the underpaid sex, we have to take advantage of the perks."

"Silencio!" the professor shouted from the front of the room and dimed the lights to begin a short film in Spanish that no one would understand. Ignoring the screen, Caroline pulled out her phone and texted her cousin.

> Hey John, how'd you and your buddies like to show my friends and me around your part of town on Friday? We're looking to change it up.

> Talked to the guys. They're down. We're still hurting from a party at our place last night. It was insane, but Friday sounds good. I'll text you later in the week to let you know where to meet us.

Caroline put her phone away and gave Amanda the thumbs-up.

Thursday, Week 1

Nikki

"Hey Lucy. How's the morning been?" I ask, looping my apron around my waist.

"Uneventful, but yesterday was interesting," she replies, mischief all over her face.

I raise an eyebrow, suspicious of both her tone and expression. "Interesting how?"

"Your hottie-patottie from Monday came in looking for you," her smile now mimicking a Cheshire cat as she waits for my reaction.

"The dark-haired guy?" My voice betrays a little more excitement than I intend.

"Yup," she nods, leaning in. "I told him your next shift is this afternoon. So, I'd say you should be expecting him." Her eyes widen. "Can't wait to see how this plays out."

Hmmmm, let's see if today is the start of Round Two, which I fully intend on winning.

Lucy and I are busy with the lunch crowd when who walks through the door, but the guy who owes me a tip. Lucy sees him at the same time I do and flashes me a knowing grin. He trains those huge brown eyes directly at me and says, "Table for one."

"Right this way, sir." I lead him to the same booth he sat in on Monday.

He doesn't sit. "I'm sure you read my note and know my name is Chris. And thanks to your co-worker, I know you're Nikki," he pauses, eyes still locked on me. "So, Nikki, I guess you don't need the money since you never texted me your Venmo name for your tip."

The nerve of this guy… "Here's a tip for *you*…," I say planting both hands firmly on my hips. "I deserved a tip and shouldn't have to give some random stranger my number to get it, even if he is handsome."

"So, you think I'm handsome?" he asks with annoying confidence, leaning against the booth and crossing his ankles getting comfortable.

"That's what you got from what I just said?" My tone sharper now. "And it's quite obvious you know you're handsome. You've got that whole chest out cocky rooster thing going. It'd be really irritating if you weren't entitled to it," I shoot back, feeling pleased with myself for holding my own, then realize I just inadvertently complimented him. Damn it!

"Thou doth flatter me too much my lady," he replies, his voice deep and sexy.

Okay that was unexpected. He is NOT winning Round Two! Think, think, think... Thanks to my mother I know my Shakespeare.

"The fool doth think he is wise, but the wise man knows himself to be a fool," I counter.

"Touché," he says conceding, "but a Venmo tip doesn't seem like a real win for Round Two. Can I take you to dinner instead?"

Wow, getting straight to it. "Okay," slips out of my mouth a little too quickly. I kick myself for not making him sweat my response a little longer, but I think I sounded casual, so it might be okay.

"Great. How about The Love Saturday night?" Chris asks uncrossing his ankles and standing up straight.

Seriously? I've never been asked out to a good restaurant since I've been in college. Usually, it's a pizza or burger joint and the expectation of something more than I'm willing to give. "The Love in Rittenhouse Square?" I ask double-checking that I've got it right.

"That's the one," he replies with a confident nod.

"I walk a dog who lives in Rittenhouse Square," I explain. "I have to take him out late Saturday afternoon, so if you don't mind making it an early dinner, I can meet you afterwards."

Chris folds his arms across his broad chest. "We haven't even had our first date yet and you're already two-timing me?"

"Yup," I say without missing a beat. "Chester will always be first in my heart. He's my favorite 'client.'" I say making air quotes for emphasis.

A smile pulls at the corners of his mouth, we're both clearly enjoying this. "Well, I'd like to meet my competition – see what I'm up against. How about I come with you, and we grab dinner afterwards?"

"Sounds like a date," I say and hand him a menu.

He puts it down on the table. "You didn't really think I came in here to eat, did you?" His eyes again fully locked on mine. "You have my number so unless I'm still 'some random stranger' text me Chester's address and I'll see you Saturday."

He leaves me standing there a little flustered but also intrigued. I think Round Two is a draw.

Friday Morning, Week 1

The Po-Po Update

Rameriz refilled his coffee cup and stopped at Batiste's desk as he passed. "So, you see anything useful following the kids?"

Tim looked up from his paperwork, the buzz of the station's activity filling the air around them. "Not really. They live together and come and go a lot, but I'd say that's pretty typical for college kids. I'll keep watching them to see if one of them slips up. You hear anything further from New York?"

"No. Like I said, I followed Rocco to I-95 and didn't have a reason to pull him over." He took a gulp of his coffee. "I let DEA in New York know he was here. So far, he's being very careful, but he'll eventually make a mistake. They always do."

"The wheels of justice turn slowly," Batiste said, crumpling up a piece of paper from his desk and tossing it into the waste basket.

"Ain't that the truth," Mike replied with a sigh.

Friday Night, Week 1

The Incident

Amanda had a busy week with classes and doing some preliminary research for 'Philly's Top 10,' but it was Friday which meant she and her roommates were getting ready to meet Caroline's cousin John and his friends in Center City. Spotify was playing while the girls pre-gamed with vodka and Crystal Light. Amanda sifted through her sweaters trying to find something to wear as Caroline put on her make-up.

"Can someone bring me another drink and turn up the music?" Maggie yelled over the sound of her hair drier. Paul Russell piped through the speaker with "You My 'Lil Boo Thang" adding to the party atmosphere until it was interrupted with an advertisement. "Jesus Amanda, can you please upgrade to Spotify without ads like a normal person or give me the aux!"

By the time all three of them were ready it was almost nine o'clock. Caroline pulled open the door to McGillin's and the three of them were immediately enveloped with the sound of bar and dinner chatter and the accompanying aroma to match. As an Irish Ale House, it had the look and character you'd expect – dark wood columns, beams and chair rails, with every inch of wall space covered in framed news articles, pictures and memorabilia collected over time. John spotted Caroline as soon as they walked in. "Hey, Cuz over here," he shouted, waving his arm. Caroline weaved around the tables and through the crowd toward the bar and greeted him with a hug before introducing her friends. Tall with sandy blonde hair, blue eyes and chiseled bone structure, there were a bunch of people hanging around him making it clear he and his friends had the whole "big man on campus" thing going on.

"John, this is Amanda, and this is Maggie," Caroline said.

"Nice to meet you, ladies. I'm John and these two clowns are Shepp and Tony." He tipped his head in the direction of his roommates behind him.

Before anyone had a chance to say hello, the guy introduced as Shepp said, "My name's Chris. These idiots have nicknames for everyone," then turned to the bartender, "six shots of tequila." The bartender was busy mixing drinks, pouring beer and talking to twenty people at once – all of whom he seemed to know, but he nodded at Chris indicating he heard him and was on it.

Amanda smiled and leaned into Caroline, cupping her hand to Caroline's ear and whispered, "So far so good on my notion of these guys financing my research." Caroline swatted her hand away and shushed her in response. The shots of tequila were passed around followed by salt and limes. Chris raised his glass, "Saluti!" The six of them air-clinked, licked the salt on their hands and swallowed the shots in unison. Maggie choked a little getting the tequila down before finding relief in sucking the lime. Chris put his glass down on the bar and got the bartender's attention by making a circular motion in the air with his finger, "Another round."

"Jesus," Amanda said to Caroline, "we might want to dial this back a bit. We only just got here," and turned to Chris, "I think I'll switch to beer if you don't mind." Caroline agreed to switch after the next shot and Maggie was too busy being flattered by Tony's flirtation to care.

"Excuse me," Amanda said, "I have to find the Ladies' room."

"It's over there," John yelled over the noise pointing in the appropriate direction. Amanda found it immediately because as usual there was a line. Seeing the line suddenly made her desperate to go and for a minute she contemplated using the Men's room but then thought better of it when she glanced in there. She had the confidence to maneuver around guys at urinals to get to a stall, but she didn't have a wing-woman and didn't think it was worth going it alone. Thankfully the line moved pretty quickly. Turned out there were more girls primping in the mirror and becoming tipsy new best friends than actually using the toilets.

John handed her a beer when she returned, and it looked like the second round of shots were already gone. Tony now had Maggie pinned between himself and the end of the bar and was commanding her full attention. Chris was scrolling through his phone oblivious to the two girls behind him who were embarrassing themselves trying to get his attention. "Thanks," Amanda said to John, and he replied with a nod.

"I was just telling John about your assignment for 'Philly's Top 10,'" Caroline said leaning in closer so Amanda could hear, "and he's got a couple of suggestions."

"Yeah. Morgan's Pier should probably make your list − it's outdoor seating on the water is awesome." Amanda nodded in agreement. "Definitely this place," John continued. "I mean it's one of the oldest bars in the country so they must be doing something right, and of course, Xfinity is the place to be on game days." He took a swig of his beer and then had another thought, "Oh, and I'm sure you know the craft beer scene in Philly is legendary. That could be its own Top 10."

"I like it. I'll have to mention that to my boss."

"Hey big dog," John said, nudging Chris. "You waiting on a stock tip or something?   You're glued to that phone."

"Sorry, I'm just expecting a text," Chris replied and put the phone in his back pocket.

The four of them shouted conversation over amplifying bar chatter and background music while finishing their drinks. They hung out a while longer before deciding to check out some other places.

"Let's go see if we can pry Maggie and Tony apart long enough to tell them we're leaving." Amanda took Caroline's hand and pulled her toward them at the end of the bar.

"Hey Mags. We're going to check out some other spots. You guys coming?"

Maggie turned toward them and looked around the room like she was seeing it for the first time. "I don't feel so good," she slurred and stumbled forward, collapsing into Tony.

"Whoa," he laughed while scooping her up in his arms, "I got you."

"Oh my God what happened to her?" Caroline gasped, "how much has she had to drink?"

"Not much," Tony said, continuing to pull her upright, "maybe it's just the tequila kicking in."

Amanda turned to Caroline, "We need to get her home. This is not normal for her."

"My place isn't far from here. I can take her there to rest," Tony suggested. "You guys go ahead."

The girls exchanged looks and silently agreed. "Sorry Tony. Girl code. She's coming with us," Amanda said and started to reach for Maggie, but Tony was already ushering her toward the door – her feet tangling and stumbling along the way.

"Tony, wait!" Amanda yelled loudly catching John and Chris's attention and startling Tony enough to give the girls time to catch up to him.

Tony saw his roommates coming in their direction concerned. "Alright, fine," he said, annoyed. "Let me call you a ride," and struggled to manage his phone while holding onto Maggie at the same time.

John and Chris were both alarmed. "What's going on?" John asked, eyes darting between them trying to assess the situation.

"Amanda and I need to get Maggie home ASAP," Caroline answered with anxious resolve. "Look at her. She can barely stand!"

"I told them I'd take her to our place, so you guys can stay out, but they want to take her home," Tony said, opening his Uber app with his thumb. He turned to Amanda, "What's the address?"

"I'll do it," she replied equally annoyed and pulled out her phone.

By the time the Uber arrived Maggie's pupils were the size of marbles. She was being held up by both John and Tony, and Chris was feeding her a steady stream of water. Amanda opened the door and got in first reaching back to grab ahold of Maggie. John helped pour her into the car and Caroline sandwiched herself on Maggie's other side.

John was clearly concerned. "Are you sure you guys are going to be okay?" he asked Caroline. "Do you want me to come with you Cuz – make sure everything's alright?"

"No. We're fine. Amanda and I can handle it."

"Okay, but text me when you get back, so I'll know you made it," John said, shut the door and tapped his hand twice on the roof of the car before it pulled away.

The girls put water on Maggie's nightstand and a trash can next to her bed, then took turns checking on her throughout the night until she finally woke up around noon the next day.

"Welcome back to the living," Amanda said as Maggie walked into the kitchen yawning and running her fingers through her hair. "How much did you drink last night?"

"I think I only had one drink after the shots. It's a little foggy. I can't fully remember, but I've never felt that way before. It almost seemed like I was hallucinating. I think someone put something in my drink."

Saturday, Week 1

Nikki

Just to keep Chris wondering and score some points toward Round Three, I wait until after noon on Saturday to text him the address where to meet me. I tell him I'll be in the lobby of the building at four forty-five and not wanting to seem too playful, purposely don't add any emojis. Next, I text Lauren to let her know my plans in case he turns out to be a psycho or I need an SOS call to end the night early. She sends back a laughy face and says she'll text me mid-dinner just in case.

In spite of doing my best to keep the upper hand, I must admit I'm excited about seeing him again and curious about what Round Three will bring. I attempt to get some homework in before getting ready but I'm too distracted to concentrate, so I open my closet to contemplate an outfit. What to wear on a date that involves both dog walking and dinner? After trying several possibilities, I settle on leather pants, black knee-high flat boots, a turtleneck, and a leopard print faux fur jacket. Casual and warm enough for walking, but also appropriate for dinner. Okay, time to shower.

To my surprise, Chris is already waiting for me in the lobby of the apartment building when I arrive. "For a minute there I thought you gave me the wrong address just to be a wise ass," he says as he approaches me, stopping so close in front of me that I think he's going to hug me, but instead he moves to the side, puts his hand on the small of my back and motions forward with his other arm, "shall we go meet this Chester character?"

"Fair warning," I smile, "you better be on your best behavior because he's very jealous."

"I'm nothing if not a gentleman." He swoops his arm in front of him and bows forward for theatrical effect. Once in the elevator I check my phone for the code to the penthouse. "Ooo, apparently Chester is a fancy guy. Maybe my competition is going to be tougher than I thought."

The elevator opens to a foyer that stores two bikes, has a hook for Chester's leash and a small table for keys and mail. I punch in the second code that opens the door to the apartment and am immediately pounced by a very enthusiastic Chester. "Awww, who's a good boy?" I coo while rubbing the back of his ears and trying to avert his slobbery kisses. "Are you ready for a walk?" With that he starts spinning in circles and making little hops between each rotation. "Okay, okay, settle down. Let me get your leash."

I step back to get the leash and Chris peaks into the apartment from the foyer. "Wow, this place is nice. Look at that view."

"I know. I dream about living in a place like this. Sometimes after Chester's walk, I just stay with him a bit to keep him company and enjoy pretending I live here. He likes to cuddle after his walks anyway. Right Chester," I turn my attention back to the dog, and he wiggles at me affectionately in return.

"How do you know these people?" Chris asks bending down to pet Chester.

I take the opportunity to hook on Chester's leash while he's distracted by Chris. "I don't know them really. I was paired with them through Uber Leash and only met them during the interview. I think he's a doctor and I'm not sure what she does, but they have wacky hours which is why they need my help with Chester."

"So how many of these 'clients' do you have?" he asks.

"A bunch. It's a good gig. I get some exercise, make some extra money, and meet handsome little devils like this guy. Right Chester? Who's my handsome boy?" I ask while giving him a kiss. Chester wags his tail and looks at me adoringly, hoping for more attention.

"Oh brother," Chris sighs, "now I'm the one getting jealous." The three of us get in the elevator and start back down to the lobby. "Do you walk other dogs in this area?" he asks.

"A few. Sometimes I walk several at once, but Chester wouldn't be caught dead walking with another dog. As you can tell, he demands my full attention and that of every other human we encounter. He's a bit of a neighborhood celebrity. You'll see."

Chester is a gorgeous, well-groomed German Shepherd with a big personality and an even bigger ego. He knows he's 'fetching,' and milks it for all it's worth. "Hey Chester," someone says in the lobby, and we wait while he stops for an ear scratch. "Have a nice walk," the guy says before heading toward the elevator. As we make our way toward the park at the center of the Square, Chester stops for head rubs from anyone who looks his way and blatantly snubs anyone walking with another dog. He really is a snob, but he gets away with it, thanks to his good looks and that undeniable, flagrant self-assurance. It's hard not to laugh at him. He practically prances as we go, looking around confidently to see who's admiring him.

Chris smiles at Chester's antics, a mix of amusement and admiration in his expression, probably seeing a bit of himself in the dog's confident swagger. "I told you he's a character," I say, bending down to give him a quick nuzzle.

"Maybe I should think about getting a dog seeing the effect this guy has on you," he says.

"There's only one Chester for me," I reply with a grin.

Chris waits in the foyer while I get Chester settled inside, giving him a quick kiss on the snout before shutting the door. "So, what do you think of my main man?" I ask while waiting for the elevator.

Chris chuckles. "I think he's the luckiest son-of-a-bitch I've met in a long time."

With my hands now free of Chester and the leash, Chris laces his fingers between mine on the walk to The Love. I'm a little startled at first, but also pleasantly surprised by the easy connection and squeeze his hand in response.

We arrive a little early for our reservation and settle into leather stools at the bar, the low hum of evening chatter around us and the 'clankering' of glasses, dishes and cutlery fills the air. The bartender, a tall guy with a tattooed sleeve and a broad chest I can't help but notice, slides drink napkins in front of us. "What can I get you folks?"

"I'll have a glass of Chardonnay," I say, hanging my purse on the hook underneath the bar and adjusting myself in my seat.

Chris glances around for a drink menu. "What kind of craft beers do you have?" he asks. The bartender rattles off a few names, his words smooth and practiced. After a moment's thought, Chris decides. "I'll take a Dogfish Head."

He swivels his stool toward me, leaning in so that his eyes lock on mine with an intensity that keeps catching me off guard. "So, Nikki," he says in a tone that is direct but also somehow flirtatious, "tell me – what do you do when you're not charming dogs or getting feisty with your customers at Mocha Loco?"

I feel a small flutter in my chest at the power of his gaze but cover with what I hope appears to be a casual smile. "Well, in my spare time, I'm a fashion student at Drexel. If all goes according to plan, I should graduate in the spring."

Chris nods and glances me up and down with a thoughtful look. "That explains your style," he says, his eyes lingering on me a moment too long. "You look great, by the way."

I'm flattered and return the compliment. "Thank you. You clean up well yourself."

Just then, the bartender returns with our drinks, placing them down in front of us before wiping his hands on the long denim apron that covers his white button-down. I take a sip, savoring the crispness of the wine before asking, "How about you?"

Chris shifts his posture slightly, leaning back more comfortably. "I'm studying Risk Management at Temple. Should be finishing up in the spring too. But since I don't have two extra jobs like someone else I know..." He shoots me a playful grin. "Staying on track shouldn't be a problem."

He raises his bottle toward me, and I clink my glass against it with a polite, "Cheers." We both take a sip and then consider one another for a moment. It feels like we're thinking the same things... *so far so good... what's next... should I make the next move...*

Before either of us can say anything else, the hostess approaches, "Sheppard. Party of two. Your table is ready." It dawns on me that I didn't even know his last name until just now.

"That was fast." Chris throws money for the drinks on the bar and we follow the hostess into the dining room. The room feels open, elegant and casual all at the same time – just welcoming – whitewashed brick and tasteful accoutrements like the small adjustable lights on the tables that offer each guest their own level of ambience – it works.

The aroma of garlic and herbs fills my nostrils as we make our way to the table. My stomach growls and I hope it's not as loud as it seems to me. Chris keeps walking so I think it went unnoticed.

The dishes being brought out look like they were prepared for a Bon Appetit photo shoot – a far cry from the freebees I'm used to at Mocha Loco or the reheated leftovers I manage on my own. The closest thing I've had to a real meal in a while was when Lauren invited me over for Asian fusion take-out.

When we arrive at the table, Chris pulls out the chair for me and I can't help but wonder if this guy is for real. Once we're both seated, I extend my hand across the table, "So Chris Sheppard, I don't believe we've been properly introduced. I'm Nikki Taylor. How do you do?"

Instead of shaking my hand, he takes it in both of his, pulls it closer to him and kisses it. "I'm charmed to formally meet you, Nikki Taylor," he says, staring deeply into my eyes, still holding my hand.

Ok swoon or barf? I'm still trying to figure out if this is my dream guy or someone impersonating my dream guy to win me over for evil intentions. Is he love bombing me right now or actually a nice guy?

We open our menus and study the selections. I consider the possibilities – nothing with spinach that might get stuck in my teeth, nothing with too much garlic or onion that will make my breath smell, and nothing with noodles that will be splashy and slurpy potentially making a mess.

"Have you decided?" Chris asks after a few minutes.

"Yes, I'm going with the Mediterranean Branzino. What are you thinking?"

"The Rigatoni and Short Rib here is really good so I'm going to have that," he replies and shuts the menu satisfied with his decision.

Jesus. How often has he been here? Is this his M.O for first dates? This guy seems like a player.

After the waitress takes our order, he folds his hands in his lap, makes that powerful eye contact again and says, "Okay, tell me all things I need to know about Nikki Taylor."

I close my eyes for a brief second to break the intensity but it's still there when I open them again. "Well, the most important things are that I take my coffee black, prefer vanilla over chocolate and can't resist a good Rom-Com."

"Good to know. The vanilla over chocolate thing is a little disturbing, but I think I can get past it. Where are you from?" he asks casually.

"I grew up in north Jersey," I start, but he interrupts with, "What exit?"

"Seriously??" I let out an exasperated sigh. "Not all of New Jersey is like the opening scene of The Sopranos. I'm actually from a very quaint little town with rolling hills, historic mansions and sought after schools, 45 minutes from the nearest onramp to the Jersey Turnpike. We don't have a single jug handle, strip club or notorious crime family," I counter.

"Still explains your spunk," he says with a smirk.

"Well, you can take the girl out of Jersey, but not the Jersey out of the girl," I say with a practiced confidence that indicates this isn't the first time I've had to explain my sass. "How about you?"

"I grew up on the Main Line," he replies with comfortable pride making it clear he enjoys being from the area.

I sit back a bit in my chair and cross my arms, a knowing smile taking over my expression. "I had you pegged for a Bryn Mawr boy."

"What makes you say that?" His voice has a curious edge now, like he's intrigued by my assumption.

"I don't know," I shrug. "You just seem to fit the mold."

He chuckles softly but isn't letting it go, "Is that a good thing or bad?"

I smile at him pretending I need more time to answer. "Hmm... I'm still deciding, but I'm leaning towards good." My phone dings and I look down at the screen, holding back a giggle as I read it.

"What's so funny?" he asks, his smile now matching mine as he watches me.

"It's my sister Lauren checking in to see if I need to be rescued," I explain and start to tap out a quick answer.

"And?" he asks curiously, leaning forward trying to see what I'm typing. I turn the phone over before finishing the text and turn my attention back to Chris. "Well, the food here looks amazing, and the company isn't bad either, so I think I'll stick it out. Let me just finish my text or she'll be calling in five minutes."

Our food arrives and Chris orders a bottle of wine. Both of our meals look delicious so we each put a small sample on the bread plates to share. As we begin eating, the volume of the conversation between the couple at the next table increases an octave or two, drawing our attention. They're oddly matched. She's dressed stylishly, like she'd planned for a night out. Her hair is perfectly coiffed, she's wearing obvious fake eyelashes, and has a French manicure. He, on the other hand, put very little effort into his attire for the evening – jeans and a flannel. Chris and I eat in silence and shamefully listen in. The guy is apparently upset that the woman has invited her mother for a week without consulting him first.

"Well, I didn't realize I needed permission to invite my own mother to stay," she says angrily.

"You don't need permission but a little heads up would've been nice. You know I have to mentally prepare for her bullshit." He's trying to keep an even tone, aware of the subject matter and his surroundings, but not really succeeding.

"This *is* me giving you a heads up and what bullshit exactly are we talking about?" she snaps.

"All of it, Ally," he says, his patience giving out, "but if you want to get specific, let's start with the fact that she's a judgmental bitch!" With that, Chris and I both put our forks down to listen a little more intently.

"Maybe if there wasn't so much to be judgmental about it wouldn't be such a problem!" She stands and throws her napkin on the chair. "I need to use the Ladies room," she hisses and storms off in a huff.

He sighs, raises his hand to get the waiter's attention and orders another drink. "Make it a double please."

I lean in, lowering my voice so only Chris can hear. "It's only halfway through our first date and we're already revealing our flaws." I rest my chin in my hand, blocking my mouth from the man at the next table. "It really isn't a very good look that both of us were so obviously eavesdropping."

"Well, in our defense," he whispers, "that show was too good to miss. She's obviously out of his league, and apparently her mother knows it." He sits back, his fingers drumming on the table as his grin widens. "And the second flaw in your case. That sharp tongue of yours is first, but I have to admit, I kinda like it."

"If we're keeping score, you're annoyingly sure of yourself," I tell him, my tone light but pointed.

"I can live with that." His grin turns more devilish, and he cocks his head, studying me for a moment, contemplating his next thought. "But is that really a flaw?"

"Maybe not," I shrug casually, not wanting to let him 'win' the exchange. "Let's just say we're even."

"Are you always this competitive?" he asks, the challenge now mutual.

"Are you?" I shoot back, trying to contain the smile that's fighting to take over my face.

"Yes," he laughs warmly. "And I think I may have just met my match!"

We enjoy our meals and 'getting to know you' conversation when the waitress approaches to ask if we're interested in dessert. "No thank you," I answer, letting out a breath and placing a hand on my stomach. "I'm too full."

"We'll just take the check when you get a chance." Chris turns to me once she walks away, "It's still early. Do you want to go somewhere else?"

"I'd like to, but I better not." I sigh, "I have to work the breakfast shift tomorrow."

His voice turns jokingly sweet. "Are you sure I can't talk you into one more drink?" he asks while over-exaggerating puppy dog eyes.

I tilt my head to meet his stare. "Are you trying to get me drunk?"

"Maybe," he admits, looking at me as if daring me to fall for it.

"Well, at least you're honest. I'll give you that." I consider it for a brief moment and let my better judgement win. "But I really can't."

He clutches his chest in mock agony. "You're breaking my heart," he pouts, then pretends to stab himself with his fork, drawing out the theatrics for all they're worth. "At least let me walk you home. How far are you from here?"

I laugh at his performance. "It's about a mile. I can just Uber."

"No." He shakes his head, his voice sincere, but insistent. "I'll walk you. I'm not ready to let you go just yet."

I let out a small, amused sigh, giving in to his charm. "Okay, if you must. But just so you know," I say with a teasing smile, "I'm not inviting you in."

He drops his head dramatically in playful defeat. "Well now you're really breaking my heart. I have one mile to try to change your mind.   Let's get started, shall we?"

Chris holds my hand as we walk and does his best to charm me into changing my mind about inviting him in. He is in fact winning me over, but I can't let Round Three go to him that easily and I do have to get up early tomorrow. "This is me," I say when we get to my apartment building.

As if reading my mind he says, "Even if you won't let me in, I still win Round Three because now I know where you live." He reaches for my other hand turning me to face him. "What time do you get off work tomorrow?"

"Noon."

"Why don't you come over to my place after work for the game. I make killer wings," he throws in at the end as if dangling a carrot.

"What game?" I ask, immediately regretting the question the instant it leaves my lips.

"What game?!" His eyes are wide with disbelief, "The Eagles game of course! Please don't tell me you're a Giants fan or worse yet, a Cowboys fan. That could be the end of our promising future together."

I laugh. "No, I'm just not much of a fan girl. Growing up in a household with just my mom and sister didn't exactly lend itself to following sports. We were more of a horse family. But since I've been in Philly, I've definitely enjoyed the craziness around the Eagles. The fans are... well, nuts."

He grins, clearly proud of it. "Yes, we are, and damn proud of it!"

"When they won the Super Bowl, did the city really have to grease the street poles to keep fans from climbing them?" I ask skeptically. I've heard the story, but it sounds like urban legend.

He chuckles. "Well, it wouldn't have been any fun if it was easy to climb them. We waited a long time for that victory, and we had *plenty* of reasons to celebrate." He seems to drift away for a moment recalling it. "The parade was insane. Kelce gave the most epic victory speech of all time – in full Mummer's regalia! I'd ask if you've seen it, but I'm betting you haven't. You should Google it. Totally worth a watch."

"Okay, I'll check it out. You Eagles fans sure are a passionate bunch."

"I'm passionate about a lot of things, Nikki," he says, daring me with his eyes.

He's smooth but I know what he's doing. It's his last-ditch effort at getting upstairs. I break his gaze and quickly steer the conversation back on track. "I've never really understood the whole Mummers thing. What's it all about?"

He shrugs, knowing the negotiations are over. "Like most Philly traditions, it's about being loud, having fun, and knocking back a few drinks with friends. We'll take any excuse to celebrate." He pauses for a beat. "So, will you come? My roommates will be home, so you don't have to worry about me trying to lure you into my evil lair to get you alone."

"Okay, that sounds fun." I start to thank him for the evening when he drops my hands, puts his arm around my waist, his other hand on my face and pulls me in for a kiss that registers about an eight on my internal Richter Scale. "Well, I'll see you tomorrow then Nikki Taylor," he says and opens the door for me.

Definitely swoon, not barf....

The Aftermath

In the Uber home, Chris texted Nikki his address for tomorrow signing off with "Go Birds," the standard greeting, goodbye or acknowledgement of any kind used in Philadelphia. She replied with a thumbs-up emoji. He started to text her back but stopped himself not wanting to seem too eager. *Slow your roll big guy. You're going to see her again tomorrow.*

Still on a high from the evening, he opened the door to his place to a scene that looked like a tornado struck. *Shit.*

John and Tony were out so he figured he was on clean-up duty – he couldn't have Nikki coming over to this tomorrow. He opened the windows to air out the smell of burnt pizza and dirty bong water and started picking up all the trash laying around. The cold winter air filled the house and made him shiver but he didn't care, it was better than the horrendous smell he walked into. They must've had people over before going out. He texted both his roommates.

> Hey dickheads. I'm cleaning up this shit hole. I have a date coming over tomorrow for the game so don't mess it up again when you get in.

> Cleaning for a date? Someone's trying to impress. I'll have to stick around tomorrow to meet her.

The three dots blinked as Chris tap, tap, tapped out his comeback.

> You already did. She's the waitress at Mocha Loco from Monday.

Tony chimed in with a fire emoji and Chris got back to work straightening up the place. When he finished with the living room, kitchen, and downstairs bathroom, he went to his bedroom, picked up his clothes and put fresh sheets on the bed. Not that he thought that was going to be necessary, but a guy could dream. He heard his mother's voice in his head... *"By failing to prepare you're preparing to fail."*

Sunday, Week 1

Nikki

Getting up early on a Sunday for the breakfast shift would normally be a bummer, but knowing I'll be seeing Chris again this afternoon has me in an unexpectedly good mood. He really did pour it on thick last night, but he seemed genuine and that kiss... I'm still having aftershocks.

I live in a studio apartment so I'm basically sleeping in my kitchen. It's really tight but is all I can afford and does have a few advantages like being able to turn the coffee on in the morning without fully getting out of bed. The smell of it brewing is enough to lure me out from underneath the covers. I pour a cup and pull out my standard waitressing uniform – black yoga pants, white blouse and denim apron – and realize this is what I'll be wearing when I arrive at Chris's house for the game. I know I don't own any Eagles gear, but I poke around my closet for something that's at least green – no luck. How is it possible there's nothing in here that works? What do I usually wear on St. Patrick's Day?

Knowing I can pick up a sweatshirt after work, I shower, dress, and begin the walk to Mocha Loco. It's early December, so the sun has only risen about fifteen minutes ago. It's peaceful this time of day; the calm before the storm. Soon the city will be yawning, stretching, rubbing the sleepy dust out of its eyes, and coming to life.

Lucy is already setting up when I arrive. "Hey, good morning," she says, "how was your date last night? Tell me *everything*."

"It was really nice."

"Details!" she demands.

"Okay, okay fine," I can't help but giggle. "We walked one of my dogs in Rittenhouse Square and then had dinner at The Love – amazing food by the way. He was so charming, which I was skeptical of at first, but I think he might be the real deal. He walked me home afterwards and gave me a kiss goodnight that would've gotten him upstairs if I were that kind of girl," I say, fanning myself for emphasis. "I'm going to his place for the Eagles game after my shift today."

"Ooo, that sounds promising. He's moving fast! You might become that kinda girl sooner than you think," she teases.

"Okay, calm down lady. It's only our second date."

By eight o'clock, customers start trickling in. It's just Lucy and me until noon, so we're balancing tables and takeout orders. We've gotten good at working in sync – bringing plates to tables, refilling each other's customers' coffees and ringing up take-out orders at the counter. And all morning, every time Lucy passes me, she throws out another question about Chris. I give her scraps of information, which only makes her more curious, and it becomes our game that helps pass the time until the lunch crew arrives.

When noon rolls around, my shift's technically over, but I've got one table still lingering. Lucy senses my eagerness to leave and offers to take over. "Thanks, Luce, you're the best. My side work's all done."

"No problem. Anything I can do to support the cause," she says with a grin. "I wouldn't mind Chris showing up in here more often with his hot friends."

"We'll see," I say, on my way to the employee bathroom to freshen up. Even though I washed my hair this morning, the smell of the café kitchen seems to cling to it like a dryer sheet on laundry. I spray it with dry shampoo, touch up my make-up, and head out in search of an Eagles sweatshirt.

Game Day

John and Tony were still asleep after a rough night. Chris, on the other hand, was showered, dressed in his Kelce jersey, and on his way to Pat's to pick up cheesesteaks for the game. They're open 24/7, so he wasn't worried about that, but there can be lines on game days, so he wanted to get there early. He ordered a few "whiz wit and a few witout," not knowing Nikki's thoughts on onions, and threw in one wit provolone in case she didn't like whiz. She was from Jersey after all, so it was anybody's guess. He had everything he needed for the wings at the house, and there was always plenty of beer in the fridge, so he thought he was in good shape.

The house was still quiet when he got home, so he had an opportunity to prep the wings in an empty kitchen without anyone giving him grief or taste-testing while he worked. Once the wings began cooking and the smell of Sunday game day started drifting through the house, John and Tony began to show signs of life.

"Hey dog," Tony said, walking down the stairs with a girl in tow. His hair was disheveled, he was shirtless, barefoot and wearing sweatpants – the stamp from last night's bar crawl still prevalent on the top of his hand. "This is Julie," he said motioning to the very embarrassed looking girl behind him.

"Julia," she corrected him but seemed thankful for the introduction all the same, as if knowing she hadn't met Chris before was helping her piece the night together.

"I'll get your coat," Tony said walking toward the entryway. She followed quickly behind clearly wanting to get out of there as soon as possible. Tony handed her the coat, "See ya around." She didn't even reply, just quickly slipped it on and dashed out the door.

"You're gonna make her take the walk of shame?" Chris said shaking his head. "Real classy dude."

Tony dropped his head in defeat, "Christ. Tell John I'm taking his car." He threw a jacket on over his bare chest, grabbed John's keys and went out the door after Julie-Julia barefoot.

John walked in a minute later and went straight to the fridge. He grabbed the Gatorade and chugged it straight from the bottle. "Ahhh," he smacked his lips once it was empty and moved toward the oven, opening the door to take a sniff.

"Leave it alone," Chris instructed, "let the master work."

"Just taking a look. It smells good. How was your night?" John asked, shutting the oven and returning to the refrigerator for further exploration.

"It was good until I got home. Looked like you guys did some serious pre-gaming."

"Wasn't me. Tony had some guys over. I think he was going to have them check out the pack before we start selling it. I met up with him after." He stared blankly inside the fridge before bending in to get a better look. "Seems like there's quite the fuss going on around here for this girl you've got coming over for the game, Shepp," John taunted from inside the fridge.

"No fuss. Just trying not to look like a bunch of Neanderthals. She'll be here for kick-off, so if you guys can get cleaned up by then, there'll be wings and cheesesteaks in it for you."

John shut the refrigerator much more interested in the game food Chris was offering. "Deal," he said and started upstairs to shower.

"Tony took your car by the way," Chris called after him. "He had to take some girl home."

John stopped on the steps. "He had a girl with him? I lost track of him last night, but he wasn't with a girl when we were together. I wonder how he pulled that off so quickly."

"Who knows," Chris answered. "He's got the charm of a bullfrog, so she must've been pretty drunk. She couldn't get out of here fast enough."

#

The guys were sprawled in the living room, absorbed in the pre-game shows as Chris bounced in and out of the kitchen, checking on the food heating up in the oven. A knock at the door cut through the buzz of sports commentary.

"I got it," Chris said, which really wasn't necessary since neither one of the others moved. He opened the door to find Nikki standing on the front porch wearing an Eagles sweatshirt. "Look at you... Thought you said you weren't a fan girl."

Nikki shrugged. "I had to pick this up on my way over." Chris smiled warmly, clearly impressed by the effort.

"Come on in." He opened the door wider and stepped to the side. "Tony, John, this is Nikki. Nikki, meet the brain trust – Tony and John." He pointed to each of them as he made the introduction, just in case there was any confusion.

"Hi guys. I remember you from the café the other day," Nikki said, offering a friendly smile.

"Yeah, hey," Tony looked up in her direction. "Sorry for being a dick that day. I was – uh – really hungover."

"We all were," Chris reminded him, "but as usual, you're the only one who owes her an apology."

Tony rolled his eyes and groaned. "Here we go again. These guys are always trying to transform me from a ghetto kid into a pathetic preppy like them. I guess I'm a work in progress."

"No worries," Nikki said with a small laugh. "As a waitress, I deal with all kinds of people, in all kinds of moods."

"Nice to see you again," John added, nodding politely.

"Here, let me take your jacket," Chris offered. She took her bag off her shoulder and tossed it on the couch to get her arm out. When the bag hit the cushion, her wallet, phone, and a ring of keys spilled out.

Tony raised an eyebrow noticing the keys. "You got a side gig as a janitor or something?"

Nikki flushed a little. "Oh sorry, let me get that," she said, slipping the rest of the way out of the jacket and shoving her things back in her bag. "No, I walk dogs for Uber Leash. The keys are to my canine customers' homes. Others have key codes I store in my phone to keep them all straight."

Chris hung her jacket on one of the hooks by the front door. "Here, give it to me; I'll hang it with your coat."

"Thanks," she said handing him her bag.

"Have a seat, Nikki. I'm gonna grab the food from the kitchen. Anyone want a beer?"

"I'll have one," John said.

"Same here," Tony added.

Nikki made herself comfortable on the couch. "I'll just have a diet coke if you have one."

"Coming right up." In the kitchen, Chris loaded the food and Nikki's diet coke on a tray he stole from the campus dining hall and balanced it on one hand while grabbing three beers with the other. He carried it all effortlessly to the living room, handing out the beers first before twirling the tray down onto the coffee table.

"Wow," Nikki's eyes widened. "You're pretty good at that. I should get you a job at the café."

John laughed. "Yeah, like he's ever put in a real day's work. Besides, I've noticed the main qualification for hire in that place is being a good-looking girl. Not sure he fits the mold."

Chris shot him a playful glare. "Hey, I can bat my eyelashes with the best of them," he said and did just that.

The game kicked off, and soon enough, the usual chaos unfolded — screaming at the TV, cursing at the refs, and jumping out of their seats. As a football novice, Nikki was asking questions that Chris found adorable and gave him a chance to flex his knowledge of the game. She asked for a knife to cut one of the cheesesteaks in half and chose a whiz wit. *I think I'm in love*, Chris thought.

They were mid-way through the second quarter when another knock sounded at the door. Tony immediately got up, like he was expecting someone. "Hey," he said, opening it for three guys Chris and John didn't recognize. "Sup?" one of them said as they followed Tony through the living room and up the stairs without further introductions. Chris gave John the side-eye and tipped his head over his shoulder, indicating for him to follow them. John shrugged and went upstairs after them.

"Another diet coke?" Chris asked.

Nikki hesitated, then shook her head. "Actually, I think I'll take that beer now." *Definitely in love.*

Chris returned with fresh beers as the three guys came back downstairs without Tony or John. One of them paused in the doorway, "What's the score?"

"10 to 3 — good guys," Chris answered, handing Nikki a beer.

"Go Birds," one of them said, as they walked out the door.

Nikki turned to Chris mildly insulted, "That was weird. Why didn't you introduce me?"

Chris shrugged nonchalantly. "I don't know them. They're probably working on a project with Tony or something. He should've introduced them. Like he said, he's a work in progress. John and I are used to it."

The Buy

John read Chris's signal and started up the stairs after Tony and the three strangers. When he reached Tony's room the deal was already going down. Tony was shoving cash in his pocket and the guys were putting bags in their jackets. When the exchange was complete Tony moved toward the door to show them out. "Guys you know the way," John said. "Tony, can I talk to you for a minute?" The three guys nodded and left the room.

"What's up?" Tony asked, pulling the cash out of his pocket to recount.

John was immediately suspicious. "Did you have that stuff checked out?"

Tony laid the cash on his desk and took a seat. "Well, I did my own little experiment and based on last night and Maggie's reaction on Friday, I'd say it's quality stuff."

John wasn't floored by much when it came to Tony, but he was floored then. "What the fuck Tony?!" he yelled, his voice hot with anger and cold with disgust. "You spiked Maggie's drink? She's my cousin's roommate you asshole! What the actual fuck were you thinking?"

Tony wasn't fazed. "Why would I rely on some shady dude when I can test it myself on a hot chick? Just taking advantage of an opportunity," he said casually and continued counting.

"An opportunity?!" John shouted and pulled him from the chair – now he had his attention. "Is that why you wanted to bring Maggie back here? And how about that girl last night... what did you do to her?" John shook him... "Huh?" he yelled louder when Tony didn't answer.

Tony slammed his arms against John's chest, pushing him toward the wall, "Back off bro!"

John stumbled backwards losing his grip on Tony. He didn't need an answer – he already knew the truth. He paused a moment and ran his fingers through his hair, letting the reality of the situation sink in. He swallowed the bile rising in his throat and cemented his resolve. This was too much, and he wanted out. "You know what man; you're a real fucking prick. I don't know what's gotten into you, but I'm out. I don't want any part of this, and I don't want you anywhere near my cousin or her friends again. Got it?"

"Relax dude," Tony said settling back into the chair ignoring both John's anger and his warning. "I didn't even get Maggie's digits and Amanda wouldn't give me the address for the Uber."

"Smart girl apparently," John said in disgust and slammed the bedroom door on the way out.

When he re-entered the living room Chris was sitting next to Nikki, his arm casually draped over her shoulder like it belonged there. He shot John a look that asked, "So?" John just shook his head knowing he couldn't explain in front of Nikki and took a seat with them in front of the TV. The game was in the third quarter, tied at 17–17.

"Why does every game have to be so close?" John sighed, slouching into the couch. "A nice, comfortable lead would be good every once in a while. I'm gonna age ten frickin' years by the end of the season."

"No shit," Tony agreed, dropping a backpack next to the chair as he joined them. Despite the tension of the game, Tony was more focused on his phone than the TV. The Eagles couldn't convert on third down, but at least they managed to take the lead with a field goal.

"Yes!" Nikki squealed as the ball sailed through the uprights. John couldn't help but wonder – *is she into the game for Chris's benefit, or is she actually enjoying it?* Either way, it was clear the two of them were enjoying each other. Chris pulled Nikki closer and kissed her on the cheek in celebration.

Hmmm, John thought, his eyes narrowing slightly as he observed them. *He's really down for the count; I've never seen him like this with a girl before.*

Nikki reached for her phone, and Tony stood up, walking behind the couch. She quickly keyed in her code, and Tony paused behind her, watching the next play. When it was over, he sat back down, as if he'd forgotten why he'd gotten up in the first place.

"I can't believe I'm saying this," Nikki said with a sigh, "I wish I could stay for the rest of the game, but I have to walk a dog on the way home."

Chris looked at her surprised. "Can you wait 'til the game's over? I'll go with you," he suggested, sounding hopeful.

"No, sorry. My 'client' needs to be let out by three-thirty, so I have to leave now." She looked at Chris with apologetic eyes, "Sorry, I had no idea how long games last." Chris smiled at her affectionately but there was disappointment written across his face all the same.

Tony looked up from his phone. "Any chance you're going down Broad Street?"

"Yeah, actually," Nikki said as she stood.

"Would you mind dropping my buddy's backpack off at his apartment building?" Tony asked, picking it up from the floor. "He can meet you in the lobby."

Nikki didn't hesitate. "Sure. No problem." She turned toward Tony and reached out for the backpack.

Chris sprang from the couch and grabbed it out of Tony's hands before Nikki could get to it. "You don't have to do that. One of us can do it after the game."

Nikki offered again, "Really, it's no problem."

"No. I don't want you to be late for your 'customer'. Can't have him peeing in the house," Chris said with a gentle smile. "Let me get your coat." He threw the backpack hard at Tony's chest and drilled him with a look. Turning back to Nikki his expression immediately softened. "Promise you'll Uber the rest of the way after you walk the dog."

"I will," Nikki said with a small laugh. She turned to John and Tony, "Bye, guys. This was fun." She gave a fist pump punctuated by "Go Birds!" and turned toward the door. Chris helped her on with her coat, laid a gentle hand on her back and walked her out, shutting the door behind them.

John was already on his feet. "God damn it, Tony!" he yelled. "I just got done telling you you're taking this too far and now you pull this shit? We only met Rocco a week ago and this is like the third bad decision you've made. If you weren't so busy cutting deals with strangers and contacting God knows who on that phone all day, you might've noticed Shepp's really into this girl. He's gonna be super pissed!"

Right on cue, the door flew open, and Chris lunged at Tony, grabbing him by the shirt and slamming him up against the wall. "You were actually gonna have her make a drop? Are you out of your mind, you crazy fuck?!" Tony raised his hands, palms out in surrender, and Chris shoved him off the wall, his anger still simmering.

"And that's not all," John grabbed Chris's attention rounding the other side of the couch. "He roofied Maggie's drink on Friday and God help the mystery girl from last night."

"What?!" Chris's voice was raw with fury, eyes wide with disbelief and hands instantly back on Tony.

This time Tony pushed back, hard, sending Chris staggering backwards. "Why are you guys being such pussies?!"

Chris righted his footing and came back at Tony, fists clenched and ready to swing. "We'll see who's a pussy!"

John jumped between them, his back to Tony and his hand out straight signaling for Chris to stop. "Whoa! I already told him *I'm* out." He locked eyes with Chris silently conveying his thoughts. "He's taking this too far!"

Chris let his fists drop, the realization that this was a choice hitting him all at once. *I don't need this shit,* he thought. John saw the awareness sink in and softened his posture in relief.

"I'm with you, man," Chris muttered, then stepped to the side to face Tony. His voice colder now, "I'm out too. I don't need your whole bad boy adrenaline rush bullshit anymore – or even the money. I'm focused on Nikki now." He paused, catching his breath and sealing his conviction. "You're on your own dude. This shit's not worth it." He stepped forward, closing the distance between them, eyes hardening, "And don't ever pull anything like that with Nikki again," he warned. "I plan on being with her a hell of a lot more and don't need to be constantly looking over my shoulder wondering about your bullshit."

Tony didn't push back with his usual attitude. He needed their help and knew fighting with them wasn't the answer. "Look, guys... you agreed to this when we met Rocco. This guy's the real deal. He's not going to just let us walk away." Tony knew the two of them could walk away. He was the only one who needed this and couldn't back out, he'd be the only one held accountable. "How am I supposed to move the whole bag myself?"

Chris scoffed, not taking the bait. "Sounds like a *you* problem." His words were curt and final. He was still pissed but also a little relieved to be done with it. "You wanted this to be your gig anyway. You've got the phone and the stash, so have at it."

Without another word, he turned his back on Tony and returned to the game. John exhaled a silent sigh of relief and joined Chris in front of the TV, leaving Tony standing there alone with the consequences of his choices.

Later that Day

Nikki

My phone buzzes almost as soon as I walk through the door. Lauren's name illuminates on the screen, so I pick it up right away while working my coat off. "Hey!"

"So, how was the date last night?" she asks curiously.

"It was great! He took me to The Love, can you believe that? Then he walked me home. And actually, I saw him again today for the Eagles game."

"The Eagles game??" I can practically hear her jaw drop. "Good God. You must be smitten."

"I know, I know, but honestly, it was fun. He explained everything – like all about the players and the rules. It's way more interesting when you actually know something about the team. And let's be real, I've been here for over three years. It's borderline criminal I haven't gotten on board sooner. I even had to buy a sweatshirt after work today." *Ding.* "Hold on, that's him texting to make sure I got home okay," I say, quickly tapping out a response.

"Let me just answer this real quick." *Tap, tap, tap...* "Okay, sorry, I'm back."

"Well, he sounds attentive," Lauren teases.

"He's definitely got my attention, if that's what you mean by attentive," I reply, smiling to myself.

She laughs. "Does he have an older brother?"

"Haha, you *really* need to start focusing on your social life. That damn column of yours eats up all your time."

"You're probably right," she sighs. "But between work and trying to see Dad on the weekends, I swear, I blink, and a month has passed. I know you usually work weekends, but I'm going to see him next Sunday if you want to come with."

"Okay, I'd like that. Let me check my schedule at work and get back to you." *Ding.* "Listen, Lauren, I'm gonna hop. That's Chris again."

"Alright, let me know about Sunday. Talk to you later, love bug."

"Shut up," I say with a smile even though she can't see it. "Bye. Love you."

WEEK TWO

Monday Morning, Week 2

Lauren

I wasn't in the office much last week because most of my time was spent gathering content for my column. I enjoy it, but it's daunting coming up with new meaningful ideas each week and researching them all. Also, I wish it was 'Philly's Top 5.' Ten gets to be too much. Five is easy, but I feel like I generally get stuck around eight with most of my lists. At some point this column is going to run its course and I better have a solid Plan B. Nikki needs help with her student loans and Dad's care is really expensive. I'm sure mom is rolling in her grave at the thought that our inheritance is being spent caring for her ex-husband. Ugh, I let out a sigh just thinking about the weight of it all.

It's been a week since I met with Amanda, and she's coming in this morning to report on her progress with the assignment I gave her. Also, Mondays are the day I have to turn in my column to Drew Davis for approval and give him a report on what ideas I have in the pipeline for the coming weeks. Usually this is all handled via email, but I feel I should be in the office on Mondays in case he has any questions that he'd like to discuss in person. That rarely happens, but I want to be available just in case. Plus, last week he asked about the intern program and he may want an update.

Amanda arrives right on time. "Good morning," she says cheerfully, taking her bag off her shoulder and putting her Starbucks down on the corner of my desk.

I'm in the middle of an idea I want to get down before I lose it. "Have a seat," I say gesturing to the side chair in my cubicle, "just give me one more sec." *Tap, tap, tap….* "Okay," I swivel my chair to face her. "So, tell me how your research is going for 'Philly's Top 10.'"

"I did a lot of online research and talked to a bunch of people. I've been compiling a list of places that meet the criteria I've developed to qualify as a college hot spot, but my in-person site visits were cut short because someone spiked my roommate's drink Friday night, and we had to take her home in a hurry."

"Oh my God. Is she okay?" I ask, startled by this unexpected turn in her report.

"Yes, but it was pretty scary. She was really out of it. She doesn't remember most of the evening. I'm just glad my other roommate and I were with her. God knows what would've happened if she were by herself."

"Wow. My younger sister Nikki is a student at Drexel. I'll have to tell her to be careful. Is this kind of thing common?" I ask while Amanda is mid-sip in her coffee.

She swallows and fans her mouth before answering. "I've heard of it happening at frat parties, but this is the first time I've experienced it up close and personal."

A thought strikes me, "Ya know what, I have an idea... add this to your research. When you're talking to students on different campuses ask if drink spiking is a prolific problem or just random incidents here and there. If we find out this is a serious issue, we can pitch the idea of a more hard-hitting story to Drew Davis and start investigating it. I've been looking for something outside of 'Philly's Top 10.'" I think about the possibilities for a moment and continue with a satisfied nod, "I'm sorry this happened to your friend, but we may have stumbled onto a story that could help raise awareness and protect other girls from the same thing happening to them. Let me just text my sister and see if she'll help out with your research."

I have a new intern who's researching college hot spots and drink spiking for me. Is it ok if I give her your number for input?

Sure. What's her name?

Amanda. She's a student at Penn. Btw, her friend got roofied last weekend at a bar. Is that a problem you hear much about?

Unfortunately, yes. I never leave a drink unattended, and I never let someone hand me a drink unless I see the bartender make it. I've heard about this happening more often recently. Frickin' scary.

OMG. Srsly be careful.

You'd know these things if you got out more often.

"Okay she's on board. Here, I'll send you her contact info."

"Two projects wrapped up in one, this is exciting!" Amanda wiggles forward a little in her seat. "I'm looking forward to talking to your sister. Sounds like she has quite a bit of experience collaborating with you on your column."

"Believe me, she'll be happy to give you her opinions – she's got a lot of them!" I say sarcastically. "But in all honesty, she'll be thrilled you're taking this on. She's not getting credits or paid when she helps me, and she already has two jobs in addition to classes."

"Well, I'm your girl then," Amanda says seeming pleased, then switches gears. "Who's Drew Davis?"

"He's the Senior Editor who approves my columns."

"The well-dressed hot guy down the hall?"

"That's the one," I nod.

Speak of the Devil - Drew

Ding. It was like clockwork. Eight o'clock every Monday morning Lauren's draft column and pipeline ideas appeared in Drew's inbox. He rarely had any comments because she was very clever and seemed to have her finger on the pulse of the city. *The Inquirer's* readers loved 'Philly's Top 10' so who was he to question it, but sometimes he'd come up with questions just to call her into his office. She was a curiosity to him. She was smart, stunningly beautiful, and must have an active city life to be able to write her column with such authority, but instead of the confidence he'd expect from her, she seemed shy around him. He was her boss after all, so he thought she'd work a little bit to impress him, but if anything, it seemed like she tried to avoid him.

Last week he called her into his office to ask how it went with the new intern, (like he cared). The sight of her in his doorway almost took his breath away -- tall and slender with long brown hair, wide eyes, full lips, and olive skin. "Come in," he said and motioned to the guest chair in his office. "Have a seat."

She was wearing a cobalt blue top that made her eyes look like the Caribbean Sea. He noticed that her eyes change color depending on what she's wearing. Sometimes they're blue, sometimes they are green and sometimes they're a grayish color.

She sat without saying a word. He asked her how it went with the new intern that morning and was so hypnotized by her presence that he didn't hear her answer. When she stopped talking, he couldn't think of a follow up comment that would make sense, so he said, "Okay then. Let me know if anything changes." She nodded, got up and left without saying another word. *Dumb ass,* he thought and got back to her email:

"Top 10 Decorating Ideas for Small Spaces"

... again, clever. Most people live in small apartments in the city, so this was actually useful information. He skipped ahead to her pipeline ideas as he really wasn't interested in decorating tips and was confident she'd make solid recommendations.

December Pipeline:

- Top 10 Things to Avoid at the Office Holiday Party

- Top 10 Holiday Recipes

- Top 10 White Elephant Gifts

- Top 10 Things to do on New Year's Eve

Later that Day

Lauren

It's been a long day, and once again, I missed my morning run. My gym bag is still under my desk from earlier in the week. Knowing I'll lose all motivation once I get home – and with the daylight already fading – I decide to run from here. Grabbing my bag, I quickly head to the Ladies' room to change. After stuffing my office clothes into the duffle, I push the door open in a rush and walk directly into Drew Davis.

"Oh my gosh. I'm sorry," I blunder, my face flushing as I regain my balance. "I'm such a klutz."

"No worries, you're fine," he says with a reassuring smile. "Going to the gym?" he asks noticing my attire.

"No." I shake my head, still feeling a little embarrassed and shove my ratty gym bag behind my back – it certainly doesn't scream professional. "I'm actually just going out for a run."

His smile fades. "By yourself?" he asks with surprise.

"Yup," I reply, regaining my composure.

I start to turn and walk away, but then his hand is on my arm, gentle but firm. "A beautiful young woman jogging through the city by herself, in the dark?" His voice is friendly but there's a note of apprehension underneath. "Doesn't sound like the best idea."

I glance down at his hand on my arm, a little surprised by the sudden contact, but shake it off. "Oh, I'm fine," I say with a small laugh. "I run all the time by myself."

He looks at me for a moment, clearly not appeased, then seems to solve the problem in his head. "Well, I have workout clothes in my office," he says. "How about I change and go with you? Just to be safe?"

I blink at him, caught off guard. The last thing I want to do is go jogging with the man. I'm uncomfortable around him when I'm at my most professional; I can't imagine working out with him. Think, Lauren, think!

I stall, trying to come up with a graceful way to decline without making it awkward or rude. "Well…" I drag it out, trying to buy a little time. "I usually only do about three miles. That's probably not enough for you. I'm sure you've got a much more challenging workout in mind, right?" I give him a sheepish smile, hoping he'll let it go.

But no, he doesn't seem to mind that idea at all. "I haven't been keeping up with my cardio lately," he admits with a shrug and half-smile. "Three miles sounds perfect. Just give me a minute to change."

Before I can protest, he turns and strides back toward his office, leaving me standing there, frozen like the proverbial deer in the headlights, trying to figure out what just happened.

Oh Lord. Running with Drew Davis?? What if he wants to talk while we're jogging? I can't talk and run; I'll hyperventilate. What if I can't keep up with his pace? What if I trip? Wait, did he just call me beautiful?

I bring my bag back to my cubicle, tuck it out of sight under my desk and wait for him in the hall. He returns a few minutes later wearing workout gear. I've never seen him in anything but perfectly tailored suits and designer shoes. He hasn't put on his coat yet and his sleeves are rolled up revealing a tattooed right forearm. Well, that's unexpected and kinda hot. Maybe Mr. buttoned up has a rebellious playful side.

"Ready?" he asks, pulling a puffer jacket over his shoulders.

I let out a long, exaggerated sigh as I press the button for the elevator, leaning against the wall. "As ready as I'll ever be."

He looks over at me, his eyes scanning my expression, trying to gauge whether I'm just being sarcastic or genuinely apprehensive. "So, how often do you run?" he asks, shifting the moment.

I didn't mean to come off wrong or make him uncomfortable. This is all just so unexpected. "Three or four times a week. I usually go in the morning before work, to get the day started right," I say hoping to end on the positive.

He nods, seeming to approve. "Good. I don't like the idea of you running alone at night."

I glance at him, surprised by the intensity of his concern. "It's fine. I've been doing it for years. It's all good."

The elevator dings and the doors slide open. I catch a glimpse of his expression – half concern, half determination – and wonder if he's going to keep pushing this. I also can't get over how different he looks wearing casual clothes and have to force myself not to stare. Of course, there are mirrors in the elevator, so I don't know where to divert my eyes and choose the floor. He has a whole new, less intimidating vibe. It's kind of sexy. Maybe I'll get through this without making a fool of myself after all. The elevator reaches the lobby, and we leave the building walking toward the Schuylkill River Trail.

"Are you planning on attending the holiday party Friday night?" His eyes look hopeful as he asks the question. "I noticed 'Office Holiday Parties' in your pipeline for 'Philly's Top 10.' Might be the perfect spot to get some content. You know how hard the open bar gets hit every year – someone's bound to make a faux pas or two," he adds with a laugh.

I nod. "Yes, I was thinking the same thing. I'll be both a guest and an observer, doing my best not to be the one to make a spectacle of myself."

"I can't imagine that happening," he says, his expression puzzled but intrigued.

"Actually, I was thinking of inviting my new intern, Amanda. Would that be okay?" I ask and then am suddenly concerned I might be over-stepping.

"Of course," he replies without hesitation. "That's a great idea. It'll be a good way for her to meet more people around the office. I noticed she got assigned to you late in the term. Do you have her next semester, too?"

"Yes," I say, nodding. "I wasn't too impressed with the few resumes I got earlier in the semester, but hers really caught my eye. She's got tons of energy and a good attitude. I think she'll be a good fit. We'll see how she handles the holiday party chaos."

When we reach the trail, I glance at my watch, "Fifteen minutes out and fifteen minutes back?"

"Sounds good," he says, already jogging in place. I set my watch to chime in fifteen and we start jogging along the path – sure enough he keeps talking. He's not just talking; he's asking questions that require answers. I keep my responses brief and am fine for the first mile or so, but I know I won't be able to regulate my breathing properly if this keeps up. Just then, like a miracle, I hear him say, "Careful, your shoe's untied."

Thank you there is a God. This gives me the perfect excuse to stop, catch my breath and re-tie my laces. "Thanks, it would be just like me to trip and fall." He continues to jog in place until I'm finished. I stand, inhale deeply, and turn to him, "Shall we?"

A few minutes later, my watch chimes, and we turn to head back. I'm relieved that the second half of the run is quiet – no forced conversation. As we approach our starting point, Drew exhales deeply and says, "Whoa, that felt great." I nod in agreement, trying not to show how much I'm struggling, and slow my pace to a walk. "We kept a good pace," he adds, glancing over at me with a grin. "I'm happy to run with you anytime."

I roll my eyes internally thinking about how badly I needed the shoelace incident, but nod again before stopping and bending over to catch my breath. "Ready to head back to the office?" I pant, "my stuff's still there."

"Sure." He's barely winded, his voice smooth as ever. "How are you getting home after that?"

"I'll just walk. It's only a few blocks."

He looks at me like I just cussed him out or something. "Don't be ridiculous Lauren. Do I have to remind you that being out alone at night is how this whole thing started," he says with weird protectiveness. "I have a car in the garage. I'll drive you."

I can't help but chuckle to myself at his insistence. I mean, how does he think I get home every other night? We make forced small talk on the walk back to the office. I'm relieved when we finally reach the entrance.

He opens the door for me and says, "I don't have anything that can't stay in my office until tomorrow, so I'll get the car and meet you out front."

I nod and head upstairs thankful for a few minutes of solitude to gather my thoughts. After grabbing my things, I catch a glimpse of myself in the elevator mirror. I tighten my ponytail, add some lip gloss, and sigh. I didn't expect any of this today…

When I reach the lobby Drew is parked out front in a Range Rover. Of course. As we start the drive he casually says, "So, tell me a little bit about yourself. We only ever talk about your column."

I look over at him, surprised. Suddenly I feel like I'm in a job interview I haven't prepared for. "Well," I pause, pulling my thoughts together. "I love writing 'Philly's Top 10.' It gives me a chance to dive into a lot of different topics, but at some point, I'd like to try my hand at something a little more... hard-hitting."

"You're still talking about work," he says with a gentle smile. "I want to know about you – who is Lauren Taylor, when she's not writing about Philly's best brunch spots?"

Crap. There goes my chance to pitch him on the story idea Amanda and I want to explore. Should I just jump right in by blurting out all my personal struggles? Well gee, my mom passed away in a freak accident, my dad is in a facility with early onset Alzheimer's, and my sister and I are barely keeping it together – so, yeah, can I have a raise?

"Not much to tell," I shrug, "typical millennial gal trying to navigate my post graduate years."

Now that it's just the two of us in the car together without the run to distract me, I'm feeling flustered again. He looks over at me and notices that my leg is shaking. "Are you cold?" he asks.

"Yes, a little," I lie hoping to explain away my nervous energy.

"The heat takes a minute," he says, turning it up. I cross my legs to keep them still. He waits a few moments and asks, "Better?"

"Yes. Thank you. I'm just a few blocks up, anyway." I try to relax knowing this will all be over in a minute and then get a random whiff of myself – sweaty from the run, ugh. Could this possibly be any more weird or uncomfortable? I slide a little closer to the car door like that's going to make a difference.

He seems oblivious to my self-consciousness, turns on the radio and casually asks, "What kind of music do you like?"

I think about it for a minute before answering. "A little bit of everything, I guess. Zac Brown, Billie Eilish, Bruce Springsteen – kind of a Jersey girl at heart, so I'm all about The Boss. This is me right up there," I say pointing to the building ahead.

He glances over with a smile. "Thanks for the exercise, Lauren. I really enjoyed it. See you tomorrow."

I open the door and hop out before turning back to face him. "Yeah, thanks for the ride." I try to sound casual and hope he can't detect my relief at this unexpected adventure being over. As the Range Rover pulls away, I shake my head and sigh... What a way to shake up a Monday.

Thursday, Week 2

Falling Hard

Chris and John stepped out of the house together, heading toward their ten-thirty Finance class. The crisp air nipped at their faces, but neither of them seemed to mind. John broke the silence first. "You wanna grab lunch after class today?" he asked, shoving his hands deep into his jacket pockets. "I didn't have time for breakfast, and I'm already starving."

Chris threw his backpack over his right shoulder. "I'm actually planning on dropping in on Nikki at Mocha Loco after class if you want to join me."

"Pfff," John laughed. "Oh, right, so I can sit there and watch you two fawn all over each other? Yeah, I'm good. Hard pass."

Chris looked at him with a challenging glare, knowing exactly where this was headed. "Shut up, it's not that bad."

"Oh, it's *that* bad, trust me." John's words came too easily, as if he'd just been waiting for the chance to say them. "Haven't you seen or spoken to her every single day since your first date?"

Chris started to defend himself, "Well yeah, but…"

John cut him off, "But what Shepp? Come on, you're falling hard. I've never seen you like this before." He punched him lightly in the arm. "Not that there's anything wrong with it, but seriously, just own it. You're totally whipped."

Chris groaned a little, rubbing his face with one hand. "It's not like that. I just... I just like her, is all." He shook his head knowing the rebuttal was weak and John was right.

John laughed and slapped him on the back. "Yeah, man, I get it. No shame."

They pushed their way through the crowded corridor and found seats in the back of the auditorium. Professor Crane had already started her lecture on improving forecast accuracy, but Chris didn't even hear her. He just sat there with his chin in his hand, his mind wondering.

John opened his tablet, looked at Chris and shook his head. Chris knew he should be taking notes, but he was too distracted with thoughts of Nikki to concentrate.

"I take it, you'll need my notes later," John said after class.

"Yeah, sorry man. I'm off my scholarly game today."

"You're off your game alright," John said with a knowing look. "Catch you later lover boy."

# # #

Nikki was busy with a table when Chris walked in. Her face lit up when she saw him in the doorway and his stomach flipped in response. *Damn this girl really gets to me.*

"Well, hello there," she said once she'd finished with her customer. "Dining with us today?"

"Yes, ma'am, but only if I can sit in your section."

"That can be arranged. Right this way." She spun around and reached back to grab his hand. She was being subtle – she was at work after all – but he just wanted to pull her into him and kiss her. She led him to a table and dropped his hand gesturing for him to sit. "Well, this is a pleasant surprise," she said with a wide smile that made him want to kiss her even more.

He didn't sit; he turned toward her instead and lifted her chin to look her in the eyes. "I'm going to have to start eating all my meals here if it's the only way I can see you. Your schedule's been really busy this week."

Nikki looked at him with a tired but affectionate expression. "My schedule is busy every week," she sighed and leaned against the table for support.

Chris wasn't easily deterred. "Well, what's it look like over the weekend? Can I take you out Saturday night?"

Nikki hesitated, biting her lip while she thought it over. "I'd like that, but honestly, I'd rather stay in. I have a lot of work to get done this weekend and I'm already exhausted."

"Miss, may we have more coffee please?" someone called from a nearby table. "Coming," she put a menu down on the table for Chris and hustled toward the coffee maker. Chris sat and watched her hurry around the room chatting with customers and making sure everyone's needs were met (except his of course) before she returned to take his order. "Sorry about that, but I know you're a bad tipper, so I have to get to my other customers first," she said with a smirk knowing she just scored a point in their playful flirtation.

"Very funny," he smiled back, appreciating her wit. "If you want to stay in on Saturday, how about I cook for you? My specialty is chicken piccata. I can do my best to find something that's both edible and vanilla for dessert and you can pick a Rom-Com."

"That sounds like heaven." She tucked a rouge strand of hair behind her ear and thought about it further. "You'll really let me pick a Rom-Com?" she asked with skeptical enthusiasm, after all their last shared viewing experience was a football game.

"Yup." Chris wouldn't have cared if she picked a documentary on the history of basket weaving if it meant she'd come to his house again on Saturday.

"Even if it's holiday themed and really cheesy?" she pushed.

"If it's the way to your heart then absolutely," Chris conceded, willingly letting her win.

"May we have our check please?" came from another table. She mouthed "sorry" and looked at him with apologetic eyes before scurrying away again. He got what he came in for, so he grabbed a napkin and wrote:

I cant be known as a bad tipper

He threw twenty bucks on top of it before heading out. The bell above the door rang as it opened, and Nikki turned to see him leaving. She gave him a puzzled look. Chris held his pinky and thumb to the side of his face indicating that he'd call her later, winked and kept going.

Tony was in the living room watching TV when Chris got home. His phone was on the coffee table so when another one buzzed, Chris knew it was the burner. Tony grabbed it out of his pocket, looked at the screen and started mad texting from his personal phone.

"Look Tony, I'm having Nikki over for dinner Saturday night and can't have any deals going down again while she's here. Why don't you run that shit out of the frat house?" he suggested. "People are always coming and going from there anyway – it'll be less suspicious."

"That's actually a good idea," Tony said looking up from his phone. "Rocco wants to meet next week and thanks to you assholes I've only moved half the pack. I can hit up more people at once at Delta." He paused and switched gears. "And another date with Nikki? Bro, you've got it bad."

Friday Morning, Week 2

The Crush

It was four days since Drew and Lauren ran together and he already knew it was a bad idea. He was thinking about her more than usual now and finding himself coming up with ways to stage chance encounters with her. He'd been dropping into the breakroom even though he has a mini-fridge and a coffee maker in his office and taking unnecessary trips to the copier. He ran into her in the breakroom yesterday and had to pretend he was looking for a spoon. *Pathetic.* Worse yet, he was so busy pretending to be in search of imaginary cutlery that he couldn't come up with anything to say to her and blew the whole encounter anyway.

I'm a grown ass 35-year-old man and I'm acting like a schoolboy with a crush. But he was so intrigued by her. They had walked to and from the River Trail on Monday, ran for a half hour together and then he drove her home, and still she said very little to him. She seemed shy around him, but he saw her interacting easily with other people in the office. He couldn't figure her out. *And why does she keep inferring that she's clumsy when she walks through the office like a supermodel on the runway? I don't know, maybe it's me.* He vowed to stop pursuing chance encounters with her, but there was the small issue of the gift he left on her desk this morning. *Crap!*

His phone rang, interrupting his thoughts. It was his mom, so he got up and closed his office door before answering. "Hey, Mom, everything okay?" he asked with some concern.

"Does there have to be a crisis for a mother to call her son?" He heard the annoyance in her voice instantly.

He sighed, leaning against his desk. "No, of course not. You usually don't call me at work is all."

"I have a doctor's appointment in the city on Tuesday." Her tone had already softened and he could tell she was moving on. "I was hoping we could meet for lunch afterward."

"That sounds nice. Is Dad driving you in?"

"No." She sounded dismissive, almost amused. "He's away next week for work. Scheduled a bunch of meetings down south to get his fill of the warm weather. I swear, he's getting soft." Her sarcasm was clear, and he could almost picture her shaking her head.

He chuckled lightly, knowing his dad well. "He's always hated the cold. You know that." He hesitated, then added more seriously, "I really wish you'd go with him more often. I hate the thought of you being home alone so much. Have you ever considered getting a dog?"

There was a brief pause on the other end, and then his mother scoffed, clearly amused. "Don't be ridiculous!" she replied, a laugh just about ready to break free. "I don't have time for a dog. Does The Capital Grille at one o'clock on Tuesday work?"

"Sure, that works," Drew conceded, knowing that pursuing the dog conversation was pointless. "See you then. Love you, Mom."

Drew spent the rest of the day hiding in his office so he wouldn't be randomly wandering the halls hoping to bump into Lauren. Besides, he knew he'd see her later at the office party, so there was that.

Lauren

I'm not about to spend the whole day at work in my party clothes, so I'll just head home, change, and go back out. I wish I had a red dress to wear — something bold and festive — but then again, I *do* have those killer red leather over-the-knee boots Nikki picked out for me. I've been looking for any excuse to wear them, and tonight's definitely it. They'll look great with my favorite little black dress and some festive jewelry. Now, the only question left is what to wear to the office today?

Once I'm dressed for work, I sift through the basket on my kitchen counter — the one where I throw all my mail and receipts for expense reports. I'm supposed to turn those in at the end of every month, and I'm already behind for November, so I need to get them done today.

As I'm sorting through the mail, I find the Save-the-Date for Tina and Todd's wedding. I hang it on the fridge and sigh. Another wedding extravaganza I can barely afford. It's never just a wedding anymore — there's the engagement party, bridal shower, an overnight bachelorette trip, and then the three-day wedding itself. Friday's the Welcome Reception, Saturday's the wedding and reception, and Sunday's the brunch. It'll be lovely, sure, but it'll also mean at least three gifts, six different outfits, and a spa overnight. Thank God it's not a destination wedding, or I wouldn't even be able to go.

I toss the receipts into my bag and head out the door. When I get to my desk, I'm surprised by a gift bag with a card. Did I miss the Secret Santa? I set my things down and open the card:

Lauren
To keep you safe when I'm not
with you
Drew

Inside the bag is a small spray bottle of mace attached to a keychain with an alarm button. Wow! That's both thoughtful and surprising. And a little weird in an overprotective dad sort of way. I don't really know how to react. I look around but there's no one there to consult. Well, thanking him would be the obvious start. I walk toward his office but see his door is shut. Phew, that buys me some time to get my response together. I'm sure I'll see him at the office party later and can thank him then.

The rest of the day flies by as I tackle my expense reports and make lists to keep myself organized for next week. I even finish early enough to squeeze in a quick manicure before going home to change.

Dressed in my party clothes I start the walk back to the office and am beginning to get in the holiday spirit. The city is lit up with Christmas lights, the store fronts are boasting their holiday window displays, and it seems like the hustle and bustle of foot traffic is beginning to pick up everywhere.

Amanda is waiting for me in the lobby when I arrive. She looks adorable in a red knit sweater dress that compliments her hair beautifully, oversized-black-rimmed glasses, and chunky patent leather loafers with sheer black ruffle socks.

"Hey, you look great!" I say giving her a hug.

"So do you," she replies warmly. "So, tell me, what can I expect at this party?"

"The usual," I chuckle. "Someone will drink too much and make a fool of themselves. There'll be some kind of entertainment or activity. If it's an activity, all the women will be scrambling to pair up with Mr. Drew-tiful, and..." The elevator dings, interrupting me.

"I assume 'Mr. Drew-tiful' is Drew Davis?" Amanda asks with a knowing grin.

"You assume correctly." I smirk. "By the way, one of my ideas for 'Philly's Top 10' in December is 'What Not to Do at the Office Holiday Party,' so be on the lookout. We might come up with all ten tonight."

The elevator reaches the top floor, and we step into the banquet room. The view of the city is stunning, and the space is decked out for the holidays with lights draped from the ceiling and pine trees decorated by children from various local grade schools scattered around the room. There's a gorgeous buffet on one side, bars at each end, and a small stage up front.

"Hey, Lauren, doesn't everything look great?" I hear as we step into the room.

I nod, "It really does. Barb, Amy, this is my new intern, Amanda." I turn toward Amanda, then introduce the others properly. "Barb and Amy work in the Sales Department. Everyone in Sales is super nice and, well... they've got the outgoing personalities you'd expect from people in sales," I add with a smile.

"Nice to meet you," Amy says, giving Amanda the once-over. "Great dress!"

"Thanks. Nice to meet both of you, too," Amanda replies, reaching out to shake both of their hands.

"So, have you heard what the entertainment is going to be this year?" Barb asks.

"No idea," I admit with a shrug. "But the magician was pretty cool last year."

A waitress approaches with a tray of assorted canapes in one hand and cocktail napkins in the other. "May I interest you ladies in an hors d'oeuvre?" she asks politely. Amy and Amanda each select one, while Barb takes a moment to consider the tray before making her choice. I avoid anything with crab or smoked salmon and take a cucumber and chive cream cheese on rye toast. What foods to avoid at the office party will also make my list.

"Oh my God," Barb says, grabbing Amy's arm dramatically, "here comes Mr. Drew-tiful. Act natural." She immediately starts acting anything but natural, faking a laugh and flipping her hair. Amanda gives me a look that clearly says, *really?* I shrug in response, silently agreeing.

Drew approaches, looking festive in a tartan plaid Christmas blazer, black turtleneck, and slacks, topped off with a Santa hat. He's carrying a clipboard. "Evening, ladies," he says cheerfully. "I've somehow been roped into signing people up for karaoke. Anyone interested?"

"Sure!" Barb blurts out before anyone else can answer. "May I see the list?" she asks, reaching for the clipboard and making her best attempt at sultry eyes and a pouty smile.

"I'll take a look too," Amy interjects enthusiastically and joins Barb in flipping through the pages, debating which song to choose.

While they're distracted, I turn to Drew. "This is my new intern, Amanda. I think you've seen each other around the office, but I'm not sure you've been properly introduced."

Amanda extends her hand. "Nice to meet you."

"You too," Drew replies, shaking it. "How's Lauren treating you so far?"

For some reason, his question makes me feel awkward, and I try to divert the conversation before Amanda can answer. "Drew, I was looking for you earlier. I wanted to thank you for the gift. It was really thoughtful." At this, Barb and Amy freeze, dropping the pen on the floor and look up at me with wide astonished eyes.

"Not at all," Drew says, brushing it off. "I just want to make sure you're safe if I'm not around to go with you." He shifts gears with ease. "So, are you going to give the karaoke a shot?" he asks with a playful grin.

"Oh, God no," I respond quickly, horrified at the idea. "I could never," I continue, bending down to pick up the pen Amy and Barb dropped and handing it back to them with a smile.

"Oh, come on, Lauren," Amanda coaxes. "We can do it together! It'll be fun. Are you guys done with the song list?" she asks Amy and Barb.

"One sec," Amy replies. "We just need to sign our names." Her hand scribbles across the song sheet before she hands the clipboard to Amanda.

I bite my lower lip and shake my head. "I don't know Amanda," I say hesitantly.

"We'll pick an easy one," she promises, flipping through the pages of the list and holding it up so I can see. As she moves through the booklet, I notice Barb has picked "Lady Marmalade" from Moulin Rouge and Amy has gone for "Before He Cheats" by Carrie Underwood. Typical.

"Here," Amanda says, pointing to a song. "How about "Sweet Caroline" by Neil Diamond? That's always a crowd-pleaser."

"Why do I feel like I'm being bullied?" I ask, hoping for a way out of this.

"Because you are," Amanda laughs, clearly enjoying my discomfort.

Drew jumps on the band wagon next. "It's important that our interns have positive experiences, Lauren," he says with grin that looks boyish under his Santa hat. "It's all about the team building, right?"

Great, now my intern and my boss are conspiring against me.

"You can lip-sync if you want," Amanda says pushing my arm with a smile – the definition of a nudge, "just come up with me. It'll be hysterical."

And Drew backs her up with, "We wouldn't want Amanda to give our mentor program a poor review with her university, would we?"

I feel flushed by the added pressure from Drew and hope it's not showing on my face. "Okay, okay," I concede, "but I'm already sorry I invited you tonight, Amanda." She signs our names next to *"Sweet Caroline"* with exaggerated strokes and a satisfied poke of the pen on the clipboard before handing it back to Drew.

"Well now that that's settled, can I get you ladies some drinks?" he asks the four of us.

We're each giving our drink orders when creepy Marv from Accounting passes by and sees an opportunity to worm his way into the conversation. "I'll help you get those Drew."

Drew turns toward Marv with zero recognition on his face. "Oh, um thanks. I'll need an extra hand."

Once they leave for the bar, Barb grabs my arm. "Dish now!" she demands. "A gift? If I can't go with you? What the what? Spill it!"

"It was nothing," I say dismissively. "He just caught me going for a jog the other night after work and didn't want me to go by myself in the dark, so he came with me." I gently release my arm from Barb's grasp.

"And then what?" Amy asks eager for more gossip.

"And then nothing," I insist. "It was actually mortifying. At one point I thought I was going to vomit trying to catch my breath. We finished the run, and he drove me home."

"He drove you home?" Barb says with shock in her voice. "You were in his car alone with him?"

Before I can answer Amy chimes in with the next question, wanting as many details as possible before the guys get back with the drinks. "So, what was the gift?"

"It was mace for my keychain. Very practical, not romantic at all so don't even go there."

Just then, Drew and Marv return with the drinks. I let out a sigh of relief. For once I'm happy to see him. I know his presence will stop the onslaught of questions. "Who has the Cosmos?" Marv asks hoping whoever answers will open an opportunity for further conversation. Amanda and I both asked for chardonnay which Drew is holding.

"Those are for these two," I answer, pointing at Barb and Amy. Drew hands the glasses of wine to Amanda and me. "Thank you so much," I say making a slight curtsey, "now if you'll excuse us, I'd like to introduce Amanda to a few more people before the humiliation of karaoke begins."

"Nice meeting all of you," Amanda says, and we make a quick getaway leaving Amy and Barb with Drew and Marv.

Once we're out of ear shot, Amanda grabs my arm and pulls me a little closer. "First observation for your Top 10 Office Party No No's: don't wear a 'boobie shirt,' especially one that's animal print."

"Yeah, but I'm sure Marv appreciated it!" We both laugh and continue around the room.

The Office Party (Take II)

Drew arrived at the holiday party early so he could be seen, make the rounds and slip out unnoticed. He hated these things. Why couldn't they have a holiday lunch during business hours instead of a Friday night party during their free time? With the money corporate spends on this shindig he was sure everyone would rather get a holiday bonus than be forced to spend more time with co-workers. He thought about suggesting it at the next Senior Team meeting but knew it would make him look like he wasn't a team player.

Audrey, the Office Manager in charge of the party, was running around frantically checking on things like a bride on her wedding day, so he asked her if he could help. She rattled off ten things that needed to be done and Drew volunteered to be in charge of signing people up for karaoke. That would be the perfect way to mingle through the party and be seen before making an early exit. Plus, it would give him an excuse to talk to Lauren. Audrey handed him a clipboard with the song list and turned to bark at a server who was apparently putting the wrong size forks on the buffet table.

Drew began working his way through the party with the song list and was surprised by how many people actually wanted to make spectacles of themselves in front of their colleagues. As he was signing people up, he noticed Lauren across the room with her intern and two women from the Sales Department. She looked breathtaking. Her long dark hair was cascading over her shoulders, and she was wearing bright red lipstick that matched the sexiest pair of boots he'd ever seen.

Well, here goes... he thought as he approached the foursome who were laughing about something. "Evening ladies. I've somehow been roped into signing people up for karaoke. Anyone interested?"

The women from the Sales Department eagerly jumped in while Lauren introduced him to her intern, Amanda. The women looking through the song list dropped the pen they were using, and Lauren bent down to pick it up for them. Drew literally had to divert his eyes from watching her bend over. *Jesus, I'm the poster boy for sexual harassment 101. Get a grip!*

Amanda was coaxing Lauren into karaoke and suddenly the evening was looking up. Drew jumped on Amanda's team encouraging Lauren to do it and eventually she reluctantly agreed. Feeling a little guilty about pushing her into it, he asked if he could get them drinks. They gave him their orders and he left for the bar flanked by some guy from Accounting. Much to Drew's chagrin, when they returned with the drinks, Lauren thanked him and excused herself and Amanda, leaving him with the women from the Sales Department and the guy from Accounting.

Drew made small talk with them for a bit and a mental note of their names before getting back to working the room. In each conversation he had, he kept one eye on Lauren. She was mingling and interacting effortlessly with everyone around her. *Why is she so reserved around me?* he wondered. Lauren was helping Amanda navigate the room and seemed to be a little protective of her, which was sweet because as far as he could tell Amanda could hold her own.

The drinks continued to flow, and people seemed sufficiently loosened up enough to start the karaoke. Audrey must have sensed the same thing and approached the stage. She picked up the microphone and gave it the obligatory three 'is this thing on' taps. "May I have your attention please?" she asked. "It's time to begin the karaoke. First up is Jay Blaken with "Tennessee Whiskey" by Chris Stapleton. Give it up for Jay everyone...."

Jay walked up to the stage while his buddies chanted, "Jay! Jay! Jay! Jay!" Audrey started the music; Jay cleared his throat and began.

He wasn't doing a half bad job, but he'd clearly picked the wrong song. Instead of Chris Stapleton's raspy tone that moves effortlessly from country to rock to soul, Jay's voice seemed better suited for a Justin Bieber song. Jay's friends sang along to the chorus, and he seemed to be pleased with his performance. When he finished everyone applauded, he bowed and returned to his friends who slapped him on the back and handed him another drink.

"Thank you, Jay," Audrey said, "next up is Barb Livingston with "Lady Marmalade" from **Moulin Rouge.**"

Barb stepped up to the stage, stumbled a little on the last step and adjusted her tightly fitting top before beginning to deliver the most inappropriately raunchy version of the song one could imagine. No one was paying any attention to her singing because all eyes were on her practically having oral sex with the microphone and slinking across the stage. Drew glanced over at Lauren who looked genuinely embarrassed for her and knew that karaoke would make her list of Top 10 Don'ts for the Holiday Office Party.

"Uh, thank you Barb for that very well *spirited* performance," Audrey said when Barb was finally finished. "Now we have Lauren Taylor and Amanda Shields with *"Sweet Caroline"* by Neil Diamond.   Ladies..."

Amanda hopped a little, clapped her hands and turned toward Lauren who was frozen in place. "Come on," she said grabbing Lauren's hand and pulling her toward the stage. Lauren reluctantly followed her up toward the riser. Amanda picked up a microphone as the music began and gave Lauren an encouraging thumbs-up. She sang the first verse by herself while Lauren silently swayed to the music. Just before the next verse, Amanda pointed the microphone at Lauren, cueing her to join in. Lauren still looked hesitant, and Drew could not believe this statuesque beauty was looking to this college kid for support. She tentatively picked up the microphone, the uncertainty on her face seeping through the redness on her cheeks.

Amanda reached out for Lauren's hand as she sang. This seemed to loosen her up to the point that she joined in. After a few lines, they caught a rhythm, and both started pointing their microphones at the audience who responded, "bah, bah, bah." They sang the next line, and the crowd shouted, "So good! So good! So good!"

Lauren was finally getting into it and put her arm around Amanda. They swayed in unison as they sang, pointing their microphones at the audience at the appropriate points in the chorus. This continued until the end of the song when Lauren took Amanda's hand and raised both their arms over head before bowing dramatically. She was smiling ear to ear and made the 'drop the mic' motion before returning the microphone to its stand.

"That was awesome," Amanda giggled as they exited the stage. "I told you it would be fun."

"Okay, okay, I admit it wasn't as mortifying as I thought," Lauren replied, her tone light with relief. "But now I need another drink."

They both started walking toward the bar, and Drew took the opportunity to follow. "That was great, ladies," he said catching up to them.

"It's all in the song choice," Amanda responded cheerfully.

Lauren just smiled and turned to the bartender to get his attention. "Two chardonnays please." She twisted back toward Drew and asked, "What'll you have Drew?"

"Scotch on the rocks," he said to the bartender then shifted his focus back to the girls. "Well, you two make quite the duo."

Lauren's playful demeanor seemed to disappear. Her expression became more serious as she met Drew's eyes. "Actually, I was hoping to talk to you about an investigative piece this duo would like to explore."

"Great," he said with an easygoing way about him. "Let's talk about it Monday morning when we're back in the office. Tonight's not about business." He hoped the conversation would continue in a casual vein. And it did, just not with him.

"Okay, thank you. I look forward to discussing it."   Lauren turned away from Drew reaching for the glasses of wine on the bar and handing one to Amanda. "Let's go back and see if anyone out does us," she said, giving Amanda a playful nudge. They walked away leaving Drew standing there with a drink he didn't even want. He almost felt like sniffing his pits to see if he smelled. He had never repelled a woman like this before. In fact, he usually had no problem with the ladies. *What is it about her?*

He endured renditions of "Dancing Queen" by ABBA and "R.E.S.P.E.C.T" by Aretha Franklin before calling it quits. Feeling that he'd been sufficiently seen, he grabbed his coat and used the exit near the bathrooms to make it less obvious that he was leaving.

Saturday, Week 2

Cooking In

Mornin' sunshine. What time can u get here today?

At the café now and have to walk a dog afterwards. Really need to study before coming over so probably not until 6:30 or 7:00.

You can study here while I get dinner ready. Come over after ur done with your "client."

The house was trashed again so Chris had to straighten up before Nikki arrived, and he wondered how long it would be until she might pop in on them and discover they were slobs. The living room wasn't in such bad shape, but the kitchen was another story. His mother's advice echoed in his head... *"The key to a successful dinner party is to start the evening with an empty dishwasher and trash can."* While tonight wasn't exactly a dinner party, the advice still held up.

Once he was satisfied with the cleanup, Chris sent a text to the guys, reminding them not to make a mess again. He knew they'd give him shit about it, but didn't care. He headed out to Reading Terminal Market, confident that its famous variety of fresh produce, meats, and baked goods would have everything he needed, even something vanilla for dessert.

Don't get your apron strings in a twist. We'll try not to leave our underwear in the kitchen.

Does this mean I have to put on pants?

Ignoring them, Chris successfully completed his shopping mission and returned home. Fortunately, both guys were out, so he could start prepping for dinner in peace. Around four o'clock, a knock at the door interrupted him. Chris opened it to find Nikki standing on the front porch, a bottle of wine in one hand, a stack of books in the other, her computer bag slung over her right shoulder, and her purse over the left. "Well, hello, beautiful," he said, reaching out to take the books and wine from her. "Come on in."

"Thanks," Nikki said quietly as she hung her coat and bag in the entryway. Chris set her books and the wine down on the coffee table before turning to give her a warm hug. She welcomed his embrace but seemed to deflate in his arms, her shoulders sagging into him.

"Everything okay?" he asked, gently lifting her face to meet his gaze.

"I'm just exhausted," she sighed. "And I still have work to do. Ugh."

Chris offered a supportive grin, "Tell ya what – how 'bout I make you a cup of coffee, and you can get set up in here with your books."

"Thank you." Nikki's voice was soft with gratitude but also a quiet determination to push through. "If I can just get an hour or so of work done, I'll be in good shape." She plopped down on the couch, pulling out her laptop and started tapping away at the keys with determined speed.

"Black, right?" Chris called from the kitchen.

"You remembered." She smiled sweetly under droopy eyes as she took the Eagles mug he handed her.

"Okay," Chris returned her smile. "I'll finish getting things prepped for later and leave you to it. I picked up some soft pretzels today if you're hungry."

"I'd love one." Her eyes perked up a little. "Do you have any mustard?"

"Do I have any mustard?" Chris repeated feigning surprise. "Do you think you're dealing with an amateur?"

When he returned with the pretzel, a generous blob of spicey brown mustard on one side of the plate and bright yellow ballpark mustard on the other, Nikki was fast asleep on the couch. He hesitated for a moment, looking down at her fondly, before setting the plate down. He bent over and gently shook her shoulder. "Nikki," he whispered softly, "babe."

Her eyes snapped open, startled. "Oh my God," she muttered, rubbing her eyes in disbelief. "I can't believe I fell asleep! Maybe I should go home and come back later."

"Don't be silly," Chris said, reassuring her. "You're here now, and clearly too tired to study. Why don't you go upstairs and lay down in my room? I'll wake you in an hour, and you can get your work done then."

"Really?" she asked, considering the offer and pushing herself upright. "Are you sure?"

"Of course," he said, taking her hand. "Come on, I'll show you which room is mine." He led her upstairs, silently high fiving himself for having cleaned earlier.

With Nikki settled in his room, Chris returned to the kitchen to get back to work. The front door opened, and he braced himself for the verbal beating he'd get from whoever walked in next.

"What are you making?" Tony asked, sucking in a deep breath. "It smells like restaurant-quality grub in here."

"Chicken piccata, roasted asparagus with tomatoes and feta, and lemon garlic herb rice," Chris answered. "And before you start giving me crap, I'm cooking enough for you knuckleheads to have leftovers."

"Jesus, Shepp. If you weren't so into Nikki, I'd date you," he joked. "What time's she coming?"

"She's already here. She's upstairs sleeping."

Tony raised an eyebrow and gave Chris a suggestive stare. Chris was immediately annoyed – *did every conversation have to go this way?* "It's not like that," he said curtly. "She's just exhausted." He had more respect for Nikki than Tony was suggesting and didn't have enough respect for Tony to try to explain it further, so he shrugged it off.

"Whatever, dude. All I know is there's a hot chick upstairs in your bed, and you're down here playing Bobby Flay in the kitchen."

Having no interest in continuing the conversation, Chris changed the subject. "I'm gonna jump in the shower while she's asleep. Leave all this alone, and I'll finish up after."

He quietly opened the bedroom door and peeked in on Nikki. The sight of her in his bed made him absolutely crazy, and suddenly he really needed that shower, a cold one. He tiptoed to the closet, grabbed some clean clothes, and shut the door quietly behind him.

When he returned downstairs after his shower, Tony was gone. Chris didn't have it in him to wake Nikki just yet, so he put in his Air Pods and got back to work. He was happily bopping around the kitchen to the music when she appeared behind him. He spun around and jumped back startled. "Huh! I didn't know you were up. You surprised me," he said pulling out his ear buds.

Nikki looked mildly upset. "You said you'd wake me in an hour."

He pulled her toward him hoping to soften her mood. "It's only been a little over an hour, and I didn't have the heart to wake you. You looked so peaceful."

"Ewww, you were watching me sleep?" She slapped him on the chest. "Gross, I was probably drooling."

"If you were, I didn't notice, and your secret's safe with me," Chris assured her, crossing his heart with his fingers.

She was still somewhat annoyed but couldn't stay that way with him pouting for forgiveness. "Okay," a smile betrayed her, "I'm going to get started on my work so I can get it over with and help you with dinner."

"Don't worry about dinner. I can handle myself in the kitchen. It's kinda my thing. You just do what you need to do so we can open that bottle of wine you brought."

"Deal." She settled back down on the couch and worked diligently until the cold air from the front door made her shiver. She turned as Tony threw his coat on the hooks in the entryway, knocking her bag off in the process.

"Oh, sorry," he apologized. "I'll pick it up."

"No worries, you can just throw that stuff back in there. There's no rhyme or reason to it." He scooped up her things, shoved them back in her bag, and started upstairs.

"Hey," Chris called to him, "where's John been?"

"He went home this afternoon, but he'll be back tonight," Tony answered, continuing up the stairs.

"How's it going?" Chris hollered to Nikki from the kitchen.

"I need about twenty more minutes, and I'll be done," she answered, her voice perking up a bit.

"Okay, dinner will be just about ready when you finish. I think it's safe to open the wine now. I'll pour you a glass."

"Great. Thanks."

Chris was pouring the wine when Tony reappeared, grabbing a six-pack out of the fridge.

"You headed out?" Chris asked.

"Yeah, going to Delta for the party tonight and to help get things set up for the game tomorrow." Tony stole an asparagus sprig off the counter. "Catch you later. Have *fun...*" he said with a lewd expression and suggestive tone.

"See you, Tony," Nikki called after him as he passed through the living room; he flashed her the peace-out sign in return and left.

Nikki uncrossed her legs and shut her laptop when Chris handed her the glass of wine. "I'm sorry you're missing the Delta party," she said. "Did you want to go?"

"I've been to enough frat parties to last me a lifetime. There's no place I'd rather be than here with you," he said with a sincere, convincing smile.

"Awww," she cooed with genuine appreciation. "So how did you meet your roommates?"

"John and I grew up together. He's my day one, ride or die." Chris sat down next to her. "Tony's one of our frat brothers. We met him once we got here. He grew up in a tough neighborhood in the Bronx and can be a little rough around the edges, but he's also a lot of fun." He paused for a sip of wine and thought about Tony for second. "He was definitely the craziest guy in our pledge class. Not much intimidates him. Tony flipped the script pretty quickly on the older guys who tried to haze us. They never messed with us again after that."

"He sounds like he's got some stories to tell." Nikki tilted her head and looked at Chris like she was waiting for more.

"Yeah," he replied with a half-smile, not wanting to go there. "Probably a few you wouldn't want to hear."

She read Chris's cues and pivoted away from Tony but was still curious about Greek life — she'd never had an interest, or the time for it. She shook her head. "I never understood the whole hazing thing. Why would you subject yourself to abuse from people who are supposed to be your friends?"

Chris shrugged. "It's not that bad. It's just guy stuff, and our class is in charge now, so we run the show."

She gave him a skeptical look. "I don't know. It seems a little... excessive."

Chris chuckled and leaned back on the couch. "It's not for everyone, I guess. But it's part of the tradition. You get through it, and you come out the other side a little stronger."

Nikki nodded slowly, considering it. "I don't really want to 'get through it' for a friendship but I think it's nice that you and John have been friends for so long. My close friends are kind of spread out at different schools all over the country. I don't get back to my hometown much since my family doesn't live there anymore, so I don't have the opportunity to see them very often."

Chris's expression softened, "What about your friends here?"

She sighed, "I go out with my freshman dormmates now and again, but between classes and working two jobs, I don't have a lot of free time. My secret's revealed..." she gave a small, self-deprecating laugh, "...I'm kinda boring."

Chris looked at her surprised. "You're anything but boring, darlin'... How about your roommates?"

"I live alone."

Chris perked up at that news, a grin forming on his face. "Well, if I knew that, I would've offered to cook at your place."

Nikki shook her head and waved her hand in front of herself. "No. It's a studio so my bed is the centerpiece of my apartment which doesn't lend itself to dinner parties or third dates."

"Sounds perfect to me," Chris said, his grin growing into a full-on frisky smile.

Nikki didn't bite at Chris's flirtation. She put her laptop in her computer bag and shoved her books to the side. "Okay, that's it. I'm calling it quits. I can finish the rest of this tomorrow."

"Speaking of tomorrow, will you come with me to The Link? My fraternity has a big tailgate at the stadium for all the home games."

"I can't," Nikki sighed. "I promised my sister I'd visit our dad with her tomorrow."

"Oh, that's nice." Chris stood and walked toward the kitchen. "Where does he live?" he asked over his shoulder.

Nikki's posture sagged as she answered, "He's in an Alzheimer's care facility in West Chester."

Chris paused, glancing over at her. "I'm sorry to hear that. How long has he been there?"

"About two years now." There was a mix of sorrow and acceptance on her face. "He has good days and bad days. We never

really know what to expect when we visit. It's such a cruel disease...
He used to be a brilliant man."

"That must be tough," Chris said softly, pulling the chicken
out of the oven and placing it on the stove.

"It is," she admitted. "On his good days, I want him to live
forever, and on his bad days, I wish it was already over. It's hard to
have those thoughts about someone you love." She forced a small
smile. "But enough about my sob story. What can I do to help?"

Chris handed her a spoon. "You can stir the rice, and I'll get
a bowl for the asparagus."

Just then John walked in. "What's cooking?" he asked, "I'm
starving."

Chris knew where this was headed and tried to shut it
down. "Weren't you just home? Why didn't you eat there?"

"I just went home to put together an IKEA thing for my
mom. You know my dad is useless with that stuff. Anyway, they had
dinner plans, so there was nothing to eat. But she did make us
cookies," John said, placing a container on the counter. "Chocolate
chip for me, and peanut butter for you."

"Awww, that's sweet," Nikki said, feeling a pang of loss
neither of them could understand. She hadn't yet shared with Chris
that she'd lost her mother.

"Yeah, Shepp's mom is a great cook. That's where he learned
his culinary wizardry, but she doesn't bake. That's my mom's
department," John explained.

"Thank God," Chris added. "Now I won't have to eat that vanilla concoction I bought at the Terminal today." He smiled and gently whipped Nikki in the rear with the dish towel he was holding.

"More for me!" she declared triumphantly as John pulled out a plate and lined up behind her at the stove.

"Seriously?" Chris asked, giving John the hairy eyeball.

"Oh, come on," John laughed. "It's not like I'm gonna sit between you on the couch later and share the popcorn. I'm going out after this." He put his arm around Nikki and shook her a little, "Right?"

Nikki smiled and stepped aside, gesturing toward the food. "After you, sir."

"Great. Now you're on his side?" Chris teased with fake annoyance.

"She's a keeper, Shepp," John announced as he filled his plate.

Nikki and Chris served themselves after John, and the three of them sat at the table. John poured himself a glass of wine, earning another dirty look from Chris. "Maybe you'd like to stay and kiss her goodnight for me too," Chris quipped sarcastically.

John deflected, raising his glass, "To the chef!"

"I'll drink to that," Nikki added, raising her glass. There was a brief moment where they were both just waiting on Chris. He let the moment hang there long enough to show he was still in control, smiled at Nikki and finally joined the toast.

As they ate dinner, John entertained Nikki with every embarrassing story he could think of about Chris. Nikki giggled, clearly enjoying herself, while Chris took it in stride, pleased to see her having fun, but then John started moving into dangerous territory.

"You've got to watch yourself with this one," John cautioned Nikki. "He's always talking me into things I shouldn't be doing because he's been blessed with the ability to wiggle his way out of trouble." Chris glared at him warning him with his eyes, but John kept going. "Like the time we were selling..." Chris wanted to choke him, and his expression made it more than clear. "Uh, selling... answers to our junior year Chemistry test," he recovered. "And he talked his way out of it by convincing the librarian's daughter to tell her mom he found them in the archives and thought they'd be a good study guide." Nikki laughed, but John knew he was on thin ice and changed direction. "Oh, and how 'bout the time we stole booze from our parents' liquor cabinets, mixed it all together so they wouldn't notice any was missing, and Shepp gave us away by puking all over his mom's velvet couch." He chuckled, "We were grounded for two weeks after that!"

Chris didn't trust John with any more stories he didn't want revealed and finally had enough. "Okay, okay, uncle already. I haven't had a chaperone on a date since junior high, much less a really annoying one who knows all my secrets. When did you say you were leaving?"

"What? We haven't even had dessert yet," John protested.

"Yours will be for your late-night munchies. Now go!" Chris insisted.

"Alright, alright," John conceded, rising from the table. He gave Nikki a conspiratorial smile. "But just so you know, Nikki, there's plenty more where that came from."

"Go!" Chris yelled, exasperated.

John chuckled as he put his dish in the sink. "Okay, you kids have fun. Don't do anything I wouldn't do," he said with a wink and finally left.

"Thank God," Chris sighed as the door closed. He turned to Nikki, who was trying to contain her smile, clearly amused by the whole exchange.

"I think it's sweet you've known each other for so long." There was approval in her voice and her expression. "It sounds like you both have nice families."

"We do. We're lucky that way," Chris nodded, knowing it was true, but not fully appreciating how fortunate that made him. It was something he'd always had and therefore took for granted. "Why don't you pick out the movie, and I'll bring dessert in there. I'm just going to put the food away."

"Okay, but let's hold off on dessert for a bit. I'm pretty full. Dinner was delicious," Nikki said, giving him a quick peck on the cheek as she carried her plate to the sink. "I'll have another glass of wine, though."

Chris poured more wine, and Nikki perused the movie selections. "The Holiday or Love Actually?" she called from the living room.

"Die Hard," he countered, testing the boundaries.

"That's not the kind of Christmas movie I had in mind," she clarified as he joined her.

"I know, but you can't blame a guy for trying." He handed her a glass of wine with a look of resigned defeat, accepting his fate. "You pick. I can guarantee I haven't seen either one."

"Thank you." She took the glass of wine in one hand and picked up the remote with the other, making her choice with satisfied determination. "The Holiday it is."

"Do you have any movie-watching rules I should be aware of?" he asked playfully as he settled in. "Am I allowed to talk?"

Nikki didn't skip a beat, "Limited speaking is permitted but it has to be at the appropriate times. If you can't get the cadence right, we're going to have a problem."

"Noted. Do you want me to grab a blanket?"

"Sure, that would be nice."

Chris found a blanket in the closet and draped it over the two of them, putting his arm around her as she snuggled into his shoulder. "Well, at least it has a good cast," he said trying to put a positive spin on what was sure to be a chick-flick.

"Give it a chance. You're going in with the wrong attitude," she scolded gently.

They watched in comfortable silence for a while, until Chris glanced down to say something at 'the appropriate time,' and found Nikki fast asleep again. He might have been insulted if he didn't feel so badly that she was this tired. Slowly, he reached for the remote, careful not to wake her, and searched for something a little more testosterone inspired. Looking down at her sleeping peacefully in his arms, he decided he was happy to hold her all night if that's what it came to.

Sunday, Week 2

Nikki

Meet me at the 104-bus line at 10:00 a.m.

C u then.

I finish my coffee – savoring the last scent of its steamy aroma, pack a photo album to show to Dad, and head out for the subway to the bus station. Lauren is already waiting for me when I arrive. "Hey, how's your weekend been?" I ask, giving her a big hug.

"It's been good," she smiles, "we had our office holiday party Friday night, so that had all kinds of antics. Amanda made me do karaoke. Has she reached out to you yet?"

I chuckle. "*You*, karaoke? That must've been something to see." I pause, then nod. "And yes, we've had several text exchanges. She's going to stop by the café this week so we can talk."

"Oh, good." Another thought strikes her. "Didn't you have a date with Chris last night?" she asks eager for details.

"Yes," I sigh dramatically. "And I would've really enjoyed it if I could've stayed awake through it. It was mortifying. First, I fell asleep before dinner trying to study, then I fell asleep again after dinner during the movie and didn't wake up until after midnight. He had to borrow his roommate's car to drive me home."

Lauren bursts out laughing. "Oh my God, that's hilarious! You're a hot date! So, did you make more plans with him, or...?"

I shrug, a little embarrassed but still smiling at Lauren's reaction. "He invited me to the stadium today for a tailgate, but that was before the second time I fell asleep on him. He was really sweet when he said goodnight, though. And I'm telling you, he's like the most unbelievable kisser – very sensual, like you're doing more than just kissing when that's all you're actually doing." I let out a breath caught in the memory of it.

"Hmmm. That sounds yummy," Lauren says with a playful grin.

The bus arrives and we look for seats. As usual I'm annoyed by the people who spread their bags everywhere to deter others from sitting down when there aren't enough seats as it is. "This seat taken?" I ask a woman trying to occupy three seats. I pick up her bag and hand it to her before she can answer, and gesture for Lauren to sit. Lauren gives me a horrified look and sits down trying not to make eye contact with the woman next to her.

"So, when am I going to meet this guy?" Lauren asks, her voice still casual but I can detect an undertone of her 'parental' voice she uses only with me.

"Oh God," I roll my eyes. "It's bad enough I'm falling asleep on him. I don't need to bring my old lady sister into the mix."

"For Christ's sake Nikki, I'm only twenty-eight," she protests and slaps me in the arm.

"Yeah, going on forty!"

We arrive in West Chester shortly after noon. It's usually a good time to visit because a meal will be in progress which provides an activity to participate in and keeps him busy. The woman at the desk recognizes us and says, "Your dad is in the dining hall."

My heart sinks when we enter the room. Dad is sitting at a table with three other people, none of whom are communicating or even seem to know where they are. He's seated in a wheelchair and hasn't been served any food yet, so Lauren and I wheel him away from the table to find a spot where we can have some private time. We stop at a quiet area in the hall and pull up chairs to sit next to him.

"How are you doing Dad?" Lauren asks and kisses him on the forehead. He grins at her affectionately but doesn't answer.

I pull out the photo album I brought, "How about we stroll down memory lane," I suggest and start showing him family photos.

He smiles as he looks at them and points at a few. We explain who the people are and what the occasions were. He nods now and again and continues to flip through the pages but doesn't say a word. Lauren and I share a look of both heartbreak and concern. Neither of us have ever witnessed him this nonverbal before. It's almost like he can't remember how to speak.

Lunch is being served so we wheel him back to the table. We sit with him, but he doesn't seem to know what to do. He just stares at the plate, his face vacant.

"Dad, can I cut your food for you?" Lauren asks and he turns his gaze toward her but doesn't respond. "Okay," she says with the patience of a kindergarten teacher, "let's try this," and starts to feed him.

Disgusted, I push my chair out and storm up to the nurse's station, "How long has he been like this?" I demand.

"Just since yesterday, dear," she replies in a practiced calming tone. "I know it's hard to see, but unfortunately this is how it goes. He could be his old self again tomorrow."

"Was anyone going to feed him if we weren't here?" I ask accusingly.

She takes my attitude in stride. "Of course. It just takes a while to get around the dining room. Many of the residents need assistance."

I know it's not her fault, but I just want someone to blame. When I rejoin Lauren and Dad, he has eaten about half of what's on his plate. Lauren doesn't seem to be having any luck getting him to take more.

She puts the fork down realizing any additional effort is pointless. "Dad if you're finished, we can take you back to your room and put the game on," she says sweetly.

He doesn't respond so we wheel him out and get him settled in front of the TV in his room. We know he won't be able to follow the game, but he used to be a huge sports fan, so we hope he'll find some familiarity in it. We both kiss him goodbye and reassure him that one of us will be back in a few days.

"Thanks for coming," Lauren says when we get outside and gives me a reassuring hug.

"Of course," I say, releasing from her embrace but still holding onto her arm. "You know you don't have to do this alone."

"I know," she squeezes my hand, "but you have enough on your plate."

We walk the rest of the way to the SEPTA stop arm in arm in silence and mutual understanding.

# # #

Once home, I settle down on the couch with my laptop to finish the work I didn't get done at Chris's yesterday. After a bit, my phone breaks my concentration.

"Hello." All I hear are a bunch of people singing, *"Fly, Eagles fly, on the road to victory. Fight, Eagles fight, score a touchdown 1-2-3...."*

"Chris?"

"Hit 'em low, hit 'em high and watch our Eagles fly...."

"Chris?" I say louder.

"Fly, Eagles fly, on the road to victory. E-A-G-L-E-S. EAGLES!" I chuckle to myself realizing he butt dialed me. At least he's having fun after what had to be a boring night last night. I put down my laptop and decide to go old school and program the Eagles fight song as Chris's ringtone in my phone. I don't know why. It just kinda feels right. Too soon?

Finished with everything I need to have done for tomorrow, I make myself a cup of tea and turn on Netflix. I know I'm the only person on the planet who hasn't seen "Breaking Bad" so maybe I'll start that, but it seems like an investment I'm not ready to commit to right now.

"Fly, Eagles fly," starts chanting from my phone and I wonder if Chris is actually calling me or butt dialing me again. "Hello."

"Hey babe," he says with a slur in his voice, "I'm in the lobby. What number are you?"

"You're in *my* lobby?" I ask, surprised.

"Yup. Remember, I won Round Three."

"Oh Lord, are we still playing that?" I ask while frantically scampering around putting things away and checking myself in the mirror.

"Only when I'm winning. I told you I'm competitive, lady," he says trying to hold his ground but not really pulling it off since he sounds like he's got peanut butter in his mouth, "what number?"

"518," I fluff my hair really quick and add some lip gloss.

"Comin' up," he says and hangs up.

I open the door to find a very glassy-eyed Chris standing there in his fan gear with a mischievous look on his face. The door isn't even fully open yet and he's already through it reaching for me. He puts his hands around my waist and pulls me toward him, but more of his body weight is on me than mine on his, so I try to turn him toward the couch, "Whoa champ, I think you need to sit down," but he still has a grip on me.

He shifts his weight and spins me around flopping me down on the bed instead. He straddles me and says, "Did I ever tell you that I'm allergic to cotton? You're really gonna have to take this off," while playfully fumbling with the buttons on my blouse.

"Okay easy tiger," I say and wiggle out from underneath him. "I think you better lay down."

He slumps over on the bed, "Lay down with me."

"I think I'll get you a glass of water instead."

When I return with the water, he's passed out cold. I take his shoes off and slide his legs under the covers. I guess falling asleep on each other is our thing – how romantic.

I let him sleep and go back to making a Netflix selection. He mumbles something, rolls over, grabs ahold of my pillow, hugs it and falls back to sleep. I can't help but smile. He's like a little boy in a man's body. Allergic to cotton – nice try.

I'm just finishing up "Bridget Jones's Diary" when Chris starts to wake. "Hey lover," I say, looking at him seductively and doing my best to sound sexy. He immediately snaps his head down to see if he is wearing pants. "Gottcha," I wink at him.

"Get over here," he says in a murky whisper. I sit down on the bed next to him and he pulls me on top of him, "Next time we sleep can it be together?" I don't answer but give him a frisky smile and lay my head on his chest. "I was thinking... my last exam before Christmas break is the 20th and then I'll be headed home. Why don't we plan our own Christmas celebration for just the two of us next Saturday night?"

"That sounds nice," I say, lifting my head to look at him – those damn eyes are so captivating even when clouded with alcohol and grogginess. "I'll have most of my exams finished by then." I return my head to his chest and dissolve in the feeling of him holding me and gently stroking my hair.

WEEK THREE

Monday, Week 3

The Calvary

Ding. Drew instinctively knew it was eight o'clock. He didn't even need to check; he was certain it was Lauren's column and pipeline ideas. Instead of reading it, he quickly emailed her:

> When you get a minute why don't you come to my office to tell me about the piece you and Amanda would like to explore.

A few minutes later, she appeared in his doorway, tapping lightly on the frame. "Come in," he invited, gesturing toward the chair in front of his desk. She settled in hesitantly, anxious about the conversation ahead. The investigative piece was important to her, and she wanted the pitch to go well.

His office screamed Harvey Specter of "Suits" – sleek, professional, intimidating – adding to her angst. None of the other offices on the floor were put together like this one. In fact, most were pretty shoddy. Drew was tidying up papers on his desk and

Lauren took in the surroundings while he finished up. She glanced at the bookcase to her left. It contained the typical 'Editor – in – Chief' type books you'd expect but there was also an assortment of hardcovers on various Presidents, some travel magazines, Stephen King and was that a bound collection of Calvin and Hobbs? *This guy really is a man of mystery,* she thought while smoothing the fabric of her skirt. She turned her head back to face him and noticed a Beatles coffee table book on the credenza behind him – that was probably just for show – a cut-glass desk clock and a box of tissues in a sterling silver case, adding to the eclectic array of accoutrements that adorned the office.

"Did you get any ideas for your column at the party Friday night?" he asked lightly as he stacked the papers to the side.

"A few." Just then her phone vibrated. She glanced at it, then back at Drew. "I'm so sorry, but I have to take this." This was not how she wanted the meeting to begin.

"Of course," Drew said as she rose and stepped into the hallway to take the call. When she returned, her face was troubled, and her eyes filled with worry. "Is everything alright?" he asked, turning to grab a tissue behind him.

"It will be," she answered, her voice cracking.

Drew was making his way around the desk to hand her the tissue when she suddenly burst into tears. Unsure what to do, he wrapped his arms around her, half expecting her to pull away. But she didn't. She sobbed into his chest, her words a jumbled mess between gasps for air.

"It's okay, Lauren. Whatever it is, I'm sure we can figure it out. It'll be okay," he assured her, gently lowering her back into the chair. He kept his hands on her upper arms, feeling that if he let go, she might run out of the office. "What's going on? How can I help?" he asked, kneeling in front of her and handing her the tissue.

"I'm so sorry," she panted trying to catch her breath, "I'm such a mess. I need to go."

She tried to stand, but Drew placed his hands on her knees, stopping her. "I don't think you should go anywhere right now. You need to take a breath and try to calm down."

She looked up and noticed her mascara had smudged on his suit jacket. "Oh no! Your jacket," she gasped in horror. "I'm so sorry. I'll have it cleaned for you."

"Don't worry about the jacket," he said calmly. "Just tell me what's going on."

Her breath caught in her throat as she struggled to find the words. "It's my dad," she managed to get out between gasps, "he's in an Alzheimer's care facility in West Chester, and he's wandered off. The police are looking for him, but I need to get there right away."

"Alright, but I don't think you should drive, Lauren." His voice was firm but kind.

"I don't have a car. I take SEPTA," she replied, wiping her eyes.

"And when you get off the bus, what then?" he asked. "Are you just going to wander around West Chester looking for him? I'll drive you."

Her eyes widened in panic. "Oh no, I've already made a fool of myself and ruined your jacket. I can't hijack your day with my problems too."

"It's no problem at all," he reassured her gently. "I've got nothing pressing today that can't wait until tomorrow."

"I really don't want to inconvenience you," she said, hesitating, looking around the room as if the empty space was going to offer an alternative. No other solution in sight, she exhaled deeply, "But I guess it doesn't make any sense to go without a car."

"Let me get you another tissue, and then we'll go." Drew stood and offered a comforting smile.

"Thank you," she managed, her voice barely above a whisper as she tried to pull herself together.

Lauren couldn't stop apologizing as they made their way to the car, her words coming out as one rapid run-on sentence. "Please, Lauren, no more apologies. I'm happy to help," Drew said almost too calmly, trying to counterbalance her emotion.

"I'm just so mortified," she stammered, her face flushed with embarrassment.

Beep. Drew opened the door for her and placed a supportive hand on her back as she climbed in. Once they were settled, he handed her his phone. "Can you type in the address, please?"

"Sure," she replied and blew her nose before taking the phone. As she typed, Drew watched her, taking her in. Even with puffy eyes, a runny nose and smudged makeup she was still the most beautiful creature he'd ever seen.

"Here you go." She handed the phone back to him. The map app connected to CarPlay, and Drew put it in drive.

"How long has your dad been in a care facility?" he asked as they merged onto the highway, trying to make conversation.

"About two years now. My sister Nikki and I were just there yesterday to see him. He wasn't having a good day, but at least he was safe," she sniffled, wiping her eyes.

"And your mom?" Drew asked, curious why Lauren was handling this situation alone.

"It's just my sister and me." She pulled down the visor and stared at her reflection for a moment, sighing at her appearance.

Way to go Drew, he thought to himself at bringing up what was clearly another sensitive topic. "Wow, the Taylor sisters against the world – that's a lot," he commented, trying to recover.

"It is, but we make a good team." Lauren fumbled through her purse for a tissue to clean up her face. "Damn it," she whispered.

"There are tissues in the glove box if that's what you're looking for."

"Thank you, Drew. You really are the savior of the day today," she said politely, still unable to meet his gaze. She found a tissue and did her best to fix her face. She had make-up in her purse but was too embarrassed to apply it in front of her boss, so this would have to do.

The drive was filled with awkward conversation, Drew trying to lighten the mood, while Lauren remained consumed with worry. They didn't know each other well enough for him to offer any real comfort in the situation, but he tried.

Forty minutes into the trip, Lauren's phone vibrated. "Oh my God, it's the facility." She answered quickly. "They did? Thank goodness. I'm about twenty minutes away. I'll be there soon." She hung up and turned to Drew. "The police found him."

"That's great news," Drew said, relieved for her.

"I just need to see him and make sure he's okay."

They pulled into the facility parking lot, and Lauren jumped out of the car before Drew even had it in park. He followed her inside as she hurried down the hall to her dad's room. A doctor was examining him when they entered. "Dad," Lauren said softly, taking his hand.

"Hi, honey." He looked up at her with a smile.

"You're talking today," she said with hope in her voice and Drew noticed it too in her eyes. Her dad gazed at her, a puzzled expression clouding his face. She smiled softly and kissed his hand.

"Well, he seems no worse for wear," the doctor announced, looping his stethoscope around his neck.

"Thank heavens," Lauren sighed with relief.

Her father turned to Drew. "Hi Jeff."

Lauren gave Drew a look that was both apologetic and embarrassed. "Dad, Jeff and I broke up in high school. This is Drew."

"So, Drew, what are your intentions with my little girl?" he asked, trying to sound stern though he couldn't mask his natural warmth.

"All good intentions, sir," Drew replied, smiling at Lauren, who mouthed a silent "thank you."

"Dad, where were you going?" Lauren asked gently.

"I was just looking for the car in the parking lot and got turned around."

"Dad, we sold the car when you moved here," she reminded him.

"Moved here? I don't live here," he said, confusion wrinkling his brow. "I'm just being checked out by the doc here."

"Okay, Dad," Lauren said, glancing at the doctor for support. "But I think the doctor wants you to stay the night."

"Yes, sir," the doctor played along, "I'd like to keep you overnight for observation."

Her father seemed satisfied with the doctor's explanation and nodded. "Dad, I need to talk to the nurses, but I'll be back to say goodbye before I leave," Lauren said, squeezing his hand.

Drew followed her down the hall to the nurse's station. "Can someone here please tell me how the hell my father wandered out of this facility??" she demanded slamming her hands down on the desk like a scene from "Terms of Endearment."

"Miss Taylor, I understand your concern," the nurse replied, trying to calm her down. "The police have already taken a statement from the aide who was with him, and she's been placed on probation."

"He was with an aide?" Lauren's voice rose in disbelief. "Then how did he wander away?"

"The aide took him outside for some fresh air," the nurse explained, "but she answered a phone call and took her eyes off him for just a moment."

"Answered a phone call?" Lauren's anger flared. "Are you kidding me?! Do you have any idea how much we pay you people for his care?"

Drew had never seen her so fiery before. It was startling. As the nurse tried to placate her, Drew decided to step in. He placed a hand on Lauren's back and addressed the nurse. "Please be aware that you'll be hearing from our attorney." Then he turned to Lauren. "Shall we?" he asked, gesturing toward the door.

Lauren looked at him like she just remembered he was even there, processed what he said and turned back to the nurse, "Yes, our attorney," she echoed, turning on her heel and storming back down the hall to say goodbye to her dad.

As she walked away, the nurse called after her, "Miss Taylor! Miss Tay—" Drew cut her off, his voice firm. "Leave her be."

Drew waited in the lobby until Lauren returned, looking more at ease. "Ready?" she asked.

Remembering their banter at the elevator before their jog together, he replied, "Ready as I'll ever be." But the joke didn't land; she didn't seem to get the reference.

"Thank you so much for everything today, especially the part about the lawyer." A small smile crossed her face. "That'll keep 'em on their toes."

"I meant it," Drew said. "My sister's an attorney, and I'm sure she'd be happy to help."

"Oh, thank you so much, but I could never afford an attorney. I was just glad you shook them up a little."

"I'm sure she'd do it pro bono if I asked," Drew reassured her.

"Let me talk it over with my sister first before inconveniencing yours," Lauren replied a little uncomfortable by the generosity of the offer. "Speaking of which, I really should call her and let her know what happened. I was in such a fit this morning I didn't even think to contact her. Will you excuse me for a sec?"

"Of course, take your time."

Lauren stepped away to call Nikki, explaining the morning's events. Drew could hear the muffled sound of her sister yelling, and Lauren looked embarrassed as she tried to end the call quickly.

"Sorry," she said walking toward him. "We can go now."

On the drive back to Philly, Lauren pitched her idea for a piece on drink spiking on college campuses. Drew gave her the green light, knowing she was eager to tackle more than just 'Philly's

Top 10.' She was bright, and he was certain she'd be good at investigative journalism.

"Drew, this whole day has been a disaster, and you've been an absolute lifesaver. Can I at least treat you to a late lunch or early dinner to make up for any of it?" Lauren asked.

"I'd love to grab a bite, but there's no way I'm letting you treat." They discussed restaurant options and settled on Estia, a Greek place in Center City.

The hostess led them to a table, and Drew pulled out the chair for Lauren. As he sat down across from her, she noticed the mascara stain on his jacket again and buried her face in her hands.

An awkward moment later, she peeked up at him. "You know, Drew, between making a fool of myself in your office, ruining your jacket, dragging you into my personal drama, and having you pretend to be my boyfriend for my dad – all before lunch – I think I've hit rock bottom on the professionalism scale. I might have just created a new list for 'Philly's Top 10.'"

Drew smiled warmly. "Today wasn't about business, Lauren. You were dealing with a personal crisis, and once you calmed down from the initial shock, you handled everything beautifully."

"Well, now I feel exposed," she said shyly, diverting her eyes for a moment. "Like I've shown you all my warts, and here you are, still the consummate professional – and my boss, no less."

If she only knew. "I don't see any warts," he said gently, "just a very capable woman handling a lot on her own."

She shook her head. "Today, I wasn't on my own at all. I don't know what I would've done without your help."

The waitress approached, filling their water glasses and reciting the daily specials. When she finished, she asked, "Can I bring you something other than water to drink?"

Lauren considered her next thought for a second and then glanced at Drew, "Is it too early for wine?" she asked. "It's been one of those days."

"In my opinion, it's never too early for wine," Drew replied with a smile. "Chardonnay?"

Lauren looked surprised that he knew her drink of choice. "Um, yes, please."

Ok, that didn't make me look too creepy. Keep it together Drew. "Make it two," he said casually, trying to cover.

They decided to share several Mediterranean appetizers. When the wine arrived, they placed their orders, asking for share plates.

"Excellent choices," the waitress said, before heading off.

Drew leaned back in his chair, taking a sip of wine. "So, Amanda seems like quite the spitfire."

Lauren nodded. "She really is. I like her a lot. She reminds me of my sister, Nikki – they both have that same spunk."

"I saw some of that spunk in you today, especially at the nurse's station. Nikki must come by it naturally."

"Oh, trust me," Lauren said with a chuckle, "there's no comparison. Nikki puts the 'F' in feisty." She raised her glass, "To a disastrous morning that somehow turned into a pleasant afternoon."

"I'll drink to that," Drew replied, smiling as he tapped his glass gently against hers.

Their food arrived, and they enjoyed sampling the dishes and sharing casual conversation. Drew had never seen Lauren so at ease – it was nice to interact with her in that way. She was clearly more relaxed now that her dad was safe. He witnessed a full range of emotions in her from hysterical, to worried, to furious and now relieved. Sitting with her then felt surreal, but there she was across the table sipping wine and talking about how she's tried to make spanakopita before but has trouble working with phyllo dough. Drew soaked in the moment, appreciating their time together. When the bill arrived, Lauren reached for her purse, but he handed his credit card to the waitress before she could pull out her wallet.

"Thank you, sir," the waitress said. "I'll be right back with this."

"Drew, at least let me split it with you," Lauren insisted.

"Absolutely not, Lauren. If it makes you feel any better, I'll expense it."

"I guess technically it's still a workday," she tried to justify, "but this was hardly a business lunch."

"We did discuss your investigative piece in the car," Drew pointed out.

"Okay. Let's go with that," Lauren said, as if she had any control over Drew's expense reports. He smiled to himself finding her 'by the book' attitude endearing.

Once the bill was settled, it seemed pointless to go back to the office, so he drove her home.

"Thank you again for everything today, Drew. Now, may I please have your jacket?"

"Lauren, I'm not giving you my jacket."

"Please, Drew. I feel terrible," she insisted.

"It's nothing, really. Don't worry about it."

"Please don't force me," she said with an uncomfortable glint of mischief in her eyes.

Drew looked at her curiously, "Force you to do what?"

Without warning, Lauren unhooked her seatbelt, leaned over Drew, and unhooked his. She placed both hands on his shoulders and began pulling off his jacket. Drew was momentarily taken aback by the unexpected physical contact but soon found himself enjoying her touch. He playfully resisted a little, savoring the moment, but eventually let her win.

"There," she said triumphantly.

"You know, I can expense the dry cleaning too," Drew said with a grin.

"On what grounds?" she asked, folding the jacket over one arm and placing the other hand on her hip. "I don't think calming inappropriately hysterical employees qualifies as a business expense."

"It falls under crisis management training," he replied with a wink.

"You're impossible," Lauren said with a laugh as she gathered her things. Before stepping out of the car, she turned to him apprehensively, "Drew, can we please forget about all of this tomorrow and go back to business as usual?"

And just like that, the wind was taken out of his sails.

The Compromise

Around noon, Tony hit the corner where Rocco told him to meet. He scoped-out the street for a minute before spotting the car, a black sedan sitting low and menacing. He walked up and gave the driver's side window a knock. Rocco cracked it just enough to peer out, his eyes bloodshot and cold. "Get in."

Tony slid into the passenger seat without a word. "Whatdaya got for me?" Tony handed him the cash he had. "What's this?" Rocco said, eyes scanning the stack before yanking Tony closer by the shirt. "Where's the rest?" he asked, his breath hot on Tony's face.

Tony put his hands up in surrender, buying some time to explain. "Look dude, my guys bailed, alright? I'm doing this alone. There's a frat party this weekend – I'll move the rest then, I swear."

Rocco's grip tightened, his voice dropping to a growl. "The people I work for don't give a shit about your problems, brah. I'm not here to listen to excuses." He pulled Tony even closer, so close their faces were nearly touching.

Tony knew he couldn't show weakness and shoved Rocco off. "Yeah, I figured you'd say that. So, I came up with something else. A side hustle."

"What kinda side hustle?" Rocco's eyes narrowed with both suspicion and intrigue but the coldness behind them never wavered.

Tony fumbled through his pocket, pulling out a key ring and a folded piece of paper. "My roommate's girlfriend walks dogs for Uber Leash. I copied all her keys and got the apartment codes out of her phone for the places with keypads. These people are never home. So, it's simple. Let yourself in, take what you can and slip back out. Clean. Plus, they can afford to have someone come take care of their mutts. Who knows what they have inside."

Rocco stayed silent for a beat, sizing him up, mulling it over. "Alright. Hand 'em over, and I'll give you another week to move the bag." He grabbed the keys and the codes from Tony with a distant nod. "This might just be the shot in the arm my game needs, but if you don't move the rest of that pack by the end of the week, I'm not the only one whose kneecaps will be broken. Got it?"

Tony heard enough about Rocco's crew in New York to know this wasn't some idle threat. This was business − Soprano style business. "Got it," he said, his pulse was racing but he kept a cool exterior.

Rocco shoved Tony toward the door, "Get out."

Tony didn't say another word. He walked home knowing that if he didn't move that bag by the end of the week, there was no telling how ugly this was gonna get. The thought of it made his stomach churn but there was no turning back now.

Tuesday, Week 3

A Mother's Advice

Drew arrived at The Capital Grille a little ahead of schedule and got a table before his mother arrived. Her doctor's appointment must have run late – *why are doctors never expected to stay on schedule*, he wondered. While waiting, he ordered two unsweetened iced teas and glanced over the menu. He was seated facing the entrance, so he spotted his mom the moment she walked in and waved to get her attention.

His mother was in her mid-sixties, but easily passed for a decade younger, she exuded the polished elegance of an interior designer, her impeccable taste reflected in her wardrobe.

"Hello, dear," she greeted him warmly as she approached the table. "Don't get up," she added, leaning in to kiss him just as he began to rise.

Drew stood anyway, embracing her. "Hi, Mom. You look great, as always."

"Thank you, honey," she replied, smiling as he pulled out her chair. "Sorry I'm late. You can never predict how long these appointments will take."

"Everything go okay?" he asked with a touch of concern.

"Oh, fine. Just routine." She opened her menu and studied it for a few moments before setting it down and turning her attention back to Drew, "So, how's work?"

"Work is work," Drew replied flatly. "I mainly keep that job for the office space. You know my real income comes from my investment properties and stock trading. *The Inquirer* has such a strong writing team that I can practically edit the columns in my sleep."

His mother paused for a moment looking at him with pride and affection. "By the way, your father and I are so proud of how well you've managed the inheritance from your Godfather," she said, unfolding her napkin and placing it in her lap.

Drew was a little surprised by the compliment. "Well, Dad helped a lot," he pointed out.

"I know he did, but you've been really smart about managing it since. You've become such an adult. Where does the time go?" She thought about it for a slight moment before snapping back to the business of the day. "And back to speaking about sleep, are you getting any? You look tired."

Drew rubbed his forehead, "Oh, I didn't sleep much last night," he admitted.

"If work is going well, then what's keeping you up?" she asked with a mixture of concern and curiosity.

"It's not what — it's who," Drew confessed. "There's a woman at the office who's driving me crazy."

"Crazy good or crazy bad?" she asked, now fully intrigued.

Drew exhaled; already sorry he opened that door – he must be tired – but now he had to answer. "Both. I can't stop thinking about her, but she works for me, so I can't pursue her either."

The waitress arrived with the iced tea giving Drew a welcome break in the conversation. "Have you decided, or do you need more time?" she asked.

"I think we're ready, Mom?" he offered her the floor to order first.

She looked at the waitress with a honed politeness, "I'll have the cobb salad with sliced tenderloin, dressing on the side please."

"And I'll have the cheeseburger, medium rare," Drew added, handing over the menus.

As the waitress walked away, Drew's mother didn't waste time getting back to their previous conversation. "You know Drew, if a woman is keeping you up at night, you'll have to find a way to address it. If she works for you, why not have her transferred to another department?"

Okay great. Drew thought. *I'm not getting out of this one so easy.* "It's not that simple, Mom. I'd still be her superior."

"Then have her promoted," she suggested in typical mom problem-solving fashion.

Drew responded flatly, trying to brush it off. "I'm pretty sure office romances of any kind are frowned upon." He hadn't discussed his dilemma with anyone and couldn't believe *this* was the topic of conversation with his mother, of all people...

"All I'm saying is you have to give love a chance."

"Love?? Don't start naming your grandchildren just yet, Mom!" Drew's head was spinning at the direction of the conversation. He was looking for any out.

"At this rate, I'll never be a grandmother. You're not dating, and your sister scares off every man she meets. Why are men so intimidated by successful, ambitious women?" she asked with irritation in her voice.

Good. Now he could deflect. "Because we're the weaker sex and need our egos stroked. But you have to admit, Jen *is* pretty scary," he added with a smirk.

"Stop that," she scolded, dismissing his comment and turning the conversation right back to him. "Back to your problem. Your father asked me out a dozen times before I said yes. What if he had given up? We wouldn't be sitting here today."

Drew took another tactic. "There's also the small issue that she's not the slightest bit interested in me."

"I can't believe that," his mother scoffed, waving the comment away with her hand. "You've never had any trouble with women."

The waitress arrived with their lunch, and he was never so relieved by an interruption. She placed the salad down first and then handed Drew the cheeseburger like a lifeline. "Well, I'm having trouble with this one," he mumbled under his breath before taking a bite.

After lunch, Drew kissed his mother goodbye and headed back to the office. As he walked down the hall, he noticed Lauren and Amanda busily working on something in the conference room. He felt a pang of guilt seeing how hard Lauren worked when he was just coasting along. Drew hadn't seen Amanda since the Christmas party, so that gave him an excuse to pop his head in. "Hi, ladies. Amanda, did you enjoy the holiday party?"

Amanda started to answer, but when Lauren looked up from what she was doing, Drew found himself again distracted by her eyes – piercing emerald-green that day. When Amanda finished speaking, he snapped back to attention.

"Well, the two of you stole the show with "Sweet Caroline." Maybe you should take your act on the road," he joked.

"It *was* more fun than I expected," Lauren giggled.

There was a little twitch in his pants at the sound of her giggle, and Drew knew he needed to make a quick exit. "Okay, I'll let you get back to it," he said, tapping the door frame before making his escape.

I can't keep up like this. Literally and figuratively.

Thursday, Week 3

Lauren

For once, I'd actually taken the time the night before to lay out my clothes, so at least that battle was already won. No scrambling, no last-minute wardrobe crises. After a brisk 30-minute jog, I pour myself a cup of coffee and hold the warm mug in my hands a minute before taking a sip. I wait for the magic brew to do its thing and give me the strength to peel off my running gear and step into the shower. As the water heats up, I find myself wondering how many hours of my life have been spent simply getting ready for the day. A disconcerting thought, but one that drifts away as the steam from the shower wraps around me.

With the morning routine finally behind me, I pack my bag and leave for the dry cleaners to pick up Drew's jacket. When I get to the office, I notice his door is open, so I tap lightly on the frame. "Knock, knock."

Drew glances up from his desk, a smile spreading across his face. "Oh, hey Lauren. Come on in."

"I just wanted to return your jacket," I say, stepping into the room, holding it out before me.

He stands up, meeting me halfway to take the jacket from my hands. "I still feel bad you cleaned it for me. It wasn't necessary."

"Oh, it was *very* necessary after Monday's fiasco. I'm still cringing that you had to witness all that."

His smile fades slightly, a flicker of concern in his eyes. "How's your dad doing now?"

The question catches me off guard, and I hesitate for a moment before answering. "Oh, um, he's been back to his usual self these past few days. It's such a strange disease," I add, suddenly feeling awkward, unsure of what to do with my hands now that they're empty.

Drew hangs the jacket on the coat rack in the corner with a quiet nod, then turns back to me. "Have you started your research for the investigative piece?"

"Amanda's got a great start on gathering facts," I reply, lacing my fingers together to keep them busy. "Once she's collected enough, I'll dive into the writing."

He leans back against the desk, looking at me with genuine interest. "Sounds like you two make a solid team. I can't wait to read it when it's ready."

"I can't wait to write it, and thanks again for giving me the opportunity."

Drew waves a hand dismissively, his smile easy and unbothered. "You don't need to thank me, Lauren. It's the next logical step in your career growth. Honestly, I should have thought of it before you asked."

"I appreciate it all the same," I say, though my voice falters a little, I'm not quite sure how to appropriately express gratitude to my boss. I stand there for a moment, awkwardly aware that there's no formal agenda, no reason for me to still be in his office. "Is there anything else you'd like to go over?" I ask, hoping to change the vibe.

Drew pauses, still leaning against the desk, lips pursing in thought as he ponders the question. His gaze lingers on me as he thinks, and I feel heat rising in my cheeks. He's never been anything but kind to me, so I don't know why I feel uneasy around him. Maybe it's his reputation around the office or maybe it's the way he looks at me – different somehow. "Not at the moment," he finally says, but I sense there's something left unsaid, like he wants me to stay but can't think of a reason why I should. He pushes off the desk and stands up straight. "I guess I'll let you get back to setting the world on fire," he says with a smile, but there's something else in his eyes, something that doesn't match his smile – could it be disappointment... No. The heat in my cheeks is now an inferno. If I'm feeling it, I know he's seeing it which only makes it worse. I quickly divert my eyes to the floor, and without another word, make a hasty exit.

Later that Day

Nikki

Amanda is meeting me at the café today after my shift to talk about the piece she's working on with Lauren. I spot her right away, thanks to Lauren mentioning her stylish, short haircut that's the same color as mine.

"Amanda?" I ask, approaching her.

"Yes, hi! You must be Nikki," she replies with a friendly smile.

"That's me. Go ahead and grab a seat in the booth over there. I've got one last check to close out, and I'll join you in a minute. Need anything? Coffee?"

"Iced tea would be great," she says, pulling her tablet from her bag and settling into the booth.

I return a few minutes later with two iced teas and slide in across from her. "So, how do ya like working with my sister?"

"I love it. She's really nice, gives me awesome assignments, and is super flexible with my schedule."

I take a sip of my tea, amused thinking about Lauren as her boss. "She told me you convinced her to do karaoke at the office holiday party. I can't believe it. She must really like you – or had a bit of liquid courage. I would've paid good money to see that."

Amanda chuckles. "How can you go wrong with "Sweet Caroline?" Did she also tell you about her hot boss who can't keep his eyes off her?"

I nearly spit my drink at this news! "What?! Tell me *everything*!"

Amanda leans forward eager to spill the beans. "His name is Drew Davis, and every woman in the office is practically drooling over him. It's honestly embarrassing. They even call him 'Mr. Drew-tiful,'" she says rolling her eyes.

"And how do you know he's into Lauren?" I ask, now fully intrigued.

"Oh, it's *sooo* obvious. At the Christmas party, he couldn't stop staring at her. And just the other day, he came into the conference room to say hi and literally went into a trance when she looked at him." She's smiling an ear-to-ear smile enjoying telling me this and I already know we're going to be friends.

I slap my hand on the table, laughing. "I can't believe she didn't tell me any of this!"

"Oh, she's completely clueless. She's all business when he's around, like she's in the middle of a performance review or something, but the second he leaves, she goes back to being herself."

"Classic Lauren," I sigh, shaking my head.

We chat a bit more before getting into the questions Amanda came here to ask me. Since I've been helping Lauren with her column for so long, I've picked up a few tricks for gathering information. I suggest Amanda look into whether there are any drink-spiking awareness programs on campus and mention I'll check the same at Drexel. I also recommend talking to a few bartenders to see if there are any measures in place to prevent this kind of thing and set up an interview with a police officer. She's nodding and typing notes when Chris walks in unexpectedly. I swear Lucy is giving him my schedule.

"Hey, you," he says as he approaches and starts to bend down to kiss me but stops midway, "Amanda, right?"

"Yup, nice to see ya again," she replies, her tone light and friendly.

I glance between them, my curiosity piqued. "Wait, you two know each other?"

"Amanda is John's cousin's roommate," Chris explains. "A group of us went out the other night."

"Small world." A twinge of suspicion creeps over me for a brief second before I brush it away. "Or small city at least."

Amanda seems eager to get more input. "Actually, that night is what inspired the piece I'm working on. Someone spiked my other roommate's drink that night."

I scooch over in the booth, patting the spot next to me. "Sit down, Chris. Maybe you can help Amanda with the research she's doing for Lauren. I've already given her a few ideas."

Chris slides in beside me, "You work for Nikki's sister?" he asks surprised.

Amanda nods, a little more serious now. "I intern for her at *The Inquirer*. I'm investigating date rape drugs on college campuses. If the story turns out to have legs, the paper is going to run it. Have you heard about this being an issue at Temple?"

Chris' expression shifts, a frown forming as he considers the question. "Of course, I know about drink spiking," he says almost cautiously. "But it's not exactly the sort of thing guys really worry about."

"But would you know where to get date rape drugs if you wanted to?" Amanda asks, fingers poised on the keyboard ready.

Chris hesitates. "No," he admits after a beat, "but like anything else, it'd probably just take some asking around."

"Yeah," Amanda says, nodding. "That's what I figured."

"Chris, I suggested she talk to some bartenders and set up an interview with the police. Can you think of anything else she might want to do?"

Chris takes a moment, chewing it over. "No, but those are good ideas," he says with a strange look that I can't place. "I'll think on it though." He scoots out of the booth, standing up to leave. "Nikki, I just stopped by to say hi. I've got class, but I'll call you later."

"We're almost done," I say peering up at him. "If you can wait a few more minutes, I'll walk with you to the subway. I have to pick up a new key at one of my dog homes. Their place was broken into, and they had to have the locks changed."

"You two finish up," Chris says, "I'm already late." He leans down and kisses me on the cheek, then turns toward Amanda, "Good seeing you again. Good luck with your story," and before I can say anything further, he's out the door.

Amanda and I chat a bit more, switching back and forth from casual conversation to ideas about her research. "I'm still deciding which hot spots to check out this weekend – there's so many. Want to join me once I've narrowed it down?" she asks.

I smile, shaking my head. "Thanks so much. Chris and I are having our Christmas together on Saturday night, but I'll definitely take a raincheck. Have you checked out South Street yet?"

"Not for a while," Amanda replies, her memory mulling it over.

"You definitely should. It's an edgy part of the city. As you know it's sort of a melting pot of multicultural groups, students, tourists, twenty-somethings and everything in between. It might yield some contenders for 'Philly's Top 10.'"

"Great, I'll add it to my list," she says, packing up her things. "I probably won't see you again until after break, so have a nice holiday."

"You too," I reply with a warm smile. "Merry Christmas, Amanda."

#

I can't wait to get home and call Lauren.

"Hey, what's up?" she answers on the second ring, as if she's expecting a call.

"I met with your intern Amanda today," I say, leaning back in my chair, getting comfortable for the conversation ahead. "She's great — really sharp, and she's got this energy that's contagious. I like her."

Lauren laughs, the sound warm and familiar. "Yeah, I knew you'd hit it off. She kind of reminds me of you, actually."

"Really?" I grin. "Well, we had a very productive meeting with lots of takeaways and next steps. But honestly, the most interesting part of the conversation was when she mentioned that you have a hot boss who is, apparently, totally enamored with you."

There's a moment of silence on the other end, then Lauren bursts out laughing, "What?? Are you kidding me? Don't be ridiculous! Where would she get an idea like that? Our relationship is completely professional — except, of course, for that one day when I had a complete meltdown in his office."

"Ah yes," I tease, "and didn't he swoop in like a knight in shining armor to save the day?"

"Well, yeah, but honestly, he was just being practical," she says with a sigh. "I don't have a car, and I needed a ride. That's all it was."

"Amanda says he can't keep his eyes off you," I press, enjoying every second of this. "Lauren, you need to start paying attention to this. Is he a guy you could see yourself dating if you, ya know, opened your mind a little? Thought about it?"

She hesitates, weighing the question. "I mean, he's the kind of guy *anyone* would date. He's handsome, has a great job, he's a perfect gentleman... thoughtful, even. But he's my boss, so what difference does it make?"

"Thoughtful?" I echo, my interest piqued. "What do you mean by 'thoughtful'?"

"The other night," she starts, "I was leaving for a run after work, and he saw me, didn't want me going alone in the dark, so he came with me. Later in the week, I found a gift bag on my desk – inside there was mace for my keychain and a note that said, 'To keep you safe if I'm not with you.' And then, of course, there was the whole Dad fiasco day."

I exhale loudly. "I swear to God, Lauren. If Prince Charming himself knocked on your door, you'd give him directions to the girl's house up the street. How are you this clueless?"

I can hear her chuckling softly, but it's the kind of laugh that makes me think she's not entirely sure I'm wrong. "Alright, alright," she says, almost sheepish. "I think both you and Amanda are crazy, but I guess I'll take that under advisement."

"You'd better," I scold.

Once Lauren and I finish our conversation, I pull out my computer and google "best gifts for a guy you've only been seeing a couple of weeks that won't weird him out." Minutes later my Instagram feed is serving me Eagles golf towels and personalized whiskey glasses. Boyfriend gifts. I swear my phone knows what I'm doing at all times. It's spooky.

whiskey glasses. Boyfriend gifts. I swear my phone knows what I'm doing at all times. It's spooky.

The Confrontation

This can't be happening. Chris left the café and rushed home, his mind reeling. Tony and John were casually tossing a lacrosse ball back and forth across the living room when Chris came flying through the door. "Okay house meeting, now!" he yelled, slamming the door behind him.

"What's up?" John asked tossing the ball back to Tony.

Chris grabbed the ball mid-air and chucked it into the corner. "I'll tell you what's up. Remember Amanda, your cousin's roommate?"

"Yeah, the red head," he answered.

"Well just so happens she's interning for Nikki's sister at *The Inquirer* and is working on a story about date rape drugs on college campuses because this asshole," he gestured toward Tony, "spiked her roommate's drink!"

"So what?" Tony said nonchalantly, putting the lacrosse stick down, "she's all the way across town."

"Oh, my fucking God Tony, what difference does that make?! She's going to be asking around and Nikki's helping her!" Chris was pacing the floor and grabbing the back of his neck with both hands. "All they have to do is talk to somebody you sold to and all roads lead back here. Nikki even suggested Amanda set up an interview with the cops! These are smart girls Tony; they're going to figure this out!"

"What do you care?" Tony shrugged, "you're not involved anymore."

"Now Nikki's involved, that's why I care! This is next level shit Tony – what aren't you getting?? This is going to blow back on us! If Rocco is part of a bigger operation like you said, you don't need *The Inquirer* investigating this. You've got to end this now!" Chris shouted, pushing Tony in the chest.

"Okay, okay. Back up man!" Tony protested, shoving Chris back half-heartedly – he knew Chris was right; the last thing he needed was a spotlight on his business. He knew no one in NY would have his back and he'd take the fall for all of it if it came out. "I can't afford to get caught or worse, expose the operation. I'll figure a way to get out," he said, shaking his head unconsciously like he was working it through in his mind, "but I've got to move the rest of this pack first. Rocco wasn't happy I didn't have all his money and threatened me. He gave me until the end of this weekend to get it done or else, and I don't want to find out what 'else' is."

Friday, Week 3

Nikki

"*Fly Eagles fly*" chants from my phone... "Hey there," I answer and pull the blinds to shield the mid-afternoon sun.

"Hey babe," Chris says sweetly, "sorry to rush out of Mocha Loco yesterday. I was really running late."

"No worries. I wasn't expecting to see you at all, so it was a nice surprise. It was pretty random that you knew Amanda."

"What are you doing tonight?" he asks ignoring the Amanda comment.

I let it go – I don't know why I think it's odd they met before. "Since we're having our Christmas at my place tomorrow, I thought I'd hang some lights to make the celebration a little more festive. Lauren and I have Christmas Eve together at her place and then we go to see Dad on Christmas day, so I never put much effort into decorating my place. After that, I was planning on getting some sleep. It's been a hell of a week with exams and work."

"How 'bout I come over and help you," he suggests. There's something in his tone. I can almost picture a glimmer in his eye as he speaks. I know he's trying to turn this into an opportunity.

I don't let on that I'm suspicious of his motives and try to set the ground rules. "Okay, but I'm serious about getting some sleep. I have dogs to walk tomorrow and a few other errands to run before I can even think about tomorrow night, and I really do want to be able to enjoy it. We have to break our streak of falling asleep on one another."

"You have my word," he says, now sounding like a perfect gentleman. "How about if I get there around six o'clock, we order a pizza and hang the decorations. I'll bring a bottle of wine and promise to leave by nine."

"You've got a deal. I'll see you later then."

I walk to the nearest CVS to pick up some lights and whatever other subtle Christmas decorations they may have that won't take up too much room in my apartment. A set of three Christmas tree candles are the first thing I spot. They'll make a great centerpiece for my coffee table which doubles as a dining table. Next, I find a whimsical 2ft. table tree that will fit on the end table next to the couch. It's perfect and we can put our gifts on the floor in front of it. I throw a box of white string lights into the cart, grab two Santa hats and leave feeling pleased with the success of my finds.

For the past few years, Lauren and my holidays have been simple. We keep the traditions from our childhood but on a smaller scale. It's nothing like the big, rowdy family celebrations I've heard about from friends. Kitchens bustling with people, mimosas flowing by nine in the morning, living room floors buried under wrapping paper, and half the adults napping by one in the afternoon knowing dinner prep will begin by three. Lauren and I have both been invited to these types of celebrations but neither of us would ever leave the other alone. Someday, we'll have families of our own and begin new traditions.

I feel more in the holiday spirit than I have in a long time. The city's decorations seem to take on a whole new meaning, like they're inviting me into the celebration and aren't just there for the retail season. I remember how much my mom loved the holidays and how she made our house feel – inviting warmth mixed with excited anticipation. I loved it as a kid.

I toss my shopping bags on the couch and rummage through my closet for something to wear. "Aha!" I pull out a knee-length black sweater dress that will look cute with the Santa hat. It's a no-shoes-necessary night, so I just need to find black tights without any runs and my jingle bell earrings from a couple of years ago. After some more rummaging – success! I get dressed, take a look in the mirror, and smile. Voila!

Opening the front door feels like opening a present. There he is – Chris: Tall, dark, and handsome, exactly as the cliché goes, wearing a black sweater that hugs his broad chest and a pair of jeans that make me take a second look.

"Hello handsome," I greet him as he steps inside.

"Hello beautiful," he replies, his eyes sweeping over me. "Well, aren't we festive?" He smiles and hands me a bottle of wine.

"I'm getting into the spirit. I have a hat for you too. What's that?" I nod toward the tube in his hand.

"Pillsbury slice and bake Christmas cookie dough," he grins. "I thought this might be about your speed in the baking department."

I smile. "Great! Let's make those first so it smells like Christmas in here before it smells like pizza. What do I need?"

Chris laughs, amused by my ignorance in the kitchen. "A baking sheet. You have one of those don't you?"

"Of course I have a baking sheet," I protest. "How else would I heat up leftover pizza?"

I peel open the dough and discover it's pre-sliced, with each cookie perfectly uniform and adorned with its own little decoration. I arrange the dough on the sheet and pop them in the oven. "Wow, if I knew cooking was this easy, I might've given it a shot sooner," I say setting the timer.

"I could tell I'd need to start you with the basics," Chris teases, stepping in closer. His eyes turn sultry as he wraps his arms around me. "Anything else I can teach you?"

I loop my arms around his neck, unable to look into those eyes, and feel the heat of his body press against mine. He pulls me closer, kissing me with a hunger that makes my knees weak. One of his hands drifts from my waist to my face, and I slide mine down to rest on his solid chest. He's still holding me gently with the other hand and I marvel at how he can feel like a wall of strength and a gentle presence all at once. His left hand moves lower, and I know it's time to pump the brakes.

"Hey," I say softly, pushing lightly against his chest, "Remember your promise?"

Chris smirks, his boyish charm showing through. "Well, I got here early, so I figured I wasn't on the clock yet."

I glance at the time. "It's about six o'clock now," I say, doing my best to sound composed while his touch is making the air feel like it's evaporating around me.

He lets me go with a knowing smile; confident he'll get his way eventually. "Okay, a deal's a deal, and I'm a man of my word. Let's get started."

I let out a breath, relieved we're back on track. "I'll order the pizza. You get the lights out and let's put on some Christmas music."

I pour two glasses of wine and join him in the living room. He's already wearing the Santa hat and untangling the lights. "If we finish early, can we pick up where we left off?" he asks with a naughty grin as he takes the glass.

"Possibly," I tease.

"I'm skipping dinner then," he says with a wink. *Ding*. The timer sounds, startling me. "Don't tell me this is the first time you've used the timer on your oven," Chris laughs in disbelief.

"Busted." I return to the kitchen and pull the cookies from the oven. The sweetest smell of 'sugar and spice and everything nice' wafts through the room as I set them down to cool.

Chris has all the lights unraveled when I return. "So how do you want these?" he asks, looking around the room.

"I guess there aren't that many choices. Let's just hang them along the molding where the ceiling meets the walls. We should have enough to circle the whole room."

"Do you have clear thumbtacks?" he asks.

"Yep, bought them with the lights," I reply, grinning as if that should be something to be proud of.

"Great. How about I hold the lights in place, and you follow behind with the tacks?" He gestures toward the tiny side chair in the living room. "Is that the only chair we've got to reach the ceiling?"

I nod, a little sheepish. "Unfortunately, yeah. But we'll make it work."

"Okay, my sexy little elf, let's see what you've got," he says grabbing the chair and climbing on.

He holds the lights up with one hand and extends the other to me. I climb on in front of him and begin tacking in the lights. Every time we need to move the chair; I find myself climbing between his arms and legs. The proximity is... distracting, and I can feel him smiling behind me. He's definitely enjoying this routine a little more than he's letting on. Just as we finish the first section, there's a knock at the door.

"Break time!" I say, hopping off the chair. I pay for the pizza and bring it back to the living room, where we eat it straight from the box.

"Perfect timing," Chris says after the first bite. "I didn't realize how hungry I was. I think the smell of the cookies jump started my appetite." He pours more wine and we each take another slice.

"Are you ready to get back to our little game of holiday Twister?" I joke, tossing the last bit of my crust back in the box.

"Right hand where?" he asks, his hand sliding down my side as he pulls me closer.

"Don't you dare Chris Sheppard!" I swat his hand away, trying to be firm. "We're on a mission here."

"Oh yes we are…," he says with a shameless grin, and I can't help but laugh.

With Mariah Carey's "All I Want for Christmas is You" playing in the background, we continue our routine – moving around the room until we're back where we started. There are still a few inches of lights left, so we loop them around the initial string until it runs out.

When we're finally finished, I turn around on the chair to face him, slipping my arms around his neck. "We did it!"

Chris smiles down at me, looking so impossibly handsome that my knees almost buckle. His deep brown eyes are filled with affection, and his dark wavy hair falls just beneath the edge of the Santa hat, making him look like he walked right out of a holiday romance novel.

He leans down to kiss me and now with neither of us holding onto the wall the chair wobbles beneath us. I grab ahold of him tighter, and he jumps off the chair with me in his arms as it tumbles over. "My hero," I say gazing up at him, my heart beginning to race.

He slowly puts me down. "Maybe I can rescue you from that pesky restraint of yours next," he says and brushes my hair away from my face. He's melting me with his eyes and pulling me backwards toward the couch. I feel myself succumbing and gently push free. "Let's plug in the lights and get a look at our handywork." I don't know why I'm resisting him. Isn't that what girls are supposed to do? I don't want him to think I'm easy, but at the same time, it's clearly what he wants, and if I'm being honest, so do I. Games suck.

He sighs softly and tries to hide his disappointment. I know he's frustrated but he's also being patient, and I appreciate it. Truthfully, I don't know why I'm holding back. His touch just scares me a little; like once the faucet is turned on, I'll never be able to shut it off. I snuggle up to him under the glow of the Christmas lights and the moon outside feeling warm and satisfied. "It's perfect," I whisper. "Thank you."

Saturday, Week 3

Nikki

When I wake up, the light in my apartment feels brighter than usual. I glance out the window and see that it snowed overnight. Not a lot, just a dusting, but it still looks dream-like. Excited, I jump out of bed, pull-on black yoga pants and Sorel boots – which are totally unnecessary, but I haven't had a reason to wear them in a while. I grab a long cable knit fisherman sweater and a pom-pom hat before stuffing some dog treats in my coat pockets and heading out to take care of my morning clients. I have three dogs today.

First up is Shady, a little Schnauzer. She's cute but not exactly ladylike – she burps and farts without a care. I unlock her door with the new key her owners made for me, and she's already wiggling with excitement and whimpering a little.

"Hey Shady-girl, ready to go pick up your buddies Jack and Russell?" Yes, you guessed it, they're Jack Russell Terriers. Original, right? I clip her leash on, and we head outside. Shady is thrilled to see the snow and immediately begins rolling in it. We walk a few blocks toward Jack and Russell's house, with Shady stopping to sniff and pee on everything along the way. "How about a poop, Shady-girl?" but nothing.

I open the door at Jack and Russell's to find them dressed in sweaters, wagging and ready to play. Shady doesn't wait for an invitation and bolts inside. I lose hold of her leash, and she races through the house with Jack and Russell in hot pursuit.

"Okay, everyone, settle down!" I call after them, laughing. "I know this is exciting, but we've got to get leashes on!"

The living room is a mess – there's a broken potted plant on the floor and mail scattered everywhere. "Who made this mess?" I ask, picking up the mail. They ignore me and continue chasing Shady. I go in search of a dustpan and hear a noise coming from the back bedroom. "Guys, come back out here," I call.

When I turn around, I'm surprised to find all three of them standing right before me eager for their walk. "How'd you guys get back out here so fast?" I clip on Jack and Russell's leashes while they circle Shady, sniffing her all over. "Okay boys that's enough. You're not gentlemen at all."

Jack and Russell are just as thrilled with the snow as Shady, sticking their noses in it and trying to eat it. "It's potty time!" I encourage. Jack responds right away and as if he gave Shady a good idea, she follows suit. Russell not so much. He's just staring up at me expectantly.

"Good job," I praise, giving Jack and Shady enthusiastic scratches hoping to inspire Russell. "Russell, you too?" He locks eyes with me clearly holding out for a treat. I pull the bag out of my pocket and dangle it before him. That does it. He squats and takes care of business.

"Good job, everyone!" I hand out treats and clean up, enjoying their happy antics as we make our way to a trash can two blocks ahead. Jack and Russell still can't resist dipping their faces in the snow and are now both sporting icicles hanging from their whiskers. I drop them off first, cleaning up their faces and paws before saying our good-byes. That's odd. I notice two pieces of mail still on the floor underneath the coffee table. I thought I had picked them all up. Oh well, I sigh putting them back where they belong. "No more house messes you little hooligans. I don't know what got into the two of you, but you know I'm going to have to report your shenanigans to the Coopers."

Shady is next. At her place, our routine is similar but just as I'm getting ready to kiss her good-bye, she lets out an epic fart. "Whoa Shady!" I laugh, retreating to catch my breath. I don't know how her owners live with that smell!

With the rest of the afternoon free, I have plenty of time to get ready for tonight. I dig around my closet looking for something special. I'm excited to get dressed up, it's been a while. I discover an emerald-green silk dress that I'd forgotten I had shoved in the back. It's a wrinkled mess but nothing my steamer can't fix. With that sorted, I prepare a small charcuterie board for later and wrap Chris's gifts.

Around four o'clock I hang my dress in the bathroom and jump in the shower, hoping the steam will get a head-start on the dress. Wrapped up in my robe, hair in a towel turban, I sift through my jewelry box searching for something to finish my look. I find a delicate gold chain with two tiny diamonds that hang from a knotted center. I try it on, and the diamonds fall perfectly into my cleavage. For a second, I consider taking it off, but who am I kidding? This is Chris, not some blind date.

My phone vibrates.

> I'm just killing time over here. Care if I come early?

> That would be great. I just need a half hour.

When Chris arrives, he's wearing a red cashmere sweater, once again just snug enough to make me notice. He's holding two wrapped packages and a bottle of Prosecco.

"Wow!" his eyes light up when he sees me. "You look incredible. The color of that dress makes your eyes look like they're painted on."

"Thank you." I bat my eyelashes up at him dramatically. "Why don't you put those gifts on the floor under my little Charlie Brown Christmas Tree and I'll open the Prosecco."

"Sure," he says, handing me the bottle and giving me another obvious once over with his eyes.

Remembering the time I almost knocked my eye out with a champagne cork, I go in search of a dish towel. *Pop!*

"That's a happy sound," Chris says, already helping himself to the charcuterie.

I join him on the couch, handing him a champagne flute. "Shall we start the gifts?" I ask, my excitement bubbling over more than the champagne.

Chris chuckles. "You're like a little kid on Christmas morning. What's the rush?"

I shrug, not trying to hide my enthusiasm. "I'm just excited. It's been a while since I've exchanged Christmas gifts with anyone other than Lauren."

"Speaking of Lauren," he says, setting down his glass, "when do I get to meet her?"

"She's been asking the same thing about you," I answer, setting my glass down next to his. "Maybe after the holidays the three of us can grab drinks. Just a heads-up, though..." I warn, grabbing his attention. "She's very sweet and lovely, but she feels responsible for me. So, she can be a little... overprotective."

"I welcome the challenge," he says confident as ever and bends down to pick up a gift. "Alright, I'll go first." He hands me a small box that looks like it was wrapped by a grade-schooler. "Merry Christmas," he says warmly as he hands it to me.

I hold it up to my ear and give it an exaggerated shake, making him roll his eyes. As I tear into the paper, I can see the faintest hint of amusement on his face. I lift the lid to find a pair of theater tickets for a show starting once he's back after the break.

"Awww Chris, this is perfect. Something to look forward to." Grinning, I lean over, grab his face and squish his cheeks together making duck lips before planting a kiss on them. "My turn!" I jump up and grab a large rectangular box from under the tree. "I hope you like it."

He takes it from my hands and is surprised by its weight. "Whoa, what'dya get me, coal?" he jokes and grabs it with two hands.

"You'll see." I can feel my smile, already anticipating his reaction.

He mimics me and holds it up to his ear and shakes it before tearing the paper off. He doesn't need to open the box because the picture on the outside reveals its contents – a portable flat-top grill. "Niki, this is awesome!"

"I noticed you don't have any grill equipment at your place. I thought you'd enjoy it in the spring and since it's portable you can bring it to your tailgates," I say, pleased by the expression on his face.

"I love it. Thank you, babe. I have one more for you." He hands me a beautifully wrapped box that's obviously been professionally done. I carefully slide off the ribbon and unwrap the paper revealing a Victoria's Secret box. I'm a little wary because if this is some over the top lingerie I'm going to be really embarrassed. Nervously, I lift the lid and find the most stunning bra and panty set I've ever seen.

I look up at him, "Chris, it's gorgeous."

"You're gorgeous, Nikki. Beautiful women should have beautiful things."

I glance at the label, a little curious. "But how'd you know my size?"

He smirks, "Nikki, I've been studying your body since the first day we met. I made an informed choice."

"Haha," I laugh, giving him a playful shove. "I have one more left for you," I say tapping my fingers together with anticipation before getting up.

"Well, let's see what this is," he says and tears off the paper. He opens the box to find grilling tools, grill cleaning tools and a leather bag to keep them in. "It's perfect, Nikki. It really is a great gift. I'll get lots of use out of it."

"I have to admit I did have ulterior motives," I say like I'm revealing a secret.

Chris raises both of his eyebrows. "Fair enough, I had ulterior motives with your gift too."

He pulls me in for a kiss that feels like another gift, maybe my favorite one. I savor the moment feeling warm and happy. He brushes his fingers down my cheek as our lips part, and a knock at the door interrupts the moment. "Oh, good, that must be the takeout."

Chris jumps up, beating me to the door. "Taylor?" the delivery guy asks.

"Yep," Chris replies, pulling out his wallet.

"At least let me split it with you," I offer.

"No way," he says shaking his head. "You paid for the pizza last night."

He unpacks the Thai containers while I grab plates and silverware. "Dinner is served!" I declare triumphantly as if I've been slaving in the kitchen all day.

After we eat, I turn off all the lights except for the string lights we hung the night before. The mood is magical. We're embraced by the warm glow of the room and the sound of "Baby it's Cold Outside" drifting through the air. Chris stands and holds out his hand, "May I have this dance?"

I take his hand, and he pulls me into him. We begin to sway back and forth in each other's arms with only the glow of the city outside and the string lights gleaming around us.

"Maybe just a half a drink more," he whispers in my ear before dipping me and pulling me back into him. We continue swaying and he moves one of his hands from around my waist up to cup my face, "Nikki, you are so beautiful, and that dress... You look amazing."

"Thank you. You look quite handsome yourself."

He breathes warm air into my ear and nibbles my lobe. My skin betrays me and rises with goosebumps that signal him to keep going. He's holding the back of my head and running his fingers through my hair while kissing my neck. The hand around my waist drops to palm my rear-end and he lifts me up slightly. I'm only an inch off the ground but feel suspended in midair, his protective arms the only thing stopping me from floating away.

My hands are on his shoulders, and I think for a second about pushing away, but I don't. I feel vulnerable, but safe with him at the same time. My hands slide down his chest and I can feel his heart pounding. Chris keeps moving his mouth slowly downward. When he reaches my clavicle, he slips two fingers under the spaghetti straps of my dress ever so gently removing them from my shoulders. The dress doesn't put up a fight at all and falls in a helpless puddle at my feet. With me now standing before him in only my underwear and heels, he eagerly pulls off his sweater and tosses it on the couch.

"Chris?" I whisper.

"Please don't make me stop Nikki," he pleads breathlessly, his hands roaming eagerly.

"Not stop, but maybe slow down," I manage to utter softly.

"Okay, slow down," he says to himself more than to me, picks me up, twirls me around and lays me on the bed.

I can feel his erection through his jeans as he climbs on top of me. He's touching my breasts over the top of my bra and discovers it has a front clasp. He makes quick work of that and now the only thing left on my top is the thin gold necklace with its tiny diamonds sparkling in my cleavage. I feel exposed and reach for the sheet but before my hand can find it, he starts licking my nipples –

now rock hard. I gasp a little and arch my back. As he continues, I start feeling the sensation between my legs. He's not even touching me there, yet my lower region is tingling.

I'm moving beneath him now and don't feel in control. My body is responding to his touch on its own. He continues sucking me and slides one hand down between my thighs, rubbing me gently over the top of my underwear. So, I guess having the tiniest piece of silk between his fingers and my private parts is what he thought I meant by slowing down. But there's no slowing down now and I know it. Silk or no silk, it feels intense, and I don't want him to stop.

There are shivers running through my whole body and small unrecognizable sounds escaping my mouth. I move my hands down his bare chest and unbutton his jeans. He handles the zipper; we pull them over his hips together and he wiggles them the rest of the way off. I can see the head of his penis peeking above the waistband of his briefs begging to be released. He grabs ahold of it and rubs it right where his fingers had just been.

"Ahhh," I gasp as my body responds to his erection touching me. He takes my moan as a greenlight to give up the panty charade and pulls them off. He gently glides his fingers around and inside me, now warm and wet. The sensation is everywhere – all over my body. My stomach constricts each time one of my internal muscles contracts, sending electricity through my body like a shock wave.

"Are you ready for me?" he whispers in my ear, his breath making me shiver.

I can barely speak but exhale, "Condom," in an airy sigh. He shifts his attention and frantically fumbles with his jeans before finding one in his back pocket. He pulls off his briefs and slides the condom over his shaft with far too practiced ease before slowly slipping inside me. I let out a little gasp and arch forward a bit. He puts his hand underneath my back and pulls me in even closer, "Just relax. Just a little bit more."

A little bit more? Are you kidding me? My whole body is already tingling, and I don't think there's room for 'a little bit more' but I tilt my hips up toward the ceiling and there it is, the 'little bit more.' "Ahhh...." He's moving back and forth inside of me, and my body has completely surrendered to him.

Otis Redding's "Merry Christmas Baby" fills the air as I feel the blood rush to my head. A tsunami of sensation floods over my body and I am not sure if I am drowning or riding the wave. I start to quiver, intense spasms vibrating through me, "Chris....!!!" I yell grabbing the back of his hair.

"Stay with me Nikki," he says breathlessly. He doesn't realize I'm already gone so I wrap my legs around his back, lock my ankles and hold on. "Stay with me...." He thrusts several more times until his body starts to tremble. He calls out my name in three desperate declarations before I feel his body relax in a satisfied triumph. His penis immediately transforms from The Hulk to Bruce Banner and makes a quick retreat like "wasn't me."

Chris exhales deeply and rolls over onto his back, "Oh my God, Nikki. That was my favorite Christmas gift ever. Roll over here and let me hold you."

I do for a minute, but I'm soaking wet and feel a little gross. "You relax here. I'm just going to get cleaned up."

The warm water of the shower feels good on my body, like a steam after a workout. While washing up, I can't stop thinking about what just happened between us. I thought I'd had an orgasm before, but maybe I never have. I certainly never felt anything like *that* before. I guess now I know what all the fuss is about.

The bra and panty set Chris gave me fits perfectly. After spraying on a dash of perfume, I wrap up in my robe, wipe the steam from the mirror and give myself a judgmental look. I exhale feeling a little embarrassed, my thoughts battling between internal lecture and pep talk around returning to Chris.

When I enter the living room, my face must be giving away my mixed feelings because he looks at me with concern. "Everything okay?"

I hesitate before answering and inhale. "Chris," big exhale… "was that too soon?" I ask in an uncharacteristically shy tone.

He looks at me with surprise. "Too soon? I thought you made me wait forever! Plus, you're my girlfriend, Nikki, we were going to sleep together at some point."

"I'm your girlfriend?" my voice again not sounding like my own.

"Of course you're my girlfriend. We've been seeing each other exclusively for weeks and talking every single day. I kinda think that's the definition of a boyfriend-girlfriend relationship." He pauses for a second, "Oh Christ, please don't tell me people still ask one another to be in a relationship." He slides over to the side of the bed where I am sitting and kneels on the floor, buck naked, one knee bent. Grabbing hold of my hands, he looks me squarely in the eyes, "Nikki Taylor, I don't want to see anyone else, and I don't want you to see anyone else, so will you please be my girlfriend?"

My whole body washes with relief. "Yes, Chris Sheppard, I'll be your girlfriend." He reaches up, taking my face in both his hands and kisses me gently before crawling back into bed. I take in the moment, no longer feeling self-conscious about what just happened between us.

"Now that that's settled why don't you get back in here with me?" he asks, his voice warm and inviting.

"I'll join you in a minute. I'm just going to get the kitchen cleaned up. Why don't you pick out a movie? It doesn't even have to be a Rom-Com." I wink at him giving him the go-ahead.

"Really?" he sits up in bed like a kid who's just been told he can stay up past his bedtime and maybe even have ice cream. "This might possibly be the best day of my life."

Chris is perusing movie selections when I return with champagne and the cookies we made last night. I hand him a glass and propose a toast, "To my boyfriend."

He raises it in response, "To my girlfriend." I kneel on the bed crawling closer to him so we can lock arms before taking a sip.

"Would my boyfriend like to see the gift he gave me?" I ask playfully.

"Hell yeah!" he says and sits up straighter.

I put down my glass and hand him the plate of cookies before slowly, seductively and playfully opening my robe to reveal the new bra and panty set he gave me.

"Nikki, you're spectacular. Come back in here with me," he says, pulling me back into bed sending the cookies flying. He rolls me around, hands roaming everywhere, kissing me while cookies crumble beneath us. He doesn't seem to notice – his attention is entirely on me. He pushes my hair away from my face and with a devilish grin suggests, "We could skip the movie and enjoy more of this instead."

"Oh my God, Chris I need a breath!" I push him off gently. "You pick out a movie and I'll clean up these cookies."

My apartment is small enough that you can see the TV from both the sofa and the bed. Since Chris is still stark naked, I assume we'll be watching from the bed. I brush the cookie crumbs onto the plate and set them aside.

"Do you want me to clean up?" he asks, putting down the remote.

"No, but you can if you'd like."

"I think I will before we start a movie. You're all fresh as a daisy and I'm raw."

"Everything you need is in the bathroom. Just make yourself at home." And when he climbs out of bed buck naked, grabs his briefs off the floor and walks toward the bathroom like he's walking to class, I realize that telling him to make himself at home really wasn't necessary.

While Chris is in the shower, I put clean sheets on the bed. He comes out of the bathroom glistening wet with a towel wrapped around his waist, his chiseled chest looking even more scrumptious shimmering with droplets of water. "Do you have a pair of sweatpants I can borrow?"

I hold my breath for a moment at the sight of him, inhale and focus on the question at hand. "I don't think I have a pair that'll fit you, but I have an extra robe if you don't mind looking like we're on a spa date together." It's obvious at this point that he'll be spending the night.

"A robe sounds great," he says, running his fingers through his hair shaking the water off.

I brush past him doing my best to ignore the glimmering wall of perfection in front of me and dig through the bathroom linen closet in search of a second robe. He steps behind me as I'm pulling it out and sees that it's hot pink.

I turn toward him reading his expression. "I can switch and give you the white one I'm wearing," I offer.

"Absolutely not," he smiles. "I'm nothing if not confident in my masculinity." He takes it from my hands and puts it on with exaggerated bravado.

"It has matching slippers," I say with a mischievous grin.

"Anything worth doing is worth overdoing. Where are they?"

I reach down to the bottom of the closet and pull out a pair of pink fuzzy slippers. He puts them on, both of his heels hanging off the ends. "Well, how do I look?" he asks posing triumphantly.

"Like Hello-Kitty." He chuckles and pulls me into him, and we hug robe-to-robe before he leads me back toward the bed. "Do you want me to make some popcorn, or will you spill that all over the bed too?" I ask jokingly.

"Popcorn would be great. I'll try to be good, but I can't promise with you lying next to me," he says with a sly smile.

Years of experience has taught me that three and a half minutes in the microwave always makes the perfect pop, nothing burnt, no leftover kernels – can I count that as a cooking accomplishment? I crawl into bed next to him and hand him the bowl. He's selected "Silver Linings Playbook," a Philly Christmas classic that is in essence a Rom-Com, but one that men – especially Eagles fans – also enjoy.

"Well played," I say grabbing a handful of popcorn. He smiles, accepting the obvious win. We both adjust pillows behind us for a better viewing angle and cuddle in to watch the show. He reaches for my hand and gently kisses my palm as it begins. It's a simple gesture but for some reason feels like so much more.

When the movie is over, I put the empty bowl of popcorn on the floor, Chris turns off the TV and I nuzzle into him to go to sleep. He wraps his arms around me, kisses the top of my head and says, "Goodnight, Nikki Taylor."

"Goodnight, Chris Sheppard," I kiss him on the chest, lay my head down and drift off to sleep.

We make love again in the middle of the night, but this time it's gentle, easy, and beautiful. We are both still half asleep and neither of us is desperate like before. He touches me tenderly and kisses me softly while slowly moving inside me. It's a whole different kind of pleasure and I wonder what other surprises Chris Sheppard has yet to reveal.

# # #

The aroma of fresh coffee fills my nose and gently welcomes me to the day. "Good morning, sunshine," Chris says. "Can I make you some breakfast?" he asks pulling a mug out of my cabinet.

I look at him a little embarrassed, "I usually eat breakfast at the café, so I only have cereal. What time is it anyway?" I ask yawning and stretching my arms overhead. "I have to be there at noon today."

"It's only nine o'clock. You've got plenty of time. What kind of cereal do you have?" he asks with a tone that suggests he's accepted that breakfast will be rudimentary.

"Special K and Cheerios," I answer, "but I also have bananas, blueberries and honey to jazz it up a little," I add with an apologetic smile.

"Wow, a girl with a wild side," he jokes.

I shimmy my shoulders as I shuffle behind him to pull out the fixings for cereal. We eat breakfast together in the living room and he actually seems to be enjoying it.

"To the chef," he says and taps his cereal spoon with mine. My heart warms looking at him in his Hello-Kitty uniform enjoying this simple breakfast. He smiles a comfortable grin and continues eating while pulling at my eyes, suggesting we might go back to bed.

Message delivered loud and clear — he can communicate a whole lot with those eyes. "No way Chris! I have to go to work." He responds with a shrug and a smirk that clearly says he thought it was worth a try — guys, do their motors ever stop running?

When we finish, I collect the bowls and take them to the kitchen. He's fully dressed when I return, and I'm strangely sad that he's no longer wearing my pink robe.

"Well, Nikki Taylor, I guess all good things must come to an end," he pulls me into him and holds me tight. "I had such an amazing time last night," he whispers in my ear, "you are perfect in every way." I remain wrapped up in his embrace, already beginning to mourn the evening past. He lets me go gently and looks me in the eye. "How am I going to make it through exam week without seeing you?" he asks, his voice tinged with a mix of affection and frustration.

"We'll figure something out," I reply, offering him a reassuring smile. "Just get home and start studying. Get a jump on it now, and maybe it won't be so bad."

He gathers his things, and we share one last kiss, the kind that lingers just long enough to make saying goodbye harder. With a promise to call later, he's out the door.

The second it shuts behind him, I collapse onto the couch, letting out a long, dramatic sigh. "Oh – my – God," I mutter to the empty room, my thoughts spinning inside my head.

After a minute, I pour myself a cup of coffee and dial Lauren's number.

She answers immediately. "Hey, how'd it go last night?"

"Well," I say, barely containing my excitement, "he bought me theater tickets and this gorgeous bra and panty set, and yadda, yadda, yadda... he spent the night, and – um – let's just say **it** was fantastic – if you know what I mean."

"Ahhh!" she screams so loudly I have to hold the phone away from my ear. "Hold on, I'm getting my coffee... Okay, I'm back. Tell me *everything*!"

And for the next half hour Lauren and I squeal and giggle as I share every intimate detail of the evening in a way only sisters can.

At Delta the Night Before

The Last Push

Tonight was the night. Tony had to move the rest of the bag. He'd bought himself some time, but this was it and he knew there'd be enough horny guys at the frat party to get it done. He pulled open the front door of Delta to the smell of stale beer and light sweat. The party was already in full swing. He stood for a second as his eyes adjusted to the light and scanned the room before spotting the guy he was looking for over by the keg serving a group of girls. "Hey Smitty," he called over the music. "Can I talk to ya a sec?"

"Sure," Smitty yelled back, handed out the last beer he was pouring and walked over to Tony, his shoes sticking to the floor with each step. "Sup?"

"I got a bag of roofies I need to move tonight. I'll give you a cut if you help me spread the word," Tony said loud enough for Smitty to hear but low enough that no one else would.

Smitty didn't hesitate, "Sure. I'm game."

"Cool. Keep it on the down-low from the guys with girlfriends. They'll try to shut it down. You know who to talk to," Tony instructed with a nod.

"K. Divide and conquer. Then meet upstairs in my bedroom at nine to exchange the goods."

"Plan," Tony said with a fist bump and the two of them separated to start working the room.

They were surprisingly smooth operators, not drawing attention to themselves while getting it done. At nine o'clock they met upstairs and started doing business. They staggered the times people were supposed to come up so it wouldn't be obvious that something was going on. By eleven the bag was gone, their pockets were full, and they went back downstairs to enjoy the party. Problem solved (ish).

WEEK FOUR

Thursday, Week 4

Lauren

There's been a series of home robberies across Philadelphia this week. Authorities warn residents to be vigilant. Sadly, many people are desperate this time of year. A house fire in South Phil… smack, I turn off the alarm on my phone. I still haven't found the right alarm tone. The original one was too 'alarming,' the second one I tried was 'easy listening' to which I 'easily' fell right back to sleep, and now the news. I guess the news is fine, but I never wake up to anything inspiring. The news is always bad, or at least what gets reported is bad. I don't like starting my day with it. What's a happy medium? Thinking for a few minutes, it comes to me like an epiphany – Gospel music! I'm not a religious person at all, but who doesn't love some good gospel music? It's perfect for an alarm tone – loud and uplifting. I busy myself in my phone for a few minutes reprogramming my alarm and set it down feeling satisfied. One little triumph to start the day. Next, the morning routine: coffee, run, shower, dress, repeat.

I've already submitted the next two weeks columns and pipeline ideas, so I can use the holiday to work on my story.

Amanda is coming in today to give me a data dump before going home for winter break, and I'm anxious to hear what she's uncovered. She won't be here for about an hour, so I browse Todd and Tina's wedding website looking for an engagement gift for the weekend. I settle on a piece of a Le Creuset cookware set they have selected and throw in a pair of pot protectors to accompany it. While I'm on the site I scroll through their photos. They really do have a storybook romance and seem to have been born for one another. So many of my friends are in serious relationships, engaged or married. It's hard not to make comparisons with my own life, but I know my person is out there somewhere waiting to be found. Two of my single girlfriends, Sarah and Emily, will be staying with me this weekend for the engagement party. They'll want to get out and about a little while they're in town, so who knows what the weekend might hold.

"Hiya," Amanda says, breaking my train of thought.

"Oh hi. Sorry, I was just finishing something up. Let's go down to the conference room. I heard there are bagels in there."

"Okay sure. I never turn down a bagel."

I'm not sure what the occasion is but there is a full spread of bagels with all the trimmings and freshly brewed coffee available. We help ourselves and settle in at the table. "So, what on earth made you think Drew Davis has a crush on me?" I ask before we get down to business.

Amanda immediately starts laughing, "Because he does – It's so obvious! He couldn't take his eyes off you at the Christmas party.

For Christ's sake, when you bent down to pick up the pen that Barb and Amy dropped, I thought he was going to hurt himself trying not to stare at your ass." She giggles some more, this time with a snort. "And the other day when he popped in to say hello, he went into a complete stupor when you looked at him and had to make a quick exit. I think the exit had to do with losing control of his lower region if you know what I mean," she snickers.

"Oh my God, you're crazy!" I chuckle. "I'm sure you and Nikki had a good time for yourselves spinning that little tale."

"It's no tale," she says with a broad smile, "but we did have a good time together. I really like her. We're going to try to get together after break."

"Good. I knew you'd like each other. You've both got that same fiery spirit, must be the red hair. Now let's turn this conversation to something based in reality. What did you find out in your research?" I ask while spreading cream cheese on my bagel.

"A good bit actually," she replies and dives right into her report. "I met with a police officer at the station yesterday and he told me that one in four college girls will experience sexual assault at some point in their college career – one in four! Isn't that astounding?" She shakes her head and holds my attention with her intensity. "Even worse, 50% of these assaults happen in students' first semester in college when they haven't yet gotten the lay of the land or established close relationships with other girls who'll have their backs."

I can't believe what she's telling me – this is a real problem. We've got a story on our hands. "What else did he say?" I ask eager to know more.

"Well, drink spiking and the use of date rape drugs are very widely unreported crimes. The officer told me that the nature of drugs like GHB or as it's known in the streets, "Liquid G," Ketamine or "Special K," and "Roofies," – formal name, Rohypnol, is that victims who unknowingly ingest them become confused, disoriented, fatigued, less in control and more uninhibited." She's rattling off facts like she's memorized them. She hasn't glanced at her notes once. "Worse yet, these drugs metabolize rapidly so the effects are quick, and all traces of the drugs leave the victim's system within 12 to at most 72 hours. They also cause memory loss, so victims often wake up unsure if they've been victimized or not. Another huge reason these crimes go unreported. I can attest to all of this based on my roommate's reaction the night it happened to her. Thank God we were with her. Lord only knows what would have happened otherwise – we're all more careful now," she pauses to catch her breath, and I slide the cream cheese toward her noticing she hasn't touched her bagel yet. "Thanks," she takes a minute to smear before taking a bite.

I nod and turn back to the conversation. "What about safeguards on college campuses?"

"Most universities have posted resources, signs to look out for, precautions to take when going out with friends…," she says as she chews, shielding her mouth with her hand. "They have offices for student health and assistance, support groups, etcetera, but since 90% of these crimes aren't reported to the universities, it's almost like the problem doesn't exist." She swallows and takes a sip of coffee to wash it down before continuing. "Also, from what I can tell from talking to people, this occurs more often at college house parties and in frat houses than in bars. Fraternities and houses in general are set up for it – lots of chaos, free flowing alcohol that no one is monitoring, young coeds eager to explore college life, and lots of available private rooms."

I can't believe what she's telling me and why more isn't being done about it. "What about the Greek Inter-Fraternity Council?" I ask, certain someone is paying attention to this.

"Well, they try to handle things as best they can on the downlow. They clearly have no incentive to collaborate with the universities on this issue for fear of being kicked-off campus, and they face the same problem other authoritative bodies do with under-reporting," she explains, wiping her mouth and going in for another bite.

"So, this is a prolific problem on college campuses... one that has no coordinated prevention or retaliation system because the victims are not reporting the crimes." I say, both as a question and a statement, shocked that no one seems to be doing anything about what is obviously a serious problem.

"Pretty much. And when these crimes are reported, they're very hard if not impossible to prove." She takes another swig of coffee and continues, eager to share what she's learned. "I also talked to some bartenders, and while there are standard protocols that come with having a liquor license, bars tend to enforce safety at their own comfort level. Some have drink testing kits on hand in case they suspect a drink has been spiked; some have training programs for staff and procedures in place if a customer is suspected of being drugged; others have policies around not leaving customers' drinks on the bar and only handing them directly to the people who ordered them, and others just play it by ear."

"This is incredible work Amanda," I say, feeling an odd sense of pride in the research she's done. "It'll give me plenty to write about over the Christmas holiday. I'm going to see if I can get your stipend increased. People are pretty liberal around here with their expense reports, so I don't see why some of that budget couldn't be reallocated to the intern program. I want to make sure you come back next semester."

Amanda smiles, her eyes lighting up. "Oh, I definitely plan on coming back – stipend increase or not. This has been such a great experience. I really enjoy working with you."

"I feel the same way," I reply. "Now, let's get you out of here and kick off your holiday break." I stand and pull her into a quick hug. "Merry Christmas, Amanda."

"Merry Christmas to you too, Lauren." She grabs her bag and starts packing up her things. "I hope you and Nikki have a wonderful holiday together. And, seriously, just text me if you need anything over the break. I don't care if I'm not officially on the clock."

We share one last hug, and I walk her to the elevator, watching her go with a smile.

Same Day

Nikki

I just finish getting ready for the day when my phone chants *Fly Eagles, Fly....* "Hi Chris."

"Hey, babe," Chris says warmly. "I've only been home one night, and I miss you already. We barely saw each other during exams, and now the thought of being apart for another week and a half... Unbearable."

I can hear the longing in his voice, and it makes me smile. "I miss you too," I sigh. "But we'll survive."

"Why should we have to 'survive.' How about you come out to Ardmore this weekend?" he suggests. "Stay at my parents' place with me. You can meet them, and all my friends will be home for break. I'll get you back to the city in plenty of time for Christmas Eve with Lauren, promise."

His invitation sounds so tempting, but as usual I have to work. "That sounds amazing, but I'm on the schedule for the weekend. I'm the only waitress and Jerry's the only cook staying in town for the holidays, so we have to cover."

"Ugh, that sucks," he says, clearly disappointed but unwilling to let it go. "Can't you talk your manager into closing a few days early? How much business can you really do with just one waitress and one cook?"

I laugh softly. "If you saw last year's sales for this weekend, you'd be right, but I don't know if my manager will go for it. Most of the dogs I walk are either home with their owners or traveling for the holidays, so it's not too bad on that end. But the café is still open until Christmas week."

Chris sounds thoughtful for a moment. "Well, if anyone can convince him, it's you. I know how persuasive you can be."

Knowing where his mind is, I caution, "Oh no, don't go there."

"Hey, I'm just saying," he teases. "But seriously, I need you here. I can't stop thinking about you... about all of you."

I laugh, shaking my head. "You have a one-track mind."

"I know," he says, sounding way too pleased with himself. "And that track is *you*."

I sigh. "Okay, okay. I'll talk to my manager tomorrow and see if I can get things worked out. I'll let you know."

"Thanks, babe. You're the best." He pauses. "So, what else have you been up to without me?"

# # #

Today is my day to shop for Lauren's stocking stuffers. I already have her main gift but since I wasn't counting on also having to get Chris a present this year, I had to wait to save up enough money for the stocking gifts.

Off I go feeling in the holiday spirit. As I walk the streets admiring the window displays and ducking in and out of shops, I can't stop hoping I can convince my manager to close on Saturday and Sunday. Lauren has plans this weekend and everyone else has already left for the holidays. It would be so nice to spend a carefree weekend with Chris and not have to worry about school or work.

Friday, Week 4

Nikki

Today is pitch day. I arrive at the café a little early, hoping to catch Jerry before Clyde gets in.

"Good morning, Jerry," I greet him with a smile.

He looks up from behind the counter grinning. "Good morning, Nick. Another day of living the dream?"

"You know it." I lean against the counter, then glance around to make sure Clyde's not here yet. "Listen, Jerry, can I talk to you about something before Clyde gets in?"

He nods, wiping his hands on a kitchen towel. "Of course, what's up?"

"Well," I start, hesitating for a moment, "last year we didn't make any money this weekend, and I'd really love to have the weekend off if I can talk Clyde into closing. But I didn't want to say anything if you were counting on working."

Jerry looks at me obviously amused. "Counting on working? Are you kidding?" He chuckles. "I'd love to be off this weekend and get the holiday started. I'll be your wingman. We can talk to him together," he says, giving me a fist bump.

We get the place set-up and wait for customers who have yet to arrive. Finally, the bell above the door rings and in walk two large, uniformed police officers. "Good morning, Officers. Sit anywhere you'd like," I say cheerfully, picking up two menus.

"We're not here to eat, ma'am," one of them replies, his voice thick with a distinctive DelCo accent. "We're looking for Nikki Taylor."

"I'm Nikki Taylor. Is everything alright? Has something happened with my dad?" I ask, my heart racing with concern.

"No Ms. Taylor, nothing like that," the officer reassures me. "We just need to ask you a few questions. Can you join us at one of these tables?"

"Sure," I reply, a little confused. "I'll just grab us some coffee and be right back."

"That won't be necessary, Ms. Taylor," he interrupts, his tone firm but not unkind. "Please just have a seat." He motions to the nearest booth.

I nod and slide into the booth hesitantly. "Okay, but if a customer comes in, I'll have to excuse myself. I'm the only waitress here today."

"That's fine. This won't take long." He takes a seat across from me and begins, "Ms. Taylor, I'm Officer Gaines, and this is my partner, Officer Burns. We're investigating a string of burglaries in the area, and while not all of them are connected, we've found one common denominator in three of the cases... you."

The blood drains from my face and my palms are immediately sweaty. I blink and try to process what he just said. "Me? How so?" I ask meekly, anxiously holding my breath unable to imagine what's coming next.

"Three of the homes that were broken into are owned by people whose dogs you walk," Officer Gaines explains, his expression all business.

"You can't possibly think I broke into those houses?" I feel the panic rising in my chest as I continue. "They're my clients! I would never steal from them. Besides, they always know when I'm going to be there, and I'm sure you're aware that Uber Leash does background checks on all of us," I add, trying to rationalize any of it.

"Yes, we're aware of that," Officer Gaines says with a small, reassuring smile, though his imposing size is still intimidating. "But while we have to consider you a suspect..."

"A suspect??" I interrupt, shocked. "Officers, I'm more than happy to bring you to my apartment right now if you want to search it. You won't find anything, I promise."

Officer Gaines seems to sympathize with my distress and tries to put me at ease. "We may want to take you up on that offer, but for now, we just have a few questions," he says.

I manage a nervous, "Okay," and brace myself for the questioning.

He pulls out a small notepad and a pen, his gaze intense as he continues. "Where do you keep the keys to your clients' homes?"

"In my purse," I answer quickly, "and the codes for the ones that have keypads are in my phone," I pause, then continue realizing what the next question will be, "which is usually in my purse, too."

"Who has access to your purse?" he asks, pen poised over his pad.

"No one."

He doesn't seem satisfied with that answer. "Do you have any roommates?"

"No. I live alone."

"Where is your purse right now?" he asks, staring me in the eyes, accessing my demeanor.

I take a deep breath before answering, feeling the pressure building. "It's hanging in the back, where all the employees hang their things when we're working."

"We'll need the names and contact information for everyone who works here," he says, releasing his gaze and turning his attention to the notepad.

"Okay," I nod even though he's not looking at me. "I can get that from my manager when he gets in. He should be here shortly."

Officer Gaines finishes whatever he scribbled on the pad and returns his focus to me. "What else do you do when you're not working here?"

I wet my lips which are suddenly dry before answering. "I'm a student at Drexel."

He continues matter-of-factly, "What do you do with your purse when you're in class?"

"I carry it with me and hang it on the back of my chair during class." I exhale and wait for the next question.

"Are your classes large lectures or smaller classrooms?" he asks without looking up from the pad.

"Both, but now that I'm a senior, my classes are more specialized, so they're usually in smaller rooms."

"Can you think of anyone else who might have access to your bag?" he presses.

"No," I answer, shaking my head. "Am I in trouble, Officer Gaines? I've never been involved with the police before, and you're really scaring me."

"Not right now," he says calmly, his expression softening. "But we're going to need a list of all your dog client addresses. We'll keep an eye on those homes and maybe we'll catch the culprit in the act."

"Okay," I say, swallowing hard. "Give me a minute and I can write those down for you. I'll need to get my phone and my keys to make sure I get them all right. Is that okay?" I ask hesitantly.

"That's fine Ms. Taylor. I'll escort you."

Just then Clyde walks in. "Oh, here's my manager now. I can ask him for the staff list."

"We'll take care of that," Officer Gaines says, motioning for me to stand. "Let's go get your bag."

Officer Gaines escorts me to the back while Officer Burns talks to Clyde and follows him to the office. I pull out a blank check from the billfold in my apron and struggle to write a list of addresses with trembling hands. Officer Gaines is standing before me just watching. Both his size and his authority are intimidating as hell. I take a deep breath and slow down trying not to show my nerves. I don't want him to think I appear guilty. "Here you go," I say, handing him the list when I finally finish.

"One more question, Ms. Taylor," he says, glancing at the list. "Did you notice anything unusual at the Coopers' house on Saturday when you went to walk their dogs?"

"Well," I begin, thinking back to Saturday, "there was mail and magazines on the floor in front of the coffee table, and the dogs had knocked over a potted plant that was broken on the floor."

"How do you know the dogs broke the plant?" he asks.

"Because they were the only ones there," I answer. "And I'm sure the Coopers wouldn't have left it that way."

"Did you walk through the apartment while you were there?" he asks, wheels turning in his head.

Static from his radio startles me and I jump slightly. Calm down Nikki... "I just went into the kitchen to get a dustpan to clean up the spilled dirt."

"Okay," he says, still jotting notes. "And did you notice anything different when you returned the dogs after the walk?"

"No," I reply, shaking my head. "Not that I remember. I wasn't really paying attention." Then it dawns on me... "Wait, there was some mail on the floor. I thought I'd picked it all up before we left for the walk, but it was under the coffee table so maybe I just didn't see it at first."

"You've been very helpful, Ms. Taylor," Officer Gaines says with a nod and the faintest hint of a smile cracking through that gruff exterior. "Here's my card in case you think of anything else. I'll be in touch if we have any more questions." He pats my hand reassuringly as he hands me the card. "Oh, and please, be cautious when entering these homes. We'll be watching, but it might be a good idea to bring a friend with you."

The officers leave and Jerry, Clyde, and I stand in stunned silence for a moment before Clyde finally speaks. "Well, that was unexpected," he says, shaking his head.

"I'll say," Jerry adds, his voice tense.

"You know I'm not involved in any of this, right?" I ask, feeling the weight of their stares.

"I'm sure it's just a coincidence Nikki," Clyde reassures me, "I don't think anyone from Mocha Loco would be involved in something like this, but the whole thing has me weirded out. Anyone else feel like throwing in the towel early for the holiday break? We didn't make any money this weekend last year anyway."

"Yes!" Jerry and I answer in unison and high-five when Clyde turns toward the door to flip the open sign to closed.

I dial Chris's number as I start the walk home, my hands still a little shaky from the whole encounter. The phone rings three times before he picks up. "Hey babe. I thought you were working this morning."

"I was, but something happened," I say, a slight quiver in my voice.

"What? You sound upset." Chris's concern comes through the line loud and clear.

"I'm still just a little shaken," I start. "The police came into the café this morning to question me about a string of burglaries in the area. Apparently three of my dog homes have been broken into."

"Wait – what?!" Chris's voice jumps an octave. "They don't think you're involved, do they?"

"They told me I'm a suspect," I say, the words feeling foreign on my tongue. "But honestly, I don't think they actually think I have anything to do with it. The officer who questioned me seemed satisfied with my answers and was more concerned about my safety than anything else."

"Your safety?" Chris repeats, his voice suddenly tight. "What did he say?"

"Well..." I exhale slowly. "He told me to be cautious when entering the homes and that, until the case is solved, I should think about bringing someone with me when I walk the dogs."

"Okay that's scary. I'm going with you on all your dog appointments from now on."

I laugh weakly, not able to muster a full chuckle knowing this is an actual situation. "I've been going into these homes by myself for well over a year, and I might remind you that I live alone. I'm a big girl Chris, but maybe until this is resolved you should come with me," I say, almost reassuring myself.

"Okay big girl," he teases, but there's a definite edge to his voice. "I'm coming with you. No arguments." I sigh with relief at his insistence. I really don't want to go into these homes alone anymore. "What did your boss say about all this?" he asks.

"Thankfully, he doesn't think I'm involved," I say, feeling a bit of relief in my own words. "But the whole thing spooked him out enough that he decided to close the café until after the holidays. So, at least there's that."

"That's fantastic!" he exclaims, all previous tension gone from his voice. "When can you get here?"

"I'll have to check the train schedule," I glance down at my watch. "But probably later this afternoon."

"Okay. Text me the time and I'll pick you up at the station. My mom is so excited to meet you," Chris says, and I can hear the smile in his voice.

"Don't talk me up too much," I sigh. "That's a lot of pressure, even for me."

"Oh, come on," he says with playful confidence. "I've only told her the obvious – that you're beautiful, smart, sexy, and sassy."

"Oh great," I groan. "So, she's expecting Emma Stone."

I call Lauren next to fill her in on the police situation and let her know I'll be spending the weekend at Chris's, so she doesn't worry. After a few deep breaths, I shake off the events of the morning and head home to pack. What a day and it's only 9:00 a.m.

Suspicion

As soon as Chris was off the phone with Nikki, he dialed Tony with a sticky feeling in his gut. "Hey dog. What's up? Miss me already?" Tony asked as he answered the phone.

Chris skipped the pleasantries and got right to it. "Do you know anything about robberies at Nikki's dog homes?"

"What are ya talkin' about?"

Chris couldn't detect guilt or innocence in Tony's voice. "Some of Nikki's dog houses have been broken into and now she's a suspect. She was questioned by the police today. Do you know anything about it?" Chris asked again, sternly.

"No. What the hell, man?" Tony shot back.

Chris wasn't convinced. "I swear to God Tony, if you're involved in this in any way, I'm turning you into the police myself. Got it?"

"Yeah, Merry Christmas to you too, douchebag." *Click.*

Later that Day

Nikki

"Hey gorgeous," Chris calls out as he strides toward me on the platform, his eyes lighting up as he gets closer.

"Hey there," I grin, dropping my bag so I can hug him. "Did you miss me?"

"Worst two days of my life," he says, pulling me closer for a kiss.

He grabs my bag and laces his fingers through mine as we walk toward the parking lot, and for a moment, it feels like we're starting a mini vacation together. The air is crisp, and the sky is just beginning to fade, making it feel like the day is holding its breath before night falls.

We drive through town, which is an urban-suburban mix of restaurants, shops, and housing. It's quaint and hip at the same time, very Main Line. I can see how growing up here would be nice.

"I'm going to take you to Longwood Gardens tonight," Chris says breaking me out of my thoughts. "Have you ever been?"

"No, but I've heard it's nearly impossible to get tickets around the holidays." I look at him a little suspiciously, "How'd you manage that?"

He smiles at my tone knowing that I think he's finagled something. "My mom booked tickets a while ago, but my dad's knee's been acting up, so he doesn't want to go. They've been a bunch of times anyway, so she gave the tickets to me. Lucky, right?"

"I'll say," I smile and immediately feel badly. "I mean, that's too bad about your dad's knee, but lucky for us. I've heard the lights there are unreal during the holidays."

"Yeah, they're pretty amazing," he says, reaching for my hand. "Our tickets are for six o'clock, so we'll need to leave around five to make sure we can park and get in before they time out."

We are driving through lovely tree lined neighborhoods with charming houses when Chris pulls into the driveway of a stone house with white dormers and black shutters, a white columned covered porch and literally a white picket fence lining the front yard. "Here we are. Home sweet home."

"Mom, we're home!" he calls, his voice echoing through the grand foyer. A towering 12-to-14-foot Christmas tree stands at the center, adorned with twinkling white lights and an array of red and gold ornaments in various shapes and sizes. The air is filled with the fresh scent of pine, giving the whole house a festive warmth that welcomes us in.

"Hey honey," says an attractive Italian-looking woman wearing jeans, black leather booties, a long white silk blouse that hangs below a shorter fitted black sweater and is accessorized with pearls. She kisses Chris on the cheek and turns to me, "You must be Nikki.   Welcome."

"Hi Mrs. Sheppard. It's nice to meet you." I extend my hand to shake hers, but she grabs hold of me and hugs me instead.

"Please, call me Marie and we're huggers. Chris, why don't you take Nikki's things up to the guest room and I'll take your coat, dear." I slip out of my coat and hand it to her.

"I just put on a fresh pot of coffee," she says while hanging my coat in the hall closet, "I hope decaf is okay."

"That's perfect. I only drink high-test in the morning."

Chris jogs up the front staircase with my bag, taking the steps two at a time and I follow Marie to the kitchen. It's an impressive, large open-concept room with a center island that leads to an eat-in kitchen-den. Beyond that is a screened in porch that walks out to a covered patio and then the backyard. "You have a lovely home, Marie."

"Oh, thank you." Marie responds, her smile warm and proud. "We've been here for years. Chris grew up in this house. How do you take your coffee?"

"Black," Chris answers joining us in the kitchen. "Do we have any iced tea?" he asks grabbing a glass from the cupboard. "I'd rather have something cold."

"I'm not sure, honey. Check and see," Marie replies while pouring the coffee. "Did you get Nikki set up upstairs?"

"If you mean, did I put her bag on the guest bed then yes," Chris answers, checking the fridge for iced tea.

Marie rolls her eyes and hands me a steaming mug with a playful sigh. "John stopped by while you were out," she says to Chris. "His mom made her famous fudge and peanut brittle, and he was out on deliveries. Would you like some?"

"I'd love some peanut brittle," I say and take a seat at the island, savoring the feel of the warm mug in my hand. "It's my favorite. My sister and I used to make it every year for our dad, but he can't eat it anymore so now we make toffee with a softer graham cracker crust."

Marie opens the tin on the counter, handing it to me with an inviting smile. "Help yourself, dear." She then turns her attention back to Chris. "Chris, I saw Joan at the club the other day, and she said Michelle is home from her semester abroad."

Chris looks over at his mom with a half-amused, half-accusatory smirk. "And I'm sure you mentioned that to John when he was here."

"Just in passing," she says lightly.

"Real subtle, Mom," Chris mutters, shaking his head.

This exchange has me curious. I take a bite of the brittle and look from one to the other. "Who's Michelle?" I ask, my interest piqued.

"She's John's high school girlfriend," Chris explains, a hint of exasperation in his tone like he's told this story one too many times. "They broke up when we all went to college, but they still have a thing for each other. Our moms are always conspiring to get them back together," Chris pauses, then adds, "it's annoying and not helpful."

"I wouldn't call it conspiring Chris," Marie says in a way that indicates she's explained this away before. "Everyone knows they want to be together. It was pathetic watching them trying not to be in love last summer."

"Awww, I think that's kinda tragic." I help myself to a second piece of peanut brittle and relax a little further into the stool thinking about John's situation. "I wondered why a nice, good-looking guy like John wasn't dating anyone."

"So, you think John is good-looking?" Chris asks, challenging me with his eyes.

"Of course, he's good-looking. Anyone would describe him that way," I start to defend my position, but Marie interjects, "Don't mind him, Nikki. He and John have been in a competition over everything since they were in the first grade." She gives her son a pointed look. "She didn't say he was better looking than you Chris, just good-looking."

Chris sighs dramatically, putting his hands up in mock surrender. "Okay, fair enough. I just like to know when I have competition, even if it is John. I'm already her second favorite Sheppard." He grins, leaning back against the counter and crossing his arms over his chest. "Her first love is a hairy guy of German persuasion who lives in a penthouse in Rittenhouse Square."

Marie turns toward me looking confused and a little annoyed that Chris is talking in riddles, "What is he talking about please?"

I laugh and answer with a smile. "I walk dogs for Uber Leash and Chester is my favorite client. He happens to be a German Shepherd and is almost as handsome as your son."

Chris wraps his arms around me from behind. I feel a little uncomfortable with the public display of affection in front of his mother, but they both seem unfazed, so I relax into it. "Marie, thank you for the Longwood Gardens tickets. I've never been and I'm really excited."

"Oh, you'll love it, dear." Chris rests his chin on the top of my head which still sparks no reaction from Marie. It makes me wonder how many girls have stood in my shoes before me. "The Christmas display is spectacular," she continues. "You'll have to bundle up though. Most of it is outdoors."

"I'll change into a turtleneck and better walking shoes before we go."

"You'll have to leave shortly." Marie turns her attention to her son. "Chris, why don't you show Nikki to her room so she can change."

Chris pulls me off the stool and I grab my coffee mug as I stand. "Thanks for the treats, Marie." She smiles warmly and shoos us away with her hands.

Chris leads me into the guest bedroom and wraps his arms around me. "This is where you'll be staying and where I'll be perfecting the QB sneak later tonight."

"The QB sneak?" I repeat.

He grins mischievously and shuts the door behind us. "Sorry, football reference, my bad. In this scenario it stands for 'quiet bedroom sneak.'"

I glance at him sideways. "The fact that you've coined a term for that is a little unsettling. I don't want to be a statistic."

Chris chuckles, his gaze locking with mine, and he leans in, his lips brushing the side of my cheek with a soft peck. "Too late. You're already number one," he whispers into my ear. "Now get changed and I'll meet you downstairs in the foyer. We've got a date with some lights and a couple of thousand other people."

Once he leaves, I glance around the room, admiring its bright, tasteful decor and the convenience of the en-suite bathroom. A bookcase along the far wall catches my eye; it's filled with family photos. I pick up a few, smiling at the images of what seems to be a genuinely happy, loving family. Of course, no one frames bad moments, but these pictures radiate warmth. Several feature Chris at different ages – he was an adorable child who doesn't seem to have experienced an awkward stage, or at least not one that was photographed – doesn't everyone have at least one picture of themselves with no front teeth? Feeling slightly guilty for "semi-snooping," I carefully put the photos back and change into warmer clothes.

Chris is waiting for me in the foyer, already bundled up and holding my coat. "Do you have a hat and gloves?" he asks.

I nod. "Yep, they're in my coat pockets."

"Okay then, let's go."

When we arrive at Longwood Gardens, illuminated traffic signs direct us to off-site parking. Following the stream of cars, we pull into a lot where attendants in reflective vests, waving what look like mini light sabers, guide us to our spot. Once parked, an attendant points us toward the shuttle stop for a ride to the main entrance.

"Wow, this is quite the production," I say, impressed before even getting started.

Chris nods, agreeing, "I'm glad we left in plenty of time."

Entering the gardens is like walking into a winter snow globe, minus the snow of course. It's truly a magical winter wonderland. Hundreds of trees are lit in different colors and huge white stars hang high from the trees that aren't lit making them appear to be suspended in the night sky.

"Let's walk toward the Conservatory first," Chris says.

The walk to the Conservatory is along a tree lit path that comes to an intersection dominated by a towering Christmas tree adorned with multicolored lights, countless oversized ornaments, and full inlaid poinsettias. A line of people is waiting to take photos in front of it, so we continue on.

At the next intersection, we have the option to head up the stairs toward the Conservatory, but instead, we detour through a tunnel of lights to the left. The colors shift and swirl around us, creating the illusion of being inside a kaleidoscope. After snapping a few selfies, we double back and head up the steps. From the top, we can see fountains below, shooting vibrant colored streams of water into the air in various formations. It's all set to music piping from outdoor speakers, and the water performs a choreographed dance that punctuates the dramatic sounds filling the air. It's quite spectacular.

We carefully navigate through the crowd, trying not to photobomb all the people taking pictures as we approach the Conservatory entrance. Inside, the atrium is filled with an abundance of plants, trees, and intricate decorations, leaving only narrow paths to walk through. The fragrance in the air is so strong that it makes simply breathing feel like a new experience.

Above us, the ceiling is adorned with massive hanging poinsettias in a range of colors, while themed trees line the pathways around a central water feature displaying floating floral and ornamental designs. It's absolutely breathtaking. We slowly wander through, taking in the beauty around us. As we near the grand tree dripping with crystal icicles at the water's edge, a young man kneels and proposes to his girlfriend. She says yes, and the bystanders applaud. This is a place where dreams are both imagined and made.

We continue through the rest of the building in silence, just taking it all in, before exiting through a side door that leads to the beer garden. There's a line for hot chocolate, but we wait so we can carry it with us on the rest of the walk outside. When we're finally served, the sweet creamy smell of chocolate mixes with the cool air and the warmth of the cups heats our hands.

"Let's go to the outdoor train display next and then we can walk to the treehouses and climb through them if you'd like," Chris suggests reaching for my hand and leading the way.

"Okay. There's so much to see."

"After the treehouses we can walk around the lake. There are more decorations in and around it and the path leads back to the entrance."

"You seem to have taken the tour guide training course so I'm following you." I joke.

When we eventually reach the lake, there are enormous, illuminated stars and oversized Christmas balls surrounding the water with floating trees shimmering in the center. It feels like the most festive and romantic date I've ever had. Even though the cold air is numbing my cheeks, I am warm inside.

# # #

"Chris we're in the living room," Marie calls when she hears the door open, "come introduce Nikki to your father."

His parents are sitting in the main living room in front of the fire enjoying a cocktail. The fireplace mantel is decorated with magnolia and nutcrackers and three stockings hang to one side. Another fully decorated Christmas tree, not as large as the one in the foyer, stands regally in the corner of the room flanked by a baby grand piano in the other.

"Dad, this is Nikki," Chris says, "Nikki, this is my dad, Bob."

Bob offers a welcoming smile and makes a movement to get up, "Please don't get up, sir. I know you hurt your knee." I extend my hand and instead of shaking it he pulls it in and kisses it, "Ahh bless you," he says and settles back in his chair giving my hand a gentle squeeze before releasing it. I can see where Chris gets his charm, this man is clearly a gentleman. "Will the two of you join us for a drink?" he asks.

"We'd like that, but we're starving," Chris says. "We kind of lost track of dinner plans tonight. Do you have any leftovers, Mom?"

Marie shakes her head apologetically. "No sorry, honey, but I can whip up a couple of grilled cheese sandwiches if you'd like."

"Thanks Mom, that's great," Chris says. "Nikki, what can I get you to drink?"

"A glass of chardonnay?"

"Coming right up."

I take a seat in a wing back chair by the fireplace and settle into the cozy atmosphere. "So, Bob, how did you injure your knee?" I ask, opening the conversation.

"Playing pickleball," he replies with an easy grin. "Do you play?"

"Afraid not, but I hear it's all the rage," I say, trying to imagine this man in pickleball attire. He seems to be overdressed for someone enjoying a Friday night in his own home.

Chris hands me a glass of wine and sets his beer down on the coffee table before pulling two wooden TV trays out of the hall closet. I don't know why this strikes me as odd, but this does not seem like a TV tray family.

"Chris, will you throw another log on the fire, please?" Bob asks, settling deeper into his chair. "I don't want to get up."

"Sure, Dad. Do you need anything else?"

"No. I'm going to enjoy the company of this lovely young lady. Why don't you see if your mother needs help in the kitchen." And right on cue Marie returns with two plates of grilled cheese sandwiches and a nonjudgmental bottle of ketchup. Thank God, I didn't want to have to ask for it.

Chris and I enjoy our sandwiches while Bob asks all the typical 'getting to know you' questions and Marie interjects pleasantries. We chat for a while longer until they finish their drinks and announce they are going to turn in. "Chris, please turn off the tree lights before going to bed."

"Will do, Mom. See you in the morning." A round of good nights is exchanged, and Chris and I are alone again.

Finally

Chris let out a sigh of relief, he'd been waiting for this moment all evening. "I thought they'd never leave," he said, turning to Nikki with a frisky grin. "Now that we're finally alone, how about we pour another drink and head down to the basement for a Christmas movie? We'll be two floors below them, so we'll have some privacy. A much better plan than the guest room."

Nikki smiled, taking his hand. "Dial it back a little big guy. I'm still hanging on to the fact that it's my turn to pick the movie. And I'm going old school."

He was more interested in her than the movie choice, but still planned on challenging her for it. He grabbed the rest of the chardonnay and led her downstairs. The basement was set up for viewing pleasure – plush sectional, big screen TV, and a basket full of soft throws. Chris snagged a beer from the mini-fridge and made a move for the remote, but Nikki was quicker, snatching it before he could get to it. "Ah, ah, ah," she teased, wagging her finger playfully. He couldn't help but smile as he poured her a glass of wine and grabbed one of the blankets, settling in beside her on the couch.

She chose "It's a Wonderful Life," and even though Chris had seen it countless times, it felt like the perfect choice to cap off a holiday evening. But as the movie started, he found it hard to focus. He was still charged up from last weekend, and all he could think about was making that happen again. Nikki seemed completely content watching the movie, but Chris was fighting an internal battle. He just wanted to feel her skin, all of it, everywhere. He made a deal with himself – if he could keep his hands where they belonged for the first half hour of the movie, then it would be okay to make a move. *Thirty minutes, Chris. You got this.*

But when Jimmy Stewart tried to stop the run on the bank, Chris's self-control gave out. He started stroking the back of Nikki's hair, and when she snuggled in closer, he turned her head toward him and kissed her. What started as a gentle kiss quickly intensified, and before he knew it, he was straddling her, kissing her hungrily. She didn't pull away, so he didn't stop. His hands found their way under her sweater, exploring the warmth of her skin as he kissed her neck. To his surprise, Nikki crisscrossed her arms grabbing the hem of her sweater and pulled it off over her head, tossing it aside.

Now there was no turning back. Chris unfastened her bra, sliding it off before taking one of her breasts in his mouth. Her nipples were hard, and so was he. The more he touched her, the more he wanted her, and soon he was unbuttoning his jeans, eager to feel more of her. Nikki helped him tug his pants off, and he kissed and licked his way down her body, stopping at the button of her jeans. Together, they worked them off. Chris's mouth continued its way downward until he was kneeling on the floor in front of her. He slid off her underwear, feeling the heat between them intensify.

He knew she was expecting his touch, but instead, Chris leaned in and pressed his tongue against her. The sound of her gasp was intoxicating, and he could tell she'd never experienced this before. That turned him on even more. He continued to pleasure her with his tongue until he felt her body begin to tremble. Nikki clutched his hair in her fists, her whimpers growing louder, and he knew she was close.

As she reached the edge, Chris pulled off his underwear, gripped her hips, and guided her down on top of him. She let out a small yelp as he entered her, and he tried to slow down, to be gentle. Their bodies maneuvered around one another for a moment until they found a rhythm. Nikki held onto Chris's shoulders and pulsed up and down. "That's it," he moaned and grabbed ahold of her hips to help intensify the movement, "that's it…" A bell rang on the TV as they moved together in perfect sync. Chris and Nikki reached the same place at the same time just as Clarence got his wings.

Saturday, Week 4

Nikki

The smell of coffee and bacon pulled Chris from his sleep, he blinked, remembering he was back home, and Nikki was just down the hall. He threw on a pair of sweatpants and a t-shirt, then knocked on her door. "Nikki, you awake?"

"Yeah, come on in. I'm just looking for something to wear."

Chris pushed the door open to find her rummaging through her bag, wearing an oversized nightshirt. "Come here gorgeous, I'll grab you a sweatshirt. I smell breakfast downstairs."

"Perfect," Nikki said, smiling up at him through thick lashes and leaning in for a kiss.

As he left the room, Chris hesitated, turning back to look at her. "Last night was amazing, Nikki," he said, holding her gaze. He noticed a hint of shyness in her expression, a rare moment of vulnerability from someone usually so self-assured. It made him feel something deeper, knowing she was experiencing firsts with him.

They walked into the kitchen together, and his mother greeted them warmly. "Good morning! Did you sleep well?"

"Like a baby," Chris replied, turning to Nikki. "Coffee?"

"I thought you'd never ask," she said with a smile.

Nikki was wearing Chris's Temple sweatshirt and a pair of leggings, her hair piled in a messy knot on top of her head. The sight of her, standing there in his childhood home, wearing his clothes, stirred something inside him. It felt right, like they belonged together.

Nikki caught him staring. "What?" she said self-consciously.

"Nothing," Chris answered with a grin. "I just like seeing you in my sweatshirt. You can keep it – it looks good on you."

She smiled back, giving him a look that he wanted to hold. She took a seat at the counter and Chris took her in, thinking she'd never looked more beautiful.

"I made scrambled eggs and bacon if you're hungry," his mom offered.

"Sounds great. Where's Dad?"

"He already ate and went to the hardware store. I swear, sometimes I think he's got a girlfriend who works there," she joked.

Chris chuckled. "He just likes to keep busy."

After breakfast, Nikki mentioned wanting to pick up a hostess gift for his mom. Chris thought it was unnecessary but didn't argue. He wasn't about to try to figure out women that morning, so they went. They were walking down Lancaster Avenue hand-in-hand when they bumped into a few of Chris's old high school buddies.

"Shepp! You going to McCloskey's tonight?"

"Yeah, we'll be there. Guys, this is Nikki. Nikki, these are a bunch of guys whose names you don't need to remember," he said, pulling her closer.

"Hi, we're Matt, Brian, and Jake. So, what are you doing with this jerk anyway?" Matt joked.

Nikki smiled, "Nice to meet you guys. I don't know, I think he's kinda cute."

"You seem like someone with better taste," Matt teased, trying to get a rise out of Chris. "But hey, we'll try to talk some sense into you later tonight. Any one of the three of us would be a better choice."

"Back off, losers. I'm standing right here," Chris said, pretending to be irritated.

Matt just grinned. "Didn't notice, Shepp. I was blinded by Nikki's beauty."

"Alright, that's enough. I know I'm going to have to put up with this later. We'll see you tonight," Chris said pulling Nikki in the direction to leave.

Matt gave him an arched eyebrow smirk as they turned to walk away. Chris shook his head and couldn't help but think, *I guess it's pretty unusual for me to be walking around town with a girl on my arm, shopping for gifts*. But it felt good – different, but good.

They had lunch in town before heading back to the house. Nikki picked out a "Dickens at Christmas" coffee table book as a gift for Chris's mom. Marie loved it and was gushing all over Nikki making Chris realize he might need to step up his own Christmas gift game this year. Maybe Nikki could help with that tomorrow. But for now, he was just looking forward to tonight – reconnecting with the old gang and showing off the girl who had quickly become so important to him.

Caught in the Act... Almost

Rocco had been making a good haul looting Nikki's dog homes. It was just like Tony said − easy in, easy out − but he was getting reckless, becoming too comfortable with the new gig. It was close to the holidays and therefore people's usual routines were no longer predictable − Rocco didn't account for that.

He was in the bedroom of a quaint brick row home in West Philly rifling through a jewelry drawer when the cockapoo who lived there ran excitedly toward the front door. He heard it squeak open, and voices greet the dog. *Fuck!*

He quickly scanned the room looking for a way out. Luckily there was a window that faced a back alley. He knew it was his only option, and he'd have to move fast. He pushed the window up quietly and kicked the screen out, not so quietly, before jumping through. It was broad daylight, so anyone could've seen him, but he had no alternative. He pulled up his hoodie as soon as his feet hit the ground and ran, hoping for the best.

Later that Night in Ardmore

Nikki

When we arrive at McCloskey's, it's already buzzing with energy. It's the oldest Irish bar on the Main Line and is known for its high-quality selection of craft beers and homestyle menu. The bar's packed with regulars and college students home on break, the air thick with laughter and conversation. Chris is greeting people left and right, his presence magnetic as always. I'm scanning the room for John, so I'll at least know one other person besides Chris. Just then, a stunning blonde weaves through the crowd and heads straight for Chris.

"Merry Christmas, Shepp!" she says brightly, wrapping him in a hug.

"Hey, Michelle. Merry Christmas to you too." Chris grins, then pulls back slightly to introduce me. "This is my girlfriend, Nikki."

"Your girlfriend?" Michelle looks at me with surprise. "Well pleased to meet *you*, Nikki. I never thought I'd see the day."

"Nice to meet you too," I say offering her a polite smile. "Are you John's Michelle?"

"Well, I used to be," she answers curiously. "What made you ask that?"

"Chris's mom mentioned that you're the one that got away. I get the impression she's a fan of yours."

Michelle laughs softly, a touch of nostalgia in her smile. "Mrs. Sheppard is such a sweetheart. She and my mom are always trying to play matchmaker. And as for being the one that got away... well, it's easy to get away when no one's chasing you."

"I'd say that's his loss, and speak of the devil..."

"Hey Shell," John says as he approaches, "I got you a drink – vodka, cranberry and a splash of 7up. Right?"

"Still," Michelle replies and takes the drink he's handing her.

John glances at me with a knowing look. "I see you met Nikki. She's making an honest guy out of Shepp."

"I can see that," Michelle says, "Nikki, there's a group of people over in the corner I need to catch up with, but I'll come back and find you to introduce you to some of the girls."

"Thank you. I'd like that." She nods with a smile, turns and walks away without saying anything further to the guys.

"John, I'm going to get drinks for Nikki and me," Chris announces, "and since Michelle just blew you off, stay here with Nikki and keep the knuckle-draggers away until I get back."

John puts his arm around me and smiles, "I'd be happy to. We'll keep 'em guessing Nikki."

When Chris leaves for the bar I punch John in the arm, "What's wrong with you? I heard about how the two of you are pining away for each other. Why don't you do something about it?"

"She left for New York and I'm not sure she's even coming back after graduation," he says, rubbing his arm.

"Well, why don't you give her a reason to?" I challenge.

He sighs, "It's not that simple, Nikki."

"I think it just might be, John. Doesn't it bother you that she's holding court with that group of guys over there?" I tilt my head slightly in that direction.

"Those idiots. No," he says dismissively. "They all know better than to make a move on Shell when I'm around."

"How about the guy who's putting his hand on the small of her back right now?" I ask.

John turns around to look, his expression hardening. "Yeah, I don't know that guy or like the looks of him. Excuse me Nikki, Chris is headed back anyway."

John walks over to the group and stands right in front of Michelle completely cock blocking the guy who's trying to get her attention. I can't hear what he says to her, but she steps backward and looks annoyed. John grabs her by the hand and pulls her away from the group giving the other guy the middle finger behind his back. Michelle looks frustrated, but she doesn't pull her hand away from his and goes with him to the corner where they continue talking heatedly.

"Are they always like that?" I ask Chris.

"Pretty much," he says and hands me a drink. "Everyone around here is used to it. They seem to do okay with their lives when they're apart, but they can't handle being around each other and not being a couple." He shakes his head. "I figure they'll wind up together again someday. John's never been serious about anyone but her."

I see Michelle storm off to the Ladies' room and notice that no one follows her, so I decide to. "Are you okay?" I ask, entering the bathroom.

"Yes," she says and wipes her eyes, "it's just so frustrating. He's the one who broke it off with me when I decided to go to school in New York, but he doesn't want me to get on with my life either. I mean what was I supposed to do, follow him to school? It's not even like New York and Philly would be a 'long distance' relationship."

"You know he's not seeing anyone in Philly," I say trying to offer some comfort.

"I didn't even think he was. I know I would've heard about it." She lets out a dramatic sigh. "Sometimes I think about coming back here after graduation and then the thought that he and I would just go on like this forever makes me never want to come back again."

There is a pounding on the door, "Shell, come out or I'm coming in," John shouts.

"Leave me alone. Nikki's with me. I'm fine."

"Nikki, is she okay?" John asks with a blend of anger and concern in his voice.

"We're fine. Just give us a minute, John." I can hear him step away from the door.

"Maybe you need to tell him how you feel," I suggest.

She pulls a hand towel from the dispenser and dabs her eyes. "If he doesn't know how I feel by now, he's dumber than I thought."

I give her a reassuring smile. "When it comes down to it, Michelle, they're all pretty stupid. You might have to hit him over the head with the truth." We chuckle at that, and she fumbles through her bag for some make-up to fix her face.

"Are you ready?" I ask after a minute.

"Yeah. Thanks for listening. Everyone around here is sick of this same old scene." She exhales loudly. "Let's do this." We walk out of the bathroom to find Chris and John standing with their arms crossed over their chests like wooden Indians in front of a tobacco store. Oh brother. Why do guys always claim women are the drama queens?

"Okay, enough nonsense," I scold. "Michelle is going to introduce me to some of the girls and you two are going to do whatever guys do when they're not being idiots."

"Which is never," Michelle adds. "Come on Nikki," she takes my hand and pulls me away.

John turns to Chris, "Oh great, now we've created a beautiful four-eyed monster."

"You did that all on your own dude," Chris shrugs, "I don't even know why I'm in trouble."

Michelle introduces me around and I'm enjoying hearing all kinds of tales about Chris in high school. Eventually the guys think they've given us the appropriate amount of space and join us again.

"Hey, Shepp," one of the girls in the group says, her tone turning a little too flirty, "we were just telling Nikki here how no one could ever pin you down in high school – not even the prom queen." She tilts her head, brushes her bangs from her eyes and flips her hair over her shoulder with a look that screams 'I was the prom queen' (and of course we hadn't been talking about that either). My antenna is up now, full 'spidey senses' on alert – everyone knows you can't trust girls with bangs!

"That's because I hadn't met Nikki yet," Chris says quickly cutting her off.

She turns to me, "Damn, girl, you really do have him under your spell. What's your secret?" she asks, her eyes scanning me up and down.

Before I can even get a word out, Chris jumps in, "No secret. If you knew her you wouldn't ask, but clearly that's not gonna change, so let it go," he says more aggressively than I expected.

I'm flattered, embarrassed, and annoyed all at the same time. This girl is obviously trying to let me know she and Chris have history and he's pushing her buttons to get her to shut up.

"Honestly, he won *me* over with his charm and persistence," I say, hoping to put an end to this little game.

"So, the mighty player has finally been played," she declares triumphantly as if she's just landed a blow.

Okay, message received – I get it, I'm not Chris's first girl – but I've had enough of this.

Chris scowls and opens his mouth to fire back, but I cut him off; I can handle this bitch. "Look, I'm not interested in being a pawn in this verbal chess match. I'm clearly the queen on the board here, so let's just call it check mate and be done."

With that, Michelle bursts out laughing. "Well, she's got you there Maura."

Maura is caught off guard both by my comeback and Michelle's reaction. With a dramatic spin, she turns and walks away, pretending to spot someone on the other side of the bar.

"That's my Jersey girl," Chris says, pulling me close and wrapping his arm around me.

Michelle is still chuckling. "Don't worry about her," she says waving an indifferent hand and turns to another girl in the group – Stacey... maybe, "OMG, did you see the look on her face?!"

"Yeah," 'Stacey Maybe' answers with a snort. "Talk about holding a grudge. Some people never leave high school behind."

There's lots of laughter, reminiscing and storytelling for the rest of the evening. Every once in a while, I catch Maura eyeing us up from across the room, so I slip my hand into the back pocket of Chris's jeans just to make a point. The bar starts to thin out around midnight and John offers to drive Michelle home. We hug and say our goodbyes and I whisper in her ear, "Tell him and use a brick if you have to." She smiles and squeezes my hand appreciatively.

"What was that all about?" Chris asks.

"Just girl talk."

"Believe me Nikki, you don't want to get involved in that relationship," he warns. "We've all seen how that turns out."

"Chris, I got this. Just offering some friendly advice. Stay in your lane."

"Sooory," he mutters under his breath.

Chris's parents are in bed when we get home, so we enjoy one more drink together in front of the fire and the Christmas tree. Part of me wishes I could stay here with this family and enjoy a traditional Christmas like the ones I remember, but I also look forward to my cherished time with Lauren and the traditions we've established together.

Christmas Eve

Nikki

I get to Lauren's in the late afternoon and immediately feel guilty when I see how much effort she's put into our little celebration. Her apartment is fully decorated for the holiday. She has a lasagna and salad already prepared just waiting to be heated and dressed, and a tin of toffee ready to bring to Dad tomorrow.

"How was the weekend at Chris's?" she asks eager for details.

"Honestly it was magical. His parents are lovely, he has nice friends except for one nasty bitch I had to straighten out, and he took me to Longwood Gardens to see the Christmas display."

"Wow, I know you think I'm a stick in the mud, but I'd really like to meet him," she says putting the gifts under the tree. It's decorated with all the ornaments from our childhood and several new ones Lauren has collected along the way. It's like a scrapbook of our lives and seeing them again always makes me nostalgic. There is a glass slipper from a family trip to Disneyland when we were kids, the Statue of Liberty to remind us of all our excursions to The City, a beach chair to signify the time we've spent at the Jersey shore and the Delaware beaches, a tiara as a nod to the countless hours I spent playing dress up as a kid, a slot machine from a bachelorette party in Vegas, and so on. More recent additions include a University of Delaware Blue Hen and a Drexel Dragon, a typewriter and a sketchbook, and two ornaments that Lauren had made from pictures of each of our parents.

"He wants to meet you too. He's coming back to the city after Christmas so we can have some time alone together before his roommates get back. Maybe we can get together for a drink then."

"That would be great," she smiles. "I'm just going to be here working on my story. The info you and Amanda dug up for me is really helpful. I've already started writing it."

"When did you have time for that?" I ask. "I thought you had friends coming into town for the engagement party this past weekend."

"I did. I started writing yesterday after they left. You know I have no life," she says with a self-deprecating tone.

"You really don't Lauren," I agree but don't let it go, wanting to make a point. "I'm in school full-time and working two jobs and still get out more than you do."

She shrugs off my comment. "Listen, I have everything for tonight, but I forgot to get rum for the eggnog. How about we go out before dinner and pick some up and we can stop somewhere for a festive holiday drink," she suggests.

"Okay but we should probably leave soon," I say glancing at the clock. "The liquor stores close early on Christmas Eve."

Lauren nods. "Let me just throw something on besides this sweatshirt and we'll go." I follow her into the bedroom and put my bag on her bed while she changes.

"So how was the engagement party?" I ask leaning against the dresser. "Any eligible bachelors there?"

Lauren's eyes roll as she walks over to her closet. "The party was great. It was so nice to see my college friends again," she says, rifling through her clothes, "but eligible is *not* the word I would choose to describe the bachelors. They all had their shirts off by the end of the night like they were still a bunch of frat boys. No thank you," she shakes her head. "Come on, let's go."

I laugh, imagining the scene. "Sounds like a good time, anyway."

We walk to the nearest liquor store and are perusing the rum choices when we hear, "Lauren?" We both turn around and there is a movie-star gorgeous man standing behind us holding several bottles of wine.

"Drew. Hi. Fancy meeting you here. This is my sister Nikki," Lauren says, gesturing her hand toward me and standing up a little straighter.

"Hi, Nikki," he replies putting the bottles down on the counter to shake my hand, "I'm Drew. Lauren and I work together. You ladies picking up some holiday libations for a celebration tonight?"

My eyes widen realizing this is the 'Mr. Drew-tiful' Amanda told me about.

"Yes, rum for the eggnog," Lauren answers, her tone is casual, but I can tell she's forcing it, "you?"

"Wine for dinner at my parents' house tomorrow. I was afraid the liquor store wouldn't be open tomorrow."

"So, no Christmas Eve plans?" I ask and Lauren shoots me a horrified look.

Drew shakes his head in an easy way. "No. I'll see my family tomorrow. I don't like to get there the night before when my mother and sister are dueling it out in the kitchen over the best way to make everything. They've both got... well, strong opinions."

I see a golden opportunity unfolding in front of me that I can't resist. "Drew, if you're by yourself tonight, why don't you join us?" I put my hand behind Lauren's back in case she needs support from the aftershock of my words.

"Oh, I couldn't crash your girls' night," he replies, but looks like he's hoping I'll insist.

Lauren is a few shades of red by now and completely speechless, so I keep going. "You wouldn't be crashing at all. Lauren already prepared a full tray of lasagna so there's plenty of food and we can grab an extra bottle of wine while we're here."

"Well, if it's really not an imposition..." Drew says, hesitating for just a second. He looks to Lauren for approval. "Lauren?"

She stammers, still processing. "Um, um, yes, of course," she manages.

"Alright then," Drew says, brightening up. "Let me just grab a couple more bottles, don't want to show up empty-handed." He heads back to the wine aisle and selects a bottle of chardonnay and a bottle of pinot noir, bringing them back to the counter with the other bottles.

Lauren is frozen in disbelief, and I have to nudge her out of it before Drew notices. "Lauren," I whisper while bumping her with my shoulder. She turns to look at me and I lock eyes with her bringing her back into the moment.

She seems to snap out of it, so while the clerk is ringing up the order I continue, "Drew, we also have a holiday tradition of eating our Christmas Eve dinner in our pajamas, so be sure to bring a pair." Lauren's color had almost returned to normal before I said that and now, she's flushed again.

"Are you serious or just pranking me?" he asks skeptically and looks at Lauren for the truth.

She's still recovering so I answer with a chuckle, "That would be a pretty big prank on someone I just met, and Lauren doesn't prank."

The clerk puts the bottles in a box and runs Drew's credit card. "Lauren, I know your address, but not your apartment number."

"It's, it's, um 412," she manages to utter.

"What time should I come?" Drew asks looking between us.

Lauren clears her throat and accomplishes a full sentence without a stutter, "How's six o'clock?"

"Perfect. Thanks so much for the invitation. This evening has just taken a pleasant turn." He takes the box from the counter and walks toward the door.

"Here, let me open that for you," Lauren says, recovering just enough to reach for the door handle.

"Excuse me sir," the clerk calls to Drew.

"Yes," he answers, turning around.

"You're under the mistletoe," he says and grins at me clearly picking up on what's going on.

Lauren again seems to be paralyzed, so Drew prods her, "Lauren, you're going to have to lean in. My hands are full." She hesitates for an uncomfortable moment and then leans forward to kiss him on the cheek, but he turns his head at the last second and her lips land on his. It's a brief, unexpected kiss and she clearly doesn't know how to react. He smiles at her for a moment too long and walks out the door. "See you both in about an hour," he shouts over his shoulder.

The door swings shut behind him, and Lauren turns to me with wide eyes, her mouth open in disbelief. "Nikki, what the hell did you just do? We've got to get out of here. Forget the holiday drink. We've got to get back. I have to change and make sure the apartment's ready. Pay for the rum please. My hands are shaking."

The clerk smiles, "No worries, ladies, the gentleman took care of it. Merry Christmas."

We rush back to her apartment, and she is in near hysterics the whole way – what about this, what about that, blah, blah,

blah... "Oh my God, Lauren, calm down. Everything will be fine. You have everything prepared and he seems perfectly nice, not to mention totally hot."

Lauren is still frantic when we arrive. "Nikki, pick me out something to wear. I can't think!" she says hurrying toward the bedroom.

I peruse her closet and jewelry box and select a pair of black leather pants and a pink silk blouse with gold jewelry. She'll look beautiful, but also like she's not trying too hard. I only have a pair of jeans and a black turtleneck with me, so I also find some festive sparkly baubles that will jazz up my outfit – tonight's not about me.

The whole time Lauren is dressing she's rattling off orders at me. "Turn the tree lights on....! Fluff the pillows on the couch...! Light the glass house candles on the mantel – and don't set the holly branches on fire doing it....! And we need to make a charcuterie board!"

After I've fluffed, lit, and pulled out the fixings for charcuterie, Lauren rushes into the kitchen and begins arranging the items on a board paying an absurd amount of attention to how she is displaying them. At this point, I don't see how we can be any more prepared, so I make us some eggnog and put on Christmas music.

"Okay, I think we're ready," she says, releasing a dramatic sigh of satisfaction. Her eyes narrow playfully. "And just because I've stopped hyperventilating doesn't mean I won't find a way to kill you when this is over."

I smile at her. "Relax," I say, handing her a glass of eggnog.

Knock, knock, knock. "Coming!" Lauren calls, her voice suddenly syrupy sweet, reminiscent of a 1950s TV mom. She glances at me with a silent 'here we go' expression in her eyes before opening the door. "Hi! Welcome to the Taylor girls' Christmas Eve extravaganza!" she says almost theatrically in a way I didn't expect − she's really pouring it on thick.

Drew steps inside, his presence filling the doorway − gym bag slung over one shoulder, two bottles of wine clutched in one hand, and a Yule log roll in the other. I can't help but chuckle; it could be the opening scene of any Hallmark holiday movie ever made.

Lauren welcomes him in, her hands outstretched for the wine. "Let me grab those for you," she says, already taking the bottles. Then, turning to me, adds, "Nikki, why don't you take the Yule log?"

"On it." I can already smell the rich chocolatey scent and even though vanilla is my flavor of choice, it's tempting me. "While I'm in the kitchen, want me to whip you up an eggnog?" I offer.

"That would be perfect," he says, carefully passing me the Yule log as if he's handing me a newborn.

"Make yourself at home," Lauren adds with a smile. "We'll be right back."

Drew steps into the living room, his eyes scanning the cozy space. "What a nice apartment," he remarks.

"Oh, thank you," Lauren calls from the kitchen and I realize that I have taken for granted what a nice job she's done decorating her place. Her furniture is modern, but not stark. She's mixed some bargain pieces from IKEA with tasteful vintage finds and some antiques that were our mother's. It's eclectic but it works – warm and inviting with its own unique personality. She also kept some of Mom's artwork which elevates the otherwise simple space and has added just the right amount of accent pieces. She's masterful at finding little treasures and repurposing them in unique ways, like the glass perfume diffuser she uses to hold dish soap in the kitchen – it adds to the charm. Well done sista, I think to myself while fixing Drew's eggnog.

Lauren has already returned to the living room trying to be the perfect hostess. "Let me take your jacket Drew," she offers.

He flashes her a devilish grin while taking it off. "Can I trust you with it?" he asks as he hands it to her.

Her face flushes with embarrassment, "Yes. I have a one jacket destroying limit."

I have no idea what they are talking about, so I raise my glass after handing Drew his eggnog and say, "Cheers!"

"To unexpected surprises," Drew adds, and Lauren finishes with, "Merry Christmas to all." *Clink, clink, clink.*

"Drew, what do you do at *The Inquirer?*" I ask as we all take a seat.

"I'm a Senior Editor," he says crossing his legs and settling in. "And frankly I really don't do much. Our writers are all so good, their work doesn't need much editing. Sometimes I offer another angle on some of the stories, but take Lauren's column as an example, I don't think I've ever touched it."

"Well, you certainly always seem like you're busy at the office," Lauren says, almost defending him.

He swirls the eggnog in his glass. "That's mainly because I have real estate holdings I keep up with and I also invest in stocks, so I follow the market closely."

"That explains it," Lauren says with some clarity, "you're known as a bit of a man of mystery around the office."

"Tell him what else he's known as around the office." I know this comment will send Lauren over the edge, but somebody's got to lighten this conversation up. It feels like a business meeting, a boring one at that.

"Oh my God Nikki!" Lauren yells and turns fire engine red (she really needs to learn how to control that).

"What?" Drew sits up straight filled with curiosity. "Now you *have* to tell me."

Lauren is squirming in her seat and fanning the color from her face. "This is so embarrassing. Please know you had this nickname before I ever started working there so I had nothing to do with it," she says, shaking her head.

"Lay it on me," Drew says planting both his palms firmly on his knees.

Lauren swallows and works up the nerve to answer. "Okay, okay. You're affectionately referred to by the women in the office as... 'Mr. Drew-tiful.'"

He laughs out a sigh, "Phew... That's actually flattering. I've been called way worse. Nikki, is there anything else I should know?"

Lauren interrupts before I can answer, "If there is, she better keep it to herself!"

Drew chuckles as he looks between us. His smile doesn't fade but he is staring at us curiously. "What?" Lauren asks self-consciously while checking her blouse for a stain or something.

He cocks his head before answering. "You're both very beautiful women, but you don't look at all like sisters."

I decide to answer so that Lauren won't start stuttering over the beautiful comment. "Well, thank you Drew. Our mother was Italian, and our father is Irish, so Lauren looks like our mom, and I take after dad."

"If you'll excuse me," Lauren says quietly, "I'm going to preheat the oven. Please help yourself to the hors d'oeuvres," and leaves the room to collect herself.

I turn to Drew, "Don't mind her. She's a nervous entertainer." He smiles, winks at me, and takes another sip of his drink.

Lauren is more composed when she returns. "Drew, Nikki and I will exchange our gifts in the morning before going to see our dad, but we do have a tradition of exchanging pajamas tonight."

She picks up a box from under the tree and hands it to me. "You first Nick."

The box is wrapped in gold shimmering paper and a red velvet bow. I tear it open and gold glitter from the paper covers my black turtleneck as if Tinker-Bell has just flown overhead. I leave it knowing we'll be changing soon. Lifting the lid, I find a throwback kelly-green Eagles top and matching plaid flannel bottoms. "Nikki has a new boyfriend who's a big Eagles guy and she doesn't have any fan gear," Lauren explains.

"It's perfect, Lauren. Thank you," I say and get up to give her a hug. "My turn." I pick up my gift from under the tree and hand it to her. I'm glad I chose something tasteful instead of lingerie that would send her into a tizzy. She's probably thinking the same thing because she's opening the box very cautiously like something might jump out at her. A mixed smile and sigh of relief crosses her face as she holds up a powder blue silk pajama set. It's a button-down top and matching pants with white satin piping and pearl buttons. "It's beautiful, Nikki. Thank you. Shall we change?"

"Wait, wait," Drew says reaching for his bag, "I have a little something for both of you." He pulls out two small rectangular boxes and hands one to each of us.

"Drew, when did you even have the time?" Lauren asks, the color again rising up her neck threatening to take over her cheeks.

"On the way home from the liquor store." He shrugs like it was nothing. "They're both the same so you might want to open them together."

Lauren and I laugh and assume our childhood back-to-back stocking opening position. Our stocking gifts were always the same as kids, so we'd sit back-to-back as not to spoil the surprise of what we were opening.

"I see you ladies have done this before," he chuckles. We unwrap the paper to discover two bottles of Chanel No. 5 perfume – Wow! Seriously?

"Drew, thank you so much. This is so very thoughtful of you... and way too extravagant," Lauren gushes.

"Well, my mother and sister won't leave the house without it, so I figured it was a female staple."

"More like a female luxury," Lauren replies, catching her breath before shifting gears. "We have something a little less spectacular for you, but it was made with love," she says and goes to the kitchen returning with the tin of toffee. I know we'll have to make more in the morning, but she pulled that one out of thin air.

Drew opens the tin and smiles, "I love toffee. Thank you, ladies. If I were a better person, I'd bring this with me to my parents tomorrow, but I'm going to keep it for myself."

"So, pajama time?" I suggest, "I'm assuming that's what you have in that bag, Drew."

"It is." He reaches for it with a smile. "I was a little skeptical but wanted to be prepared."

"The bathroom is down the hall, Drew." Lauren says pointing in that direction. "Nikki and I will change in the bedroom and meet you back here."

When we're alone in the bedroom I turn to her, "Lauren, he's literally like the perfect guy and Amanda's right about the way he looks at you."

"Shhhh!" she whispers, putting her finger to her lips. "We're not having this conversation now! Just get changed and help me get the dinner out."

"But..." she grabs my hand, squeezes it hard and spears a glare through me. Message received.

The pajamas look gorgeous on Lauren. They not only fit her perfectly and compliment her eyes, but they are respectfully appropriate. She definitely looks like the sophisticated older sister with her college student younger sibling, but it's perfect for tonight. We return to the living room to find Drew wearing a black silk pajama set with a Hughe Hefner silk robe and slippers. I have to choke back a laugh. The only thing missing from his look is a glass of brandy and a pipe. This guy is a character.

Lauren puts the lasagna in the oven, and I dress the salad. "What can I do to help?" Drew asks joining us in the kitchen.

"How are you with garlic bread?" Lauren asks.

"One of my specialties," he replies with enthusiastic pride that I can't tell is real or not. I mean, whose specialty would be garlic bread? Even I can handle that.

"Okay you're on bread then," Lauren says and directs him toward the counter where she has everything laid out.

We've all finished our eggnog by now and that is definitely a one drink cocktail, so we decide to open a bottle of wine.

"Lauren, have you started writing your story yet?" Drew asks, brushing melted butter and garlic onto the bread.

"Actually yes," Lauren responds, all-business now. "Amanda and Nikki really helped me out with some of the research."

I cut in with a half-joking, half-serious tone, "Yeah, and speaking of help, any stipend left in the budget for me? I've been helping Lauren with her column since she started, and I nearly passed out when I heard Amanda's getting both credits *and* a stipend."

Lauren shoots me an exasperated glare. "Nikki, maybe focus on your manners for just a minute. Good grief." Drew's grin deepens at our back-and-forth.

"I'll see what I can do, Nikki," he says, wrapping the bread in tin foil before sliding it into the oven beside the lasagna.

Lauren brushes the front of her pajama top even though there is nothing there. "Let's have our wine in the living room while dinner is heating up," she suggests.

Drew settles in on the couch, casually crossing his ankles. "I'm glad you're delving into a news story, Lauren. Recently I've been thinking about exploring something more challenging too. Maybe editing for a book publishing company or finding a writing assignment that would allow me to travel." He pauses for a moment and then adds, "I feel like now's the time for that when I'm not in a relationship and don't have a family."

"Wow," Lauren's eyes widen with surprise. "I had no idea you were thinking about leaving *The Inquirer*."

"I'm just toying with the notion right now," he says. "How about you, Nikki. What do you do when you're not volunteering your time for Lauren's column?"

"I'm a fashion student at Drexel. I also waitress in a café and walk dogs for Uber Leash."

"Busy lady," he comments with a nod and a tip of his glass.

"Nikki had something scary happen to her recently with some of the dogs she walks," Lauren motions to me, "tell him what happened."

"Apparently several of my dog clients' homes have been broken into recently, so the police came into the café and questioned me about it. They told me they had to consider me a suspect, but also seemed concerned about my safety when entering the homes."

"That *is* scary." Drew's casual tone now replaced with concern. "You ladies really need to be careful. I don't like Lauren jogging alone at night either."

I try to lighten the conversation, "I only have one dog to walk this week, and my boyfriend is going to come with me. Hopefully the case will be solved soon, and I won't have to worry about it anymore."

Ding. The timer on the oven goes off and Lauren jumps up to check on the lasagna and garlic bread. "I think we're ready," she calls from the kitchen, "Nick, can you set the table?"

"Sure," I reply, and Drew gets up to help me.

When we're alone in the dining room, he turns to me and asks, "So how about your sister, is there anyone special in her life?"

I pull the plates out of the hutch and open the silverware drawer for Drew. Lauren found the piece at a flea market and painted it a cool forest green color but left the wooden legs untouched giving it a contemporary look. I turn to Drew while laying out the plates, "Believe me, she's one step away from being an old lady living with twelve cats. I'm always trying to encourage her to get out more."

He laughs but is clearly pleased to learn Lauren isn't dating anyone, it's written all over his face. It dawns on me that the 'not being in a relationship' comment was for Lauren's benefit, though I'm certain she didn't pick up on it.

"You two are certainly a pair," he says, following me with the silverware.

Lauren brings out the lasagna and Drew and I go to get the salad and bread. Once we're settled, Drew proposes a toast, "To an unexpected Christmas Eve with two of the loveliest ladies I am privileged to share it with." We air clink and dig in.

"This is delicious, Lauren," Drew says, wiping his mouth and looking at her with way too much admiration. "You've really outdone yourself." (Not that he'd have any idea of what out-doing herself would mean).

"Thanks," she says, smiling. "I learned to cook from our mom. Somehow, that talent skipped Nikki."

I grin, shrugging. "Lucky for me, I work at a café, so I eat there most of the time."

We continue to chat throughout the meal and if Lauren isn't noticing how Drew is completely captivated with her, she's more clueless than I thought. He hangs on her every word and can't keep his eyes off her. I've also never seen Lauren so on edge around someone before. She blushes like a schoolgirl every time he gives her the slightest compliment and her voice doesn't even sound normal to me. It's almost painful to watch. When we finish, I clear the dishes and tell Lauren I'll put the coffee on. "I can help with that," she says.

"You cooked, so I'll clean. Sit." I really just want to give them some time alone together, so I busy myself in the kitchen putting the food away, loading the dishwasher and pulling out dessert plates. Lauren is laughing in the other room, so something must be going well. I stall for a few more minutes before returning with a tray holding everything we'll need for dessert and making a second trip for the coffee.

After finishing dessert, it feels like the evening is winding down, so I again try to make myself scarce. I retreat to the bedroom to give them space, but after about fifteen minutes of doing nothing, I start feeling like my absence might seem rude and head back out.

Drew stands when I enter the room, "Well ladies it's been a wonderful evening. I can't thank you enough for including me in your special traditions, PJs and all."

"It was our pleasure," Lauren says but there's something new in her expression. It's obvious to me that she's considering him in a different light, even if she hasn't realized it yet herself.

"Speaking of which, I guess I should change again before leaving. A guy in silk pajamas and a leather jacket might draw some attention." He grabs his bag and goes to the hallway bathroom coming out a few minutes later in his clothes.

"Don't forget the toffee," Lauren says, handing him the tin.

"I wouldn't think of it." He takes the tin from her hand but also unexpectedly pulls her in for a hug. "Merry Christmas, Lauren."

She seems a little shocked but hugs him back, "Merry Christmas to you too."

Drew holds the embrace for a moment too long before slowly releasing her, his hand gently gliding down her arm. He looks into her eyes and for a second I think he is going to kiss her, but then it's almost like he remembers they're not alone and turns toward me instead. "Nikki, it was great to meet you, and I'll check on that stipend for you," he says walking toward the closet for his jacket and winking at me again in both an appreciative and conspiratorial way that tells me he knows I'm on his team.

Once he leaves, Lauren collapses on the couch with an exaggerated sigh, toppling the throw pillows to the floor. "Well despite your best efforts, we survived that."

I raise an eyebrow, unable to hide my grin. "I'd say you way more than survived it. Lauren, in case you haven't noticed he's really hot and more than enthralled with you."

"He *is* really charming, isn't he?" she says in the voice I recognize again.

"Uh yeah, and I'm pretty sure he wants you to have his babies!"

She laughs, swatting at me playfully. "Oh, stop it, Nikki. I already told you, he's my boss. I guess I'll just have to join the ranks of the other pathetic office gals who have a crush on him."

I lean in, looking at her more seriously. "Keep your options open, Lauren. He seems like a guy who knows how to get what he wants. And, by the way, he asked me if you're seeing anyone."

"What? When?" Lauren's eyes snap to mine, her feet hitting the floor as she sits up straighter.

"When we were setting the table. He's definitely interested."

She freezes for a moment. "Maybe he was just curious," she says, but then puts her hand up to her mouth and looks at the ceiling for a second and I know she's considering it.

I plop down beside her, nudging her with my elbow. "Lauren, don't be an idiot – you *have* to pursue this."

She looks at me, a little lost. "I wouldn't have the slightest idea how to pursue it, given our circumstances," she admits with a sigh.

"I'd leave it up to him. He seems pretty determined to me. Just keep an eye out for his cues. Didn't you notice how he *purposely* let you know he's not in a relationship?" I nudge her leg with my foot, making sure she's really hearing me.

Lauren shakes her head. "He was just talking about his career," she says brushing it off, but I can tell she's not entirely convinced.

"Maybe," I say, "but maybe he was trying to let you know that he's considering making a change – so he won't be your boss anymore. Just saying." I shrug, waiting for her reaction.

"That's ridiculous!" she scoffs, but there's an edge of uncertainty in her voice. "He's not going to quit his job just to ask me out. Now, let's get a new batch of toffee cooking and open up our stockings."

"You were quick on your feet with that one by the way."

"Well, who doesn't love toffee?"

Determined

On the drive home, Drew replayed the evening in his mind, still amazed by how everything had unfolded. That trip to the liquor store felt like a Christmas miracle – or maybe Lauren's fiery sister was the real miracle. Either way, he wasn't complaining. And the mistletoe? That was just the cherry on top. The memory of her lips on his sent chills down his spine, and then some.

Spending time with her only made him want more. She was sweet, reserved, and so put together, but he could sense a playful side lurking just beneath the surface, especially in the way she interacted with her sister. He needed to find a way to be with her.

Maybe once she finished her news piece, he could arrange for her to be transferred to the News Department, so she'd report to someone else. Hell, Amanda could take over writing 'Philly's Top 10' for all he cared. Or maybe he should seriously consider pivoting away from *The Inquirer* in the new year. The idea of changing jobs for a woman was something he never thought he'd consider, but there was something about Lauren that he couldn't ignore. What if she was *the* one, and he let something as stupid as a job keep them apart? His mom was right – he'd never forgive himself if he didn't at least try.

Christmas Day

Lauren

I wake up with the familiar yet unfamiliar feeling of someone else in my bed. It's Nikki of course and we've shared beds on every childhood vacation, trip to our grandparents and numerous sleepovers with friends. Waking up with her next to me just reinforces that today is a special occasion. I slip out from underneath the covers gently and grab my robe at the foot of the bed. Since we no longer wake up at five o'clock on Christmas morning to see what Santa brought us, I let her sleep in. We don't have a hard schedule today for our visit with Dad, and we stayed up too late last night opening goofy stocking stuffers and giggling about Drew. And there it is, my first thought about Drew Davis today. Going back into the office and assuming our professional roles is going to be difficult. I push it out of my mind.

Usually, the newspaper gets dropped outside my front door, but today the delivery person managed to shove the whole thing through my mail slot – must be a light edition. I know it seems silly to have it delivered when I work there, but I'm not always in the office and I keep a portfolio of all my columns. I slide off the rubber band and unroll the paper, briefly skimming the headlines. There's one just below the fold that catches my eye: Update on Burglaries in Society Hill.

Sitting with a cup of coffee and the paper, I chuckle at the stocking stuffers Nikki and I exchanged. A bell for the bar cart that says: "Ring for Tequila," day glow running socks, mini boxes of sugary cereal we were never allowed to eat as kids, old fashioned dish towels, organic honey, and bar napkins that read, "Cheers Bitches!"

"Good morning," Nikki says.

"Oh hi. I hope I didn't wake you."

"No, the smell of coffee did. Merry Christmas," she says and bends down to give me a hug.

I return the hug. "Nikki there's an update on the burglaries in today's paper. I hope this gets resolved before your dog walking appointments pick up again after the holidays."

Nikki picks the paper up from the coffee table and quickly scans the article.

"I have fixings for bagels for breakfast. Do you want eggs too?" I ask.

She looks up from the paper, "I'll pass on the eggs but if you have bacon let's make that. It's Christmas, so it's a cheat day – carbs and grease!" We high five in agreement and head to the kitchen.

After breakfast Nikki and I exchange gifts. She opens hers first and smiles as she pulls it out of the box, "It's gorgeous, Lauren.

And you had it monogrammed. Thank you, I love it," she says and smells the leather.

"Well, you'll be starting work in the real world soon and need a proper computer bag."

"Open this one first," Nikki says, handing me a rather large flat box. I tear off the paper to find a cardboard box that has to be opened on the ends, not from the top.

"I'll get a pair of scissors." She hops up and hurries into the kitchen to my junk drawer. I can tell she's excited about the gift and now I'm really curious. I work the end open and pull out a matted and framed charcoal sketch of an old-fashioned typewriter on vintage paper. "Oh my God, I love it. It's beautiful!" I exclaim admiring it. "It'll look perfect in here!"

"Do you really like it?" she asks a little sheepishly, and I take a closer look noticing her initials in the lower right-hand corner.

"Nikki, did you sketch this?" She nods and smiles, and my eyes start to well up. "It's the nicest gift anyone has ever given me, Nick." I put it down to give her a hug. "I'll treasure it always, just like you." I pick it up again to admire it some more. "You've gotten so good. I can't believe it! This is my new favorite thing. Hmmm..." I look around the room and consider where it should go. "Once I take these Christmas decorations down, I think I'll put it over the fireplace. It deserves to be front and center. Now, this is nothing compared to the gift you just gave me, but here's one more small present for you."

Nikki opens it and laughs, "A sketch book and charcoal pencils. I'll never have too many of these." She puts them down on the coffee table. "I have one more small gift for you too." She hands me a gift bag with tissue paper and ribbon. I reach inside and pull out a t-shirt that reads:

Writer's Block
When my imaginary friends won't talk to me

"I love it!" I say with a laugh and hold it up to my chest to check the sizing, "it's perfect."

We clean up the wrapping paper, then get dressed for our trip to West Chester. As I open the apartment door to leave, I spot a gift bag hanging from the door handle. A note is attached that simply reads:

For Nikki

"What the heck is this?" I ask, handing the bag to her.

"Beats me. Who even knows I'm here?" She reaches inside pulling out a mace alarm for her keychain and holds it up for me to see. "Is this Drew guy some kind of magician or something?"

"I don't know, but I'm definitely impressed," I reply. "And with these robberies going on, you should definitely keep that on you."

"Noted," she replies and puts it in her coat pocket.

On the bus, Nikki can't stop talking about Chris, and I'm genuinely happy to see her so excited. She's dated a bit in college, but it's been a while since she had a serious boyfriend – and her last one, from high school, was kind of a jerk.

We don't know what to expect when we get to the facility. It could be a good day, or it could be a tough one, so we brace ourselves for whatever is to come.

When we arrive, Dad is in the community room with a few other residents, listening to Christmas carolers. He waves when he spots us, and we both exhale with relief. We wait for the carolers to finish before joining him.

"Merry Christmas, Dad," I say, smiling. "Let's wheel you out into the hall where we can talk."

"So, what's new, girls?" he asks, looking at us expectantly.

"Wait until I show you the sketch Nikki did for me." I pull out my phone and show him a picture of it.

"Wow, Nick. You've really gotten good. Do you have any photos of your designs?"

Nikki and I exchange a hopeful glance. "These are a few of my latest," she says, scrolling through her phone to show him several pictures.

Dad nods, his eyes gleaming with pride. "Your name will be on labels all over the world one day. And how about you, Lauren? Still with that fine young man you brought last time?"

Nikki and I smile at each other. "In fact, we saw him last night."

Having Dad lucid and engaged like this is a gift, one that comes less often these days. So, Nikki and I stay a while longer, reminiscing about the good times while he can still remember them. Before we leave, we give him the tin of toffee. He smiles that familiar, wide grin we've missed in recent weeks and says affectionately, "You remembered."

WEEK FIVE

Tuesday Afternoon, Week 5

Playing House

Chris's mom was a little irritated he was going back to Philly so soon after the holiday, but he needed to get his place in order so Nikki could stay with him for the next couple days before the guys got back. She didn't have to work that week, and they were both on break, so he wanted to take as much advantage of the time as they could.

> I'm headed back to Philly now. Can you come to my place tonight?

> Sure. Lauren wants to meet you. Do you want to do drinks first?

> That would be great. U girls pick the time and place, I'll bring the charm.

> There's that self-confidence issue rearing its ugly head again.

Ugly looks good on me. 😵‍💫 😵‍💫.

The house wasn't too bad considering everyone left in a hurry for Christmas break. He just shut the doors to Tony and John's bedrooms and focused on the main living spaces and his bedroom, of course. It was only about three o'clock, so he had time to stock up the fridge too before meeting the girls for drinks.

Did you decide on a place?

Writer's Block Rehab at 5:30. Tinsel afterwards to check out the decorations.

It's a date.

Nikki

Lauren and I are a little early, so we get a table and look at the cocktail selections. I place my overnight bag under the chair and take hold of Lauren's hand, "Look, I've already told you all about Chris and his family, so can you please not grill him with a million questions?"

"I'll behave," she says squeezing my hand, "but I don't know why after your performance on Christmas Eve."

"Oh, here he comes," I say, waving my hand.

"Wow, Nick he's cute," she whispers before he reaches the table.

"Hey babe," Chris leans down and kisses me on the cheek. "And you must be the infamous Lauren," he says, reaching out to shake her hand.

"Hi, Chris. It's a pleasure to finally meet you." Lauren smiles warmly, taking his hand in both of hers. "I've heard a lot about you."

"The pleasure's mine," Chris replies, flashing a teasing smile. "Should I be nervous about what you've heard?"

Lauren grins. "Considering the source, yes, but so far, it's been all good. I heard about your spectacular visit to Longwood Gardens."

Chris takes a seat, his demeanor sure and confident as if impressing women is child's play. "It was almost as beautiful as your sister."

I roll my eyes. "Okay Chris, you don't have to lay it on *that* thick. She's my sister, not my father and you're not asking for my hand in marriage."

"Not yet," he says with a warm knowing smile. Those two little words hit me harder than I expected, like he just announced how serious he is about us – even before we've had that conversation. He places his hand gently on my knee under the table, his touch grounding me. "So, how was your Christmas, ladies?"

"Christmas with Dad was a good day," I answer, resting my hand on top of his. "We were both thankful for that. But Christmas Eve was... well, more interesting than it's been in a while."

"Interesting how?" Chris asks, clearly intrigued.

I lean in and shoot Lauren a grin. "Well, Lauren has a hot boss who definitely has a crush on her. We ran into him in the liquor store, so I invited him to dinner and Lauren almost had a heart attack."

"Nikki, this is supposed to be about Chris and I getting to know one another, not about you rehashing every embarrassing moment of the Christmas Eve you ambushed me with," she says with a pointed look.

"I don't know," Chris laughs, "it sounds pretty interesting to me."

"I'll tell you about it later," I say to Chris. "So, we don't have to spend the next hour watching Lauren blush."

Just then, a waitress approaches the table. "Welcome to Writer's Block Rehab. May I bring you something other than water to start?" she asks while filling our water glasses.

"The Lady Boss looks good to me," Lauren says, closing the drink menu.

"I'll have an Espresso Martini please," I add.

"That sounds good," Chris agrees. "Make it two."

"Okay, I'll be right back with those."

The waitress nods, taking the drink menus and heading off. As soon as she's out of earshot, Lauren turns to Chris, her expression curious. "Chris, you're in a fraternity, right?"

"Yeah, but I don't spend much time there anymore." He turns his eyes toward me, "Especially now that I have Nikki to occupy my time." He squeezes my leg under the table.

Lauren nods. "I ask because I'm writing a piece for *The Inquirer* about drink spiking. How common is that sort of thing at frat parties?"

Chris shifts slightly in his seat. "Parties usually have kegs of beer and if there's a mixed drink available it's spiked with alcohol, not drugs."

"Are drugs available at the parties?" she continues questioning.

"Pot sure, but not so much anything harder," he answers, his tone a little more guarded.

Lauren isn't deterred and presses further. "Would you know how to get something harder if you wanted to?"

Chris shifts in his seat again, obviously uncomfortable with the direction the conversation is taking. "Lauren," I interrupt gently but firmly, "I thought we agreed this wasn't going to be an interrogation. Chris already talked with Amanda and me about this."

Lauren pauses, softening. "You're right. I'm sorry. It's just that the more I dig into this, the more I think it might be... bigger than I expected."

The waitress returns just in time, placing our drinks on the table. "Would you like to see food menus?"

"Just drinks for now," Lauren replies.

Chris raises his glass relieved the conversation has shifted and returns to his comfort zone – charming, "To the two most beautiful women in Philadelphia and to spending the next few days with one of them, Chin Chin!"

We chat while enjoying our drinks and Lauren seeks a little revenge on me by telling Chris stories of our childhood. I don't bother stopping her because I know I deserve it, and Chris seems to be enjoying it. Plus, in perfect Lauren fashion she's choosing stories that are more cute than embarrassing. She really is a nicer person than I am.

After finishing our drinks we walk to Tinsel, a pop-up Christmas bar that is decked out in gift wrapped chandeliers, multiple decorated trees, huge ornaments hanging from the ceiling, a few nods to beloved Christmas characters and villains alike, and blinking lights galore. It's something to see, but almost sensory overload, so we decide not to stay.

"Can I take you ladies to dinner?" Chris asks once we're outside.

"Oh, you two go ahead," Lauren answers, "I want to get back to my story and I have leftover lasagna at home. It was really nice to meet you, Chris."

"You too Lauren." This time instead of shaking her hand he gives her a hug.

She pats him on the back and blows me a kiss over his shoulder. "Call me tomorrow, Nick," she says when Chris releases his embrace.

"Alright. Good night then... talk in the morning."

Chris takes my hand as we walk away. "Well, I see what all the fuss is about. She seems lovely."

I sigh pensively, "She is, and she doesn't even know it." I turn to him considering the rest of the evening, "Do you really want to go out to eat or should we just grab something to bring back to your place?"

"I like that idea better," he agrees.

There's a Honeygrow on the way back, so we stop and get takeout. Chris brings the food into the kitchen when we get to his place, and I run upstairs to put my bag in his room. Last time I was in this room I was too exhausted to take much notice of it, but now I see it is really well appointed for a college room. I'm sure his mother must have decorated it. Or an ex-girlfriend with very good taste. Either way, the budget had to have come from his parents. They clearly adore him. I guess there are some benefits to being an only child, though I'm thankful every day that I'm not. I toss my bag on the bed and can see why I slept so soundly in it. It has a hotel quality comforter with multiple plush pillows. I walk around a bit more and notice a black and white photo of his parents sitting on the dresser which I think is sweet, but the most interesting thing is the leather butterfly chair in the corner with a guitar leaning against it.

I walk into the kitchen, where Chris has the food laid out. "Chris, do you play the guitar?" I ask, leaning against the counter, watching him search his kitchen drawer for serving spoons.

He pauses, glancing over at me with a half-smile. "Yeah, sometimes. Haven't practiced much lately, so I'm a little rusty." His voice trails off as he pokes the spoons into the containers.

"Will you play something for me later?" I ask, curious.

He shrugs with a playful glint in his eye. "I can try, but I can't guarantee the quality." He digs into the food, filling his plate.

I follow behind him filling my plate and then take a seat across from him at the counter. "I'll take whatever I can get."

We eat in a comfortable silence for a moment, the aroma of the meal filling the air and the food filling our stomachs. "Now that I've met your sister, when do I get to meet your father?" Chris asks.

I look up, suddenly aware of the shift in the air. "We can go visit him one day over break, if you really want to," I say, trying to keep it light, but even I can hear the hesitation in my voice. "But... it's unpredictable. Sometimes he remembers, sometimes he's barely even aware we're there."

Chris doesn't flinch. "I'll take my chances," he says without hesitation and then his expression softens. "Is it okay if I ask about your mother?"

I'm not quite sure how this conversation turned so serious, so suddenly, like meeting Lauren opened the door for him to step squarely into the center of my personal life. I take a slow breath before answering, contemplating whether I have the energy to go there. After all, he's welcomed me into his personal life, but let's face it, it's pretty perfect – mine is far from it. Chris is looking at me patiently and reading my thoughts. "I honestly don't mind talking about her," I finally say. "It helps to keep her memory alive; you know? But... it's hard sometimes. Usually, those conversations are just between Lauren and me. We lost her together, and that's something we... well, we share. That horrible bond is sacred in a way."

There's a long pause, and I can see the empathy in Chris's eyes. He's not rushing me. He's sizing me up trying to determine if he just overstepped an emotional line. "I'm sorry, Nikki," he says gently, looking down at his plate for a moment before meeting my gaze again. "I didn't mean to take you there. You don't have to say anything more."

"No, it's okay," I reassure him. I can tell he wants the emotional intimacy, like he feels I've been keeping something from him, so I relent. "I want to tell you. I do. It's just a lot." He reaches for my hand but doesn't say another word. He waits for me to decide what to do next. I swallow and begin, "As you know, my parents divorced when I was young, so my mom raised Lauren and me. My dad was involved, but the day-to-day was just the three of us, so we were very close. We were a team. My mom worked and Lauren and I were both in school, so we all pitched in to do our share. Sometimes Lauren and I would surprise her with a clean house and a hot dinner when she got home from work." I pause, "Of course, Lauren did the cooking."

"Of course," he smiles.

"We learned a lot from her. She was beautiful, smart and funny, but she was also very strong and independent. She had a big sense of adventure and a big heart, and in the end that's what killed her." I take a moment. That word always lands hard on me.

"What do you mean?" he asks. My eyes well up and my voice cracks when I begin to answer. "It's okay Nikki. You don't have to go on." He gets up and walks around to my side of the counter taking me in his arms.

I rest in his embrace for a moment before taking a deep breath, continuing. "I'm okay. I just needed a minute." I exhale and start again. I'm in it now, for better or for worse. "My mom grew up with horses and loved to ride. She taught Lauren and me as well. Lauren was actually pretty well trained. She rode dressage and competed in shows. I was more of a trail rider. I loved to run."

"I can believe that," he says and wipes my eyes with his sleeve. He looks at me reassuringly giving me the option to stop or continue.

I take a breath and choose. "My mom volunteered at an Equine Therapy Center that provides physical and occupational therapy for people with disabilities. She was there one day when a severe pop-up thunderstorm rolled in. There were horses out in the pasture that needed to be brought to the barn right away, so she and several of the employees went after them." A tear escapes down my cheek, but I keep going. "The horses were spooked and ran into the pasture shelter for cover, but it wasn't going to be enough to protect them against the wind. The employees grabbed the first two and my mom went for the last one just as the shelter collapsed. It fell on her and in the horse's attempt to get away it kicked her in the head as she was falling."

"Jesus, that's awful," Chris says, the reality of what I've been through sinking in.

The one escaped tear is now joined by dozens, but I manage to choke out, "The worst part is that she survived, but was declared brain dead. Lauren and I had to make the horrifying decision to take her off life support."

He pulls me in close and holds me in his arms, rubbing my back and kissing the top of my head, "I am so, so sorry, Nikki. I can't imagine going through something like that." I can't respond, so I just stay there in his arms for another few minutes, sobbing softly until my tears finally dry up.

When he hears my breathing steady, he lifts my head from his chest and says, "That's a whole lot to carry around lady. What can I do to help?"

"Maybe get me a tissue and play me a song on your guitar?" I sniffle.

"That I can do." He kisses my forehead and goes upstairs, returning with the guitar and a box of tissues. I blow my nose and settle into a chair in the living room awaiting his performance. "Okay, now don't judge," he says, sitting down across from me with the guitar.

"I can't promise," I reply with a small smile.

He tunes it for a minute and then starts strumming. I recognize the chords but can't place the song until he starts singing. It's "Brown Eyed Girl" by Van Morrison. I'm stunned by his voice. It's smooth and sexy and when he gets to the chorus, he changes the lyrics to 'green-eyed girl,' giving me goosebumps. He keeps strumming and singing and looking up into my eyes every time he sings the chorus until he finishes. I'm mesmerized.

"So, how'd I do?" Chris asks, slapping his hand down on the frame of the guitar and looking at me matter-of-factly.

I'm on my feet applauding before I even answer. "Well, you had me at hello with 'green-eyed girl,' but I'm blown away – truly, it was amazing! You have to keep up with it, Chris. You're really good." I join him on the couch, the cushions sinking softly as I sit down beside him.

"It's only a few chords, so it's not that hard," he mutters, sounding almost embarrassed. There's a strange vulnerability in his voice, and I can't help but smile at how *real* he's being. I love it.

"Are you being bashful, Chris Sheppard?" I tease with a playful smile. "I've never seen this side of you."

He looks over at me, a little flushed, his usual confidence nowhere to be found. I reach for the guitar, gently pulling it from his hands, and without warning, start tickling him – just enough to make him squirm.

"Stop!" He bursts into laughter, his body jerking away from me as he grabs my wrists. "Okay, okay! You win! I've just... never had an audience before."

I stop, sitting back slightly, studying him with newfound curiosity. "Wait... What? You've *never* sung for anyone before?"

Chris shifts uncomfortably. "Not really. I mean, I've played, but... I've never had a beautiful girl I wanted to serenade before." He glances at me with a soft smile that feels almost shy. "I think you inspired me."

My heart does something strange in my chest, and I can't help the smile that takes over my face. "You can serenade me anytime, Chris Sheppard. That is *definitely* my new favorite song." I give him a playful nudge, my fingers grazing his thigh in the process.

His grin widens, that familiar glint of mischief in his eyes. "Next, I'm going to learn "Jersey Girl" for you," he says, his ever-confident tone restored. "I won't be able to sing it like Bruce, but I'll put my own spin on it."

I can't resist teasing him further. "Are you trying to make me fall in love with you?"

He pauses for a moment, tilting his head with a grin that's both cocky and sweet. "Is it working?" he asks, his voice almost daring me to answer.

"Maybe," I say, leaning in until my lips are just a breath away from his before climbing into his lap wanting more.

Wednesday, Week 5

The Altercation

Chris was up before Nikki, so he showered, dressed, and got the coffee brewing. When she finally appeared in the kitchen wearing his shirt, he couldn't hold back his smile – he loved seeing her in his clothes. "Morning, gorgeous," he greeted her.

"Good morning, handsome," she replied, leaning in for a kiss.

"What do you want to do today with all this newfound freedom?" he asked, curious about what she had in mind.

"Honestly, I'd love to do all the touristy things we never have time for. Like the double-decker tour bus, the zoo, skating at Riverside Village, maybe even a historic walking tour. We could run up the Art Museum steps and do the Rocky victory dance at the top. I bet I could beat you…," she teased.

Chris was reaching for a coffee mug and stopped mid-way to look over his shoulder at Nikki, "The only way you could beat me up those steps is if my leg was broken," he said and turned back toward the cabinet, "but I'm game for touristy. Where should we start? You pick."

"How about the zoo? I just need to be back by four to walk Chester," she said, mentally calculating the time.

"That works. Go ahead and get dressed; I'll whip up some eggs," Chris offered, handing her a cup of coffee to take upstairs.

The zoo would be both indoors and out, so they bundled up and walked to the bus stop. Chris was getting a kick out of Nikki's enthusiasm; she was practically bouncing with excitement.

"Let's grab a map and plan our route. I want to see everything!" she said when they arrived.

"So, I guess they don't have any zoos in New Jersey?" he teased lightly.

"Of course we do!" she scoffed. "I just haven't been to one since I was a kid."

The Philadelphia Zoo is the oldest zoo in the country, so there was plenty of time to get it right. It really did have a lot to offer. There are mesh and wire enclosed trails above and around the property that allow the animals to roam and explore and spectators to see them up close. Nikki had a strategy laid out, so Chris followed along. The big cats strolled majestically through the overhead trails; the polar bear displayed himself proudly on the rocks intermittently slipping into the water to entertain the children in the glass tunnel below, and the monkeys swung like acrobats through the trees.

They spent hours there, marveling at the animals. Nikki seemed more pleased with every new exhibit they encountered. Chris was enjoying himself, but he was enjoying Nikki's child-like excitement more. When it was time to leave, she asked him which was his favorite exhibit. "Personally, I liked the monkeys," he said, reaching for her hand.

"Yeah, they're so cute and playful," she agreed, "but so are the river otters and how can you resist the giraffe and elephants?"

# # #

They caught a different bus back since they were going to Rittenhouse Square for Chester's four o'clock walk. Chris was being playfully flirtatious, and Nikki chuckled at him as she punched in the code to the penthouse door. She opened it cautiously expecting Chester's usual enthusiastic greeting, but he wasn't there. "Where's my handsome boy?" Nikki called as she walked into the apartment.

Chris grabbed for her arm, "Nikki, wait!" he called out, "something's not right..." But she was already inside, heading toward a whimpering sound in the other room. Chris walked after her anxiously looking around for trouble, assessing the situation, an uneasy feeling already creeping up the back of his neck. Nikki reached the dining room and was shocked to find Chester tied to the leg of the table with his leash. He began whimpering louder at the sight of her and fear swept through her body at the realization someone else could be in the house. "Chris," she whispered over her shoulder and knelt by Chester's side working to untie him and trying to quiet him down. "Shhhh..." she whispered and stroked his thick fur while she worked.

Chris heard a noise in the hallway and turned to see a shadowy figure emerging from the corner of the room. The sun was streaming brightly through the floor to ceiling windows keeping the figure in silhouette until it stepped closer, coming into view. Rocco stopped dead in his tracks at the sight of Chris and in one rapid instinctual motion pulled a gun out of the back waistband of his jeans.

Chris put his hands in the air, "Easy man. You don't need that. We're not looking for any trouble."

"Shut up!" Rocco yelled. "From where I'm standing, I decide what happens next." Chester growled in a low rumble and Rocco turned his attention to the dining room with the gun still pointed at Chris. He looked at Nikki like an animal about to overtake its prey. "Umm, umm... who do we have here?" Nikki pulled Chester closer into her chest, her eyes wide with terror. "Damn, you're fine girl. We could have some fun."

"Get away from her!" Chris screamed and started to move toward Nikki.

Rocco snapped his head back to Chris, "Take another step and it'll be your last!"

Chris stopped where he stood and tried reasoning with him, forcing himself to appear calm. "Look man we'll take the dog for a walk, and you be gone by the time we get back. No harm, no foul."

Rocco sized him up for a minute before putting the pieces together in his head. "Hold up, you're that college fuck boy who screwed over my runner Tony. What made you think you could walk away from this without any blowback? That's not how this shit works."

Chris watched the love and trust drain from Nikki's body as Rocco's words hit her ears. "It's not what you think, Nick," he said, desperately trying to handle the multiple crises erupting at once.

"It's exactly what you think sweetheart," Rocco grinned, his eyes narrowing into menacing slivers. "He owes me now. And you baby girl are gonna be the price. I'm gonna show you what it's like to be with a real man." Turning the gun toward Nikki he demanded, "Leave the dog and move over there with him."

"Nikki, stay put!" Chris yelled frantically, his pulse quickening and mind racing. "Rocco, point the gun at me." Rocco quickly shifted his aim back to Chris, the sound of the safety clicking off on the gun. In that moment, Chris felt the full weight of their reality – had his reckless choices brought them to this? He'd do whatever it took to protect Nikki. But how? He was in no position, their situation dire. "We'll just walk away," he begged trying to sound confident, like there was an easy solution to all of it. "You just slip out as easy as you slipped in," he panted, his heart hammering in his chest. "No one needs to get hurt and no one needs to know. Think about it man, this doesn't have to escalate. It can be just like nothing happened."

"And how's that gonna work?" Rocco sneered. "You can both identify me."

"We don't want any part of this. Why would we tell anyone?"

Nikki had freed Chester from the leash and shouted, "Get him!" releasing him from her grasp. Chester bounded forward and sprung through the air going for Rocco's throat. Rocco turned just as the dog landed on him and threw his hands up to protect his neck. Chester missed the bite but knocked Rocco over onto the glass coffee table which shattered into huge pieces on the floor. The pistol went off and Chester yelped at the same time. Nikki screamed as the chaos erupted and Chris seized the opportunity to dive on top of Rocco, punching him repeatedly with everything he had. The gun had been dropped, but Chris couldn't see it.

"Nikki, get the gun!" he yelled while struggling with Rocco.

Rocco and Chris were pretty evenly matched in size, but Chris had the advantage being on top. Rocco was rolling on broken glass trying to avoid Chris's blows while searching the floor with his hand for a weapon. He managed to grab a shard of glass and quickly, violently stabbed Chris in the arm with it to stop the beating.

"Ahhh!" Chris screamed in pain but knew he couldn't let up. It was clear if Rocco regained the upper hand, he had no intention of letting them walk away. Grabbing the wound on his arm with one hand, Chris used his leg to knee Rocco as hard as he could in the balls. Rocco groaned and took the shard that was cutting his hand open and thrusted it forcefully into Chris's thigh. Chris fell backwards, rolling off him and grabbing his leg in agony.

"Stop right there!" Nikki yelled loudly pointing the gun at Rocco, but her voice trembled, and he knew she wasn't a threat.

"Oh, the sorority girl is gonna shoot me," he challenged with a malicious sneer, and started toward her, completely unintimidated.

"Okay wait!" she shouted, putting her hands in the air. "Don't come any closer and I'll put the gun on the floor."

Rocco stopped and Nikki began to bend slowly to the floor with her eyes trained on Chris. She placed the gun down carefully, but then shoved it toward Chris with her foot as she stood. Chris quickly grabbed it from his position on the floor and aimed it at Rocco. "She might not shoot you, but I'll blow your fucking head off. Get in that chair over there, now!" he yelled, motioning with the pistol. "Nikki, grab Chester's leash and tie him up." Chris pushed himself backwards with his good leg until his back hit the wall and he steadied himself, his aim never faltering.

Rocco started to move toward the chair but turned suddenly, grabbing Nikki and pulling her in front of him as a shield with the shard of glass pressed tightly against her neck. "How good of a shot do you think you are, tough guy?" he taunted. "Cuz I've got her pretty close and I know I can slit her throat before you can aim your shot. Now put the gun down!" he demanded, spit flying from his lips.

Chester was still whimpering, and Nikki was sobbing, her hands trembling by her sides as Rocco dragged her backward. "Okay Rocco, calm down. No one needs to get hurt here. I'll put the gun down if you let her go," Chris tried to negotiate, the gun still trained on Rocco.

"That's not how this works. I'm gonna count to three and if that piece isn't on the floor, you're gonna watch hottie here bleed out." He gripped her tighter and began the countdown, "One…"

Nikki gasped in horror, her eyes wet with fear while slowly inching her hand into her coat pocket.

"Okay, okay!" Chris yelled desperately and slowly started to lower the gun when suddenly Nikki's hand flew up behind her head spraying Rocco in the face with pepper spray Chris didn't even know she had.

"Ahhh you bitch!" he screamed, doubling over, falling onto one knee and grabbing his eyes as Nikki scrambled from his grasp.

Chris aimed the gun at him again from his position on the floor, "Get in the chair now!" he yelled loudly.

Rocco started to crawl toward the chair still covering his eyes, "Fuck! Get me water. Fuck!"

"She'll get you water once you're tied to the chair. Now move!" he shouted, his voice firm and unyielding.

Rocco made it to the chair and Nikki tied him up with the leash before running to the kitchen. Chris held the gun steady with his good arm and painfully reached into his back pocket for his cell phone. "911 what's your emergency?"

"There's been a home invasion. We're in the penthouse at 1830 Rittenhouse. I've been stabbed and a dog has been shot. We have the intruder restrained," he winced.

"Is anyone else hurt?"

"The intruder's hand is bleeding, and he's been sprayed with mace."

"Okay sir, help is on the way. I'm sending police and paramedics. I can stay on the line with you until they arrive."

Chris put the phone on speaker and laid it down so he could have both hands on the gun. Nikki rushed back with a dish towel and was trying to stop Chester's bleeding. He was shot in the hip, whimpering through the pain. "It's okay boy," she said while petting him and kissing him on the head, "help is on the way."

"Water!!" Rocco screamed. Nikki scrambled back to the kitchen returning with a glass of water that she threw in Rocco's face infuriating him even more. "I'm gonna kill you bitch!" he threatened, shaking his head violently, nearly tipping the chair over. Nikki ignored him and ran to the bathroom returning with gauze and an ace bandage.

Chris was still on the floor propped up against the wall with the gun aimed at Rocco as Nikki knelt in front of him. "Nikki, I don't have anything to do with this. You know that, right?" She put the gauze on Chris's leg and started to wrap it. She was breathing heavily between soft tears while she worked. "Nikki, please look at me," Chris pleaded. She didn't answer him and shifted her attention to his arm. "Nikki, I can explain. Please look at me!"

Chris begged trying to lift her head to face him while she worked, but she refused to look up. She finished wrapping his arm and turned her attention back to Chester, pressing the dish towel against his wound.

Thump, thump, thump, "Police! Open up!"

"Coming!" Nikki yelled and ran for the door. Two police officers entered the room with their guns drawn. "Drop your weapon!" one of them shouted at Chris. He put one arm in the air and slowly lowered the gun to the floor with the other before kicking it away.

"It's his gun," Chris said pointing at Rocco, "he attacked me." Several paramedics followed the police officers. Rocco was still screaming for water, and Chester was whining a painful whimper from the floor. One of the paramedics approached Chris and another went to get a wet towel for Rocco. "Are you cut anywhere else?" he asked.

"No, just my arm and leg," Chris said and sucked in a strained breath as he tried to sit up straighter.

The paramedic pulled back the bandage on Chris's leg. "Okay, your friend did a good job stopping the bleeding, but we need to get you to a hospital. This wound looks deep."

A third police officer entered the room, and Nikki ran into his arms, "Officer Gaines!" He was a big burly guy who looked more than just a little intimidating.

He wrapped his arms around her, "It's okay, Ms. Taylor. It appears to be over." She wept softly into his barrel of a chest as he rubbed her back gently.

Chris couldn't believe his eyes. "Nikki...," he pleaded as the paramedics loaded him onto a stretcher. "Nikki please!"

Nikki looked up from the officer's chest, catching her breath. "Which hospital are you taking him to?" she asked, refusing to meet Chris's eyes.

"Jefferson," the paramedic replied.

The EMT wrapping Rocco's hand piped in, "This one doesn't need a hospital. You can take him to the station."

Chris was shocked to hear what came out of Nikki's mouth next, "Officer Gaines, can you take Chester and me to the animal hospital please? He needs help right away."

"Of course, Ms. Taylor. I can take your statement there. Guys, take this one to the precinct," he instructed motioning toward Rocco, "I'll get her statement at the animal hospital, and he can be questioned at Jefferson," he said pointing at Chris.

What's happening right now? She's more concerned about the dog than me? Chris' thoughts spinning in his head.

The other officers helped get Chester onto a gurney while Gaines led Nikki toward the entryway with his arm around her.

Chris was more pained watching this man comfort his girl than he was by his wounds. "Wait, Nikki, wait!" he yelled, his voice heavy with panic. "Nikki, please. I love you!" he shouted desperately as she stepped onto the elevator without even turning around.

Rocco finally stopped screaming and turned to Chris, "And I thought I was fucked."

Nikki

I ride in the back seat of the police car with Chester in my arms. I'm petting him and whispering to him gently while holding the dish towel over his wound. I try to remain calm, but the sound of the siren has me on edge. The blood is seeping through the towel and puddling around my fingers.

"I'll need your account of what happened once we get him inside," Officer Gaines says from the front seat. "We're almost there."

I look away to gather my thoughts. I've already texted his owners, and they're going to meet us at the animal hospital. The squad car comes to an abrupt stop, the door opens suddenly, and arms are lifting Chester from my lap. "We'll take it from here ma'am," someone says, and he's gone.

Officer Gaines and I take a seat in the waiting room. "So, tell me what happened," he says, gently placing a hand on my knee.

I take a deep breath and begin, "I went to take Chester out for his four o'clock walk and brought my boyfriend with me, like you suggested. Chester didn't greet me when I opened the door, but I could hear him in the other room, so I walked inside."

Officer Gaines interrupts, "When I questioned you at the café, you didn't mention you have a boyfriend."

"Well, why would that be relevant?" I ask, confused.

"Because he would probably have access to your bag."

"I don't understand, Officer Gaines. Chris wouldn't be involved in something like this, but he knew the guy. It doesn't make sense." I bow my head in my hands bewildered.

"How do you know he knew him?" he asks.

"Because the guy recognized Chris – not right away, but eventually. And he was implying Chris was involved in something shady with him. Also, Chris knew his name – it's Rocco. I don't know what to believe. Chris did everything he could to protect me." I realize I'm crying again as I speak.

"Sometimes people aren't who they seem," he says suspiciously and rubs my back again to comfort me.

Cold air washes over me and I turn to see Chester's owners walk in. I stand to greet them. "Mr. and Mrs. Murphy, I'm so sorry," I say wiping the tears from my eyes. "Chester is in surgery right now. We haven't received an update yet. This is Officer Gaines," I say waving my hand in his direction.

"Hello Mr. and Mrs. Murphy." He shakes both of their hands. "We're still sorting through the details, but Ms. Taylor and her boyfriend walked in on a robbery when she went to walk your dog today."

"Oh my God!" Mrs. Murphy gasps in horror, raising her hand to cover her mouth. "What happened? Are you all right, dear?" she asks, her shock turning to concern.

"I'm fine, but Chester....," I choke back a sob to stop my emotions from pouring out in front of them.

Recognizing that I can't complete my sentence Officer Gaines takes over for me, "he was shot in the hip. They're taking care of him now." Mrs. Murphy gasps again and turns to her husband for support. "We'll need you to come down to the station later to file a report," Officer Gaines continues. "The robbery was stopped so nothing was stolen, but a coffee table was broken in the struggle and there are some blood stains on your carpet."

"Blood stains. Good Lord," Mr. Murphy says and reaches for his wife's hand.

"Now that you're here, I need to go to the hospital to question Nikki's boyfriend. Here's my card and the address of the precinct," he says and turns to me, "Ms. Taylor, I'll need you to come with me. I'm not done taking your statement."

"Okay," I say, my voice cracking as I speak. "Mr. and Mrs. Murphy, will you please text me as soon as you hear anything about Chester?"

"Of course, dear. You go along and take care of what you need to."

Officer Gaines and I drive to the hospital, and I share all the details of what happened on the way. He asks a lot of questions about Chris – he's clearly suspicious of him. When we arrive at the ER, he offers me a seat and hands me a pad of paper and pen. "Please write down everything you just told me. I need to speak to Chris alone before you can see him." He looks at me with comforting eyes before turning toward the nursing station. "What room is Chris Sheppard in?"

The nurse looks at a chart and answers, "They should be done stitching him by now.   He's down the hall in curtain 12."

I write everything down the best I can with trembling hands and take another deep breath to try to calm down. Between the adrenaline, fear, and confusion about Chris, I'm a mess. I know I have to call Lauren but need to pull it together first or I'll scare her. There's a vending machine down the hall, so I purchase a bottle of water and drink half of it in one gulp. Ok Nikki, you've got this. I dial Lauren.

"Hey Nick. What's up?" she answers cheerfully.

"Okay, don't freak out but I'm at the hospital."

"What!? Are you okay?" she asks, her cheerfulness replaced with alarm.

"Yes, I'm fine," I exhale. "But Chris and I walked in on a robbery at one of my dog houses today and he was stabbed by the intruder."

"Stabbed?" she gasps. "Oh my God. Is he going to be okay?"

"Yes, but Lauren, he's somehow involved," my voice now a whimper. "He knew the guy."

"What?" Lauren yells. "Which hospital?"

"Jefferson. I'm in the ER waiting room."

"I'm on my way!"

The Interrogation

Chris was lying in a hospital bed, LED lighting overhead walled in only by a retractable curtain. His wounds were stitched but throbbing and his mind was a wreck about Nikki. As the curtain pulled back, he had a fraction of a second's hope it would be her. Instead, Officer Gaines was standing there, his face unreadable. "Where's Nikki, sir?" Chris asked, trying to keep his voice steady.

"She's in the waiting room," Gaines replied abruptly.

"Is she okay?"

"Physically, yes. But she's emotionally shaken, and with good reason," Gaines said with an expression that told Chris he thought he was responsible for everything that happened.

"When can I see her?" Chris pressed, more eager to straighten things out with Nikki than with the police.

"After you answer a few questions." Gaines adjusted his belt in a way that made sure Chris noticed the holstered gun. It was a subtle reminder of who was in charge. "What's your connection to this Rocco character?"

Chris didn't hesitate. "He's a drug dealer. I only met him once. My roommates and I thought we could make some extra cash with him, but as soon as we realized how dangerous it was, we backed out. I never sold anything to anyone."

Gaines's expression didn't change. "I'm going to need the names and contact information of your roommates."

"No problem, but they're both home on break right now," Chris said, wincing slightly as pain shot through his leg.

"Where do they live?" Gaines continued.

"John's in Ardmore, and Tony's in the Bronx."

"How were you introduced to Rocco?" Gaines asked without looking up from his pad.

"Through someone Tony knows in New York."

Gaines probed further. "So, Rocco's operating out of New York as well?"

"I have no idea. That's something you'll have to ask him," Chris replied, growing impatient.

"We will. But we need to corroborate your story." Gaines paused, his eyes boring into Chris. "Did you give Rocco Ms. Taylor's keys?"

"No! I'd never put her in danger like that. I love her. I told you, I only met Rocco once, and Nikki never met him until today's fiasco. I don't know how he got her keys," Chris insisted.

Gaines ignored Chris's reaction and was already on to the next question. "Do your roommates have access to her purse?"

"Well, she's brought it to our house before, but I don't see how anyone could have copied her keys or gotten the codes from her phone without anyone noticing," Chris said, trying to piece together the situation himself.

Gaines looked up from his pad making direct eye contact with Chris, "One of the three of you is an accomplice in this crime, Mr. Sheppard, and someone *will* be charged."

"I have nothing to hide. I'm not the bad guy here. In fact, I stopped the robbery today and saved my girlfriend. As you can see, I've got the injuries to prove it," Chris argued with growing frustration.

"It's my understanding Ms. Taylor saved herself with the mace and stopped you from bleeding out," Gaines shot back.

This guy is a real pain in my ass. "When can I see her?"

"Write down your contact information and your roommates' as well as your account of what happened. I'll tell her you want to see her, but that'll be entirely up to her," Gaines said, handing Chris the pad and pen.

Chris quickly scribbled down the information and handed it back. Gaines gave a curt nod. "I'll be in touch, Mr. Sheppard," he said before pulling the curtain back and stepping out.

Chris could hear him talking on the phone, "Hey Rameriz, I think I've got a break in the case you're working with DEA in New York. We've got a guy down at the precinct connected to some local robberies, but I have reason to believe he might be involved in running drugs through the Northeast corridor."

D-fucking-E-A. Just great. God only knows what Robo Cop is gonna tell Nikki, Chris thought, panic starting to rise, but he knew he had to warn John. He fumbled for his phone and quickly dialed.

"Hey, dude," John answered casually. "How's married life treating you?"

"Not well. Listen, I don't have much time. Nikki and I walked in on Rocco robbing one of her dog homes today. He had a gun, and we struggled. He stabbed me twice," Chris explained, trying to get it out quickly.

"What?! Are you okay? How's Nikki? And how the hell was Rocco at one of Nikki's dog houses?" John asked rapid fire.

"We're fine, and I have no idea. It had to be Tony, but I don't know how he could've copied her keys. The cops questioned me and asked for your info and Tony's. We've got nothing to hide, but I wanted to give you a heads-up. They'll be contacting you," Chris warned.

"Holy shit, man!"

"Yeah, and it gets better. The DEA is involved. They think Rocco's part of a bigger operation. It's the cops' job to gather evidence, so I didn't throw Tony under the bus, but it had to be him. I just don't understand how," Chris said, his mind racing.

"Are you going to call Tony?" John asked.

"Hell no. He's on his own. His bullshit almost got us killed today!" Chris snapped.

"Crap. I've got another call coming in and I don't recognize the number. It's probably the cops. I'll call you back." *Click.*

A nurse entered the 'room,' informing Chris that he'd be released soon and asked if he had a ride home. He lied, saying he did. His only priority was sorting things out with Nikki and he didn't want to hold up his release. He couldn't shake the worry that she hadn't come back to see him yet, and he definitely didn't trust whatever Gaines might have said to her.

Impatience got the better of him and he decided to go in search of Nikki. Getting out of bed wasn't so bad, walking was another matter. The nurse was probably going to bring him crutches with the paperwork, but he couldn't wait any longer. Despite the throbbing in his leg, he could use it if he didn't put too much pressure on it. He limped out from behind the curtain, steadying himself against the wall as he made his way down the hall.

Halfway to the nurses' station, he spotted Nikki sitting with Lauren, who was holding her close. "Nikki!" he called out.

The nurse at the desk looked up, "Mr. Sheppard, you shouldn't be out of bed."

Nikki and Lauren turned toward him. Lauren raised her hand, signaling him to stop. "Don't, Chris," she said sharply.

"A drug dealer, Chris? How could you?" Nikki cried; her voice filled with hurt.

"I don't know what the cops told you, Nick, but I'm not involved. That's why I'm free to go," Chris desperately tried to explain, but he saw the pain in her eyes and knew he was losing.

"Whatever you're mixed up in, Chris, I don't want Nikki anywhere near it − or you. She could've been killed! I'm taking her home with me," Lauren said, her voice firm as she tightened her grip on Nikki.

"Wait! I can explain. Nikki, Lauren, please!" Chris pleaded, but Lauren turned Nikki toward the door, and they walked away without looking back.

The Arrest

Once the paramedic finished wrapping Rocco's hand, the police handcuffed him and read him his rights. At the station, the officer emptied Rocco's pockets and discovered a set of keys and the paper with the codes written on it. They took his mug shot, fingerprinted him, and put him in a holding room for questioning.

The police left Rocco alone for about 20 minutes to let him sweat but this wasn't Rocco's first run in with the law, he knew the drill. Eventually Officer Burns entered the dimly lit room and pulled out the metal chair across the table from Rocco, turned it backwards and straddled it. "My name is Officer Burns and what's yours?"

"Rocco Brown," he answered with indifference, slouching in the chair.

"So, Mr. Brown," the officer said, leaning his elbows on the back of the chair and lacing his fingers, "how did you obtain the codes and the keys?"

"I found them," Rocco answered flippantly, almost like a challenge.

"Where?" Burns asked.

"On the street. Someone must have dropped them."

Burns was growing impatient with Rocco's attitude. He'd dealt with plenty of thugs before and wanted to skip all the bullshit and just get down to business. "That's awfully convenient. Thing is, those keys are copies of keys the young woman who walked in on you today owns and the codes were taken from her phone. So, who do you suppose would've done that?"

Rocco nonchalantly sat further back in his chair before he answered. "Beats me," was all he said.

There was a knock at the door. "Sit tight Mr. Brown. I'll be right back." Burns stepped into the hall closing the door behind him. Mike Rameriz and Tim Batiste from the DEA were waiting to speak to him. The buzz of fluorescent lights hummed overhead, cutting through the low murmur of the voices around them. "Hey Rameriz – hey Batz. What's up? I'm in the middle of an interrogation."

"Gaines called and said the kid your guy stabbed gave him up as a dealer from New York," Rameriz said. "We have reason to believe he's connected with the operation we've been trying to take down and he could be just the leverage we need."

"Okay. We've got him on the robberies. We still need to find out who his accomplice is but go ahead and question him on the drug running if you want." Burns offered.

"The kid who was stabbed has two roommates. The accomplice has to be one of the three of them. Gaines already questioned the one kid at the hospital and has the contact info for the other two," Batiste added.

Rameriz and Batiste followed Burns back into the room where Rocco was being held. "Mr. Brown, we're with the DEA," Rameriz said. "We're less concerned with you than we are with your boss. You're going down for these robberies unless you cut a deal with us to expose your network."

Finally, they had Rocco's attention. "Look man, I'm not looking to get myself killed. I want a lawyer!" Rocco demanded.

Lauren

Nikki's been through a hell of an ordeal, and I don't want her to be alone. She collapses on the couch when we get to my place, and I make her a cup of tea. *Fly Eagles fly...* "Jesus Nikki, is that Chris? Just turn it off."

"I can't," she murmurs, her words heavy with exhaustion. "I'm waiting to hear about Chester."

"Okay, well don't answer it. There's plenty of time to hear what he has to say. Right now, you need to rest."

She rubs her hand over half-lidded eyes. "You know he'll just keep calling," she says, her voice trailing off.

"Then give it to me. I'll answer if he calls back." She hands me the phone and not two minutes later, *Fly Eagles fly...* "Chris, she's resting, and I won't give her the phone. She'll call you if and when she's ready to speak to you."

"But..." *Click.*

"Nikki, get some sleep. I'll wake you if you get a text about Chester." I put a blanket over her and she's sound asleep five minutes later. A text comes through on Nikki's phone and I check to see if it's news about Chester.

> Nikki, I know you're resting, and Lauren won't give you the phone, but I'm begging you to call me when you wake up. Or text me Lauren's address and I'll come over to speak to you face-to-face. I have to talk to you. I can explain. PLEASE!

I put the phone down. Nikki can read that later. I'm not going to wake her.

I've been working on my article most of the day yesterday and today before this whole fiasco happened. With Nikki resting, I decide to pull out my computer and get back to it. I should be able to finish it by tomorrow or the next day. Drew isn't expecting it until the new year, but I'd love to get it to him early. And there he is in my head again. Do I want to finish it early just so I'll have a reason to speak to him? Crap, I might be in trouble.

I write for a while to distract myself from thoughts of Drew and order a pizza, so we'll have something for dinner when Nikki wakes up. *Ding.* It's Nikki's phone.

Hi dear, it's Mrs. Murphy. Chester is out of surgery and doing well. Apparently, the bullet went straight through his hip. They've sewn him up and dressed his wounds. He's going to be fine but won't need walking anytime soon. We'll be back in touch when he's fully recovered. So glad you weren't hurt.

The knock on the door when the pizza arrives wakes Nikki. "How long have I been asleep?"

"About an hour and a half. You needed it. Good news just came through about Chester," I say and hand her the phone.

She reads it, "Oh thank God he's okay." She looks back at the phone and then up at me. "When did this text from Chris come in?"

"Just after you fell asleep. Are you hungry?" I ask.

"Starving."

I pull out paper plates and open the box. "No mushrooms," Nikki says looking at me through sleepy eyes before we both start to laugh. When we were kids, our dad told us that all pizza came with mushrooms because that's the way he liked it. No kid likes mushrooms, so we always had to pick them off. It wasn't until we started eating over at friends' houses that we discovered you could order pizza with any toppings you want.

"Lauren, what am I going to do about Chris? Why would he know a gun toting drug dealer?" she asks with sadness and confusion washed all over her face.

My chair creaks across the hardwood floors when I push it out to reach for a napkin. "You're going to have to hear him out at some point, but it's up to you to decide when."

Nikki takes a slice of pizza out of the box but plops it down on the plate without taking a bite. "I was actually falling in love with him, Lauren. He's everything, and now this."

"Maybe there's an explanation for all of it, but if he's responsible for putting you in danger, I don't want you to ever see him again. I mean it, Nick," I say looking at her sternly.

"Speak of the devil, he's texting again."

> Nikki, if ur awake, *please* call me. I'm going
>
> out of my mind!

"What should I do?" she asks, staring at her phone like it's a crystal ball that is going to provide her with some magic solution.

"Why don't you give yourself the night. Text him back and tell him you'll call him in the morning and then turn off the phone."

Her shoulders slump and she exhales a deep breath. "I don't even know if he got home from the hospital alright. Am I being heartless? He got stabbed twice trying to protect me."

Even though she said she was starving she hasn't touched her food. All of this is weighing too heavily on her. "Let's decide after dinner," I suggest. "This is all too much on an empty stomach."

Nikki takes a few bites of pizza and decides to call Chris. "I gave him your address," she says. "He'll be here in about 20 minutes. He wants to talk in person." She sits back at the table and pushes the half-eaten slice around the plate deep in thought. I know she's hoping his explanation will satisfy her concerns, but she doesn't look confident. The tension emanating from her body is palpable, making me almost equally uneasy while we wait.

The knock at the door breaks our tense silence. Chris is standing there on crutches with one leg lifted off the floor looking more than a little panicked.

"Are you alright?" Nikki asks at the sight of him.

"I'm fine. May I please come in?"

She lets him in, and I offer to give them some privacy, knowing full well I'll be able to hear them through the bedroom door – my apartment is not that big.

Nikki doesn't waste time, "So how do you know Rocco, Chris?"

"Tony got his contact info from a guy he knows in New York and set up a meet to talk about making some extra cash selling drugs," he says and leans against the wall for support.

"So, you were selling?" she asks with unblinking eyes, pinning him to the wall with her glare.

"No. John and I realized right away that Tony was being reckless, and this Rocco dude seemed like the real deal, so we both bailed out. Neither one of us sold a single thing or wanted any trouble." Her eyes stay glued on his and he does his best to remind her of what they share with his expression, but she can't see it – she's pissed!

"What about Tony?" Nikki asks, her intensity fierce.

"He sold for a few weeks, but John and I talked him into stopping. He was done with it when he went home for break." Chris moves both crutches into one hand and reaches out for Nikki's hand, but she steps back.

"So, you knew he was selling, and you were okay living with him?" It's a question, but it comes out more like an angry statement. This conversation is clearly not going the way Nikki had hoped.

"No," he says, dropping his hand back to his side and readjusting the crutches. "I told you. John and I talked him into quitting." It's clear he's being honest but it's also clear it's not giving Nikki much comfort – after all he was okay with it.

"Did you tell all of this to Officer Gaines?" she asks with both exasperation and irritation.

"No. I gave him John and Tony's contact information and figured that's for him to sort out." He smiles at her, eyes wide with misguided hope, and tries to lighten the mood. "By the way, I think Robo Cop has a crush on you."

Nikki throws her arms up in frustration or maybe anger – or both. "Don't do that, Chris! This isn't funny, and we're not done talking," she says sharply.

Chris seems to deflate – nothing is working for him. Even his superpower, his charm, is failing him. "I'm sorry Nikki. I just want this to be over," there is an air of defeat in his tone and the hope that was just apparent in his eyes is gone completely. "What else do you want to know?"

"This is far from over, Chris! How did Rocco have keys to my homes?" Nikki demands.

"I have no idea, Nick. I really don't. The only connection is Tony, but I don't understand how."

"Wait…, was Tony with you the night you met Amanda?" Nikki asks, putting the pieces together in her head.

Chris has the look of a caged animal. He knows where this line of questioning will lead and that there's no way out. "Yes," he answers warily, his voice a sad whisper.

Shock and disbelief cross Nikki's face. "So, was he the one who spiked her roommate's drink?"

"Yes, but John and I didn't know it at the time. I swear," Chris replies desperately trying to defend himself, "and we made sure those girls got home safely."

Nikki starts to pace back and forth in front of him. "What the hell, Chris? You're literally living with a sexual predator drug dealer who somehow figured out how to break into my dog homes!" she shouts, her anger at a full boil.

Chris tries to reach for her but she's moving too quickly and he's having trouble managing with the crutches. He slumps in frustration, "I know, babe, but I'm done with him now. I didn't realize how far off the rails he was. John and I don't want anything to do with him anymore."

"Don't call me babe," Nikki says firmly stopping straight in front of him. "Let me get this straight... my sister is writing a news story based on the fact that your psycho roommate drugged Amanda's roommate with bad intentions?"

Chris grasps at an answer that will appease her but it's evident in his expression he knows there isn't one. "Yes, but I *promise* you I didn't know it at the time. *I swear.*"

At this point I've heard enough and come out of the bedroom. "Are you kidding me, Chris? You actually live with the guy who roofied Amanda's roommate?"

Chris turns his attention to me desperately hoping to gain an ally, "I know it looks bad, but Lauren you *have* to believe me," he pleads. "Neither John or I knew about it at the time."

Before I can respond Nikki is shouting again, "But you knew he was selling date rape drugs all semester and you were okay with it?!"

"I wasn't okay with it, Nick. John and I talked him into stopping." He's begging for forgiveness with his eyes, his voice, his expression, his body language but Nikki's fury is blinding her to all of it.

"Weeks later Chris!" she yells, "how many girls were assaulted in the meantime?"

"I don't know, Nikki… *Please…* I really wasn't thinking about it. I was focused on you – on us." He tries again to move closer to her, but she starts pacing again. Running out of options, he repeats, "I wasn't thinking about what Tony was doing. I was thinking about us and how I was falling in love with you."

The words don't hit Nikki's ears; she's caught in her thoughts. "So, the day you stopped into the café when I was meeting with Amanda, you lied to us."

His shoulders seem to slouch even with the crutches under his arms propping them up. "I didn't lie to you, Nick. I just didn't tell you what I knew. I couldn't. I knew I had to put a stop to it, and I did."

"Chris, I think you need to leave," I say firmly.

"Please Lauren. I'm not done explaining," he pleads.

"What else is there to explain?" Nikki cries. "You knew what was happening and you didn't do anything about it. It took *The Inquirer* doing a news story about drink spiking and date rape drugs for you to come to your senses? I don't even know who you are right now!"

"You've said enough, Chris. Let's not make this a bigger scene than it already is," I say calmly but firmly, "please just leave."

Chris turns to Nikki with one last desperate attempt, "But I love you, Nikki. Tell me what I can do to fix it. I'll do whatever it takes. Anything, just tell me."

"My heart is broken, Chris. I don't know if it *can* be fixed. Just go." Nikki wipes a tear from her eye and spins around running down the hall toward the bedroom. Chris tries to go after her, but I stand in his way, and he can't get by me with the crutches.

"Lauren *please,*" he begs.

"She needs time, Chris. Just go."

Friday, Week 5

Wheels in Motion

Drew thought about Lauren all week and how he might be able to see her again before they returned to the office. He drove around her neighborhood hoping to run into her and even stopped back into the liquor store where they met on Christmas Eve, but no luck. His mother asked him about her at Christmas dinner which sent his sister Jen into a tailspin. She's been sending him HR policies all week and finding loopholes to legitimize office romances, which was of course, just furthering his resolve to pursue Lauren.

Just as if he willed it to happen, an email from Lauren showed up in his inbox. The subject line was: One in Four No More. *This must be her article*, he thought. He opened it up and started to read. It was a very powerful piece. It wasn't just factual and bringing attention to a serious issue, it was a call to action much like Nancy Reagan's 'Just Say No to Drugs' campaign in the 80s. She challenged student groups to unite in 'One in Four No More' campaigns across the country. She called out university administrations for not doing more to educate students on how to protect themselves and suggested standardized national materials for student orientations. The article went further to task state's Liquor Control Boards to develop a seal of approval that bars could attain by adhering to certain safety protocols and she challenged Interfraternity Councils to do a better job policing themselves with 'spotters.' It was informative, well written, eye-opening and persuasive. Drew couldn't help but feel proud of her. He knew the news team would eat it up, so he forwarded it to his counterpart in the News Department and suggested they consider a role for her. The wheels were now in motion. He emailed her back:

> Congratulations, Lauren. Your article is excellent! I know you were planning on working remotely until next week, but I'd like to talk to you about it before then. Are you free for dinner tonight?

He stared at his inbox anxiously tapping his fingers on the desk. *Come on, come on, come on...*

Lauren gasped and looked up from her computer, "Oh my God. Drew just read my article and wants to meet me for dinner!" she said to Nikki who was still staying with her. They both felt more comfortable being together for now.

Nikki jumped up from the couch. "No way! Okay, so you're definitely going – this is huge Lauren, on so many levels!"

Lauren hesitated for a moment before responding and then nodded. "Yes, yes, I'll go. I just don't know what to expect... I'm nervous," she said tentatively but also with excitement.

Nikki grabbed her by the arm and pulled her into the reality of the moment, "I'm sure it's good news," she said with reassuring eyes. "Why would he want to see you before you were back in the office if it was bad?"

Lauren contemplated it for a minute. "I guess you're right. Let me just email him back and then I need you to pick me out something to wear... I feel like this is an important night."

"On it," Nikki said and hustled to the bedroom closet while Lauren returned Drew's email:

> Hi Drew. I'm so glad you liked it! I'd love to hear more of your thoughts. I'm available to meet you for dinner. When and where?

"Yes!" *Tap, tap, tap...*

> I'll make a reservation at Lacroix and pick you up at six.

The Silent Treatment

It was two days since Chris had last seen or spoken to Nikki, and he was losing his mind. He left her countless messages, apologizing over and over, until he finally promised to give her some space. But if she didn't respond by New Year's Eve, he was ready to show up at her apartment, no matter what.

John returned to town yesterday because the police wanted to question him in person. He backed up Chris's story – that they'd only met Rocco once and never sold anything for him. Neither of them had heard from Tony. As far as they knew, the police didn't have any solid evidence against him, but with both Chris and John identifying Rocco as a dealer, who knew what he'd say to save his own ass.

After his interview with the police, John went back to Ardmore to spend time with Michelle before she left again for New York. Watching their relationship always gave Chris a headache, but he'd take that over the torture he was going through with Nikki right then. It was unbearable.

Chris's mom begged him to come home with John and even threatened to come to the city herself, but he couldn't leave – not when there was a chance Nikki might finally respond. Desperate to keep himself busy, he passed the time watching video tutorials on how to play "Jersey Girl" on the guitar and practicing it. He was determined to win her back, no matter what it took.

Still Friday

First Date?

As Drew pulled up to Lauren's building, he saw her waiting in the lobby. He quickly parked and jumped out to open the door for her as she approached.

"Hi, Drew," she greeted him, and leaned in for a very awkward hug; neither of them knew how to navigate the boundaries of their relationship since Christmas Eve. Drew's nerves were already on edge because of the conversation he planned to have with her, and the hug only made things worse.

"Drew, how on earth did you manage to find mace for Nikki on Christmas Eve?" she asked as they walked to the car.

"When I ordered yours, I got one for my sister too. I just went home, grabbed it, and brought it back that night."

"Well, thank God you did, because it might have saved her life."

Drew stopped in his tracks. "What? What happened?" he asked, alarmed.

On the drive to the restaurant, Lauren filled him in on Nikki's ordeal in vivid detail. It was clear how deeply affected she was by what Nikki had been through. The way she was talking was as if it had happened to her. He couldn't help but be moved by the bond Lauren and Nikki shared. He'd never seen anything quite like it before. Lauren's love and concern for her sister warmed his heart, making him wish he could just hold her. *Not yet, Drew.*

Once inside the restaurant, Drew offered to take Lauren's coat. "Yes, thank you," she said. Beneath it, she wore a long black dress that hugged her figure perfectly, paired with black leather high-heeled boots. Her long dark hair was pulled up in a dramatic high ponytail – if you can describe a ponytail as dramatic. She looked stunning, and Drew's nerves ratcheted up a notch as he thought about the conversation ahead, but he maintained a cool exterior.

"Have you eaten here before?" he asked as they sat.

"I've been here for drinks but never for a meal. It has wonderful reviews," Lauren replied.

"Yes, it's one of my favorites." As they settled in, the hostess handed them menus and mentioned their waiter would be with them shortly.

"So, your article," Drew began.

Lauren anxiously interrupted, "Be honest. What does it need?"

"It needs to be published," Drew replied without hesitation. "It exposes a serious issue that a lot of organizations, agencies, and businesses are ignoring. It's shocking, well-researched and courageous. It's a call to action that can't be ignored."

"Do you really think so?" she asked, excitement in both her expression and tone.

A waiter approached just then, asking if they preferred sparkling or tap water. "Tap will be fine," Drew answered, then turned to Lauren. "Would you like something else to drink?" purposely not assuming she'd have chardonnay.

"A glass of chardonnay would be nice," she said pleasantly.

Drew nodded. "May we see the wine list, please?"

"Of course, sir. I'll be right back."

Turning back to Lauren, Drew continued, "I've already sent your article to the News Department and recommended they consider you for a role there if that's what you want. You can keep 'Philly's Top 10' as long as you like, but you could start handing more of it over to Amanda as she gets more experience, freeing you up to delve into more substantial stories."

"Drew, I don't know what to say. I'm a little shocked," she said, briefly covering her mouth with her hand. "I'd love to work on more news stories!"

"Lauren, you're an exceptional investigator and writer. Your talents are wasted on 'Philly's Top 10.' I'll set up the meeting for next week if you want to pursue this."

Lauren's face lit up, and she clapped her hands in delight. "This is so exciting! Thank you so much, Drew."

The waiter returned with the water and wine list. Drew was pulling out all the stops tonight and ordered one of their finest bottles. "Excellent choice, sir," the waiter commented.

"Drew, that isn't necessary," Lauren said, sounding a bit self-conscious.

"Lauren, we're celebrating. Besides, you already know I fudge my expense reports," Drew said with a wink.

The waiter smiled and nodded. "Very well then," he said, and walked away.

Drew took a deep breath, preparing himself for what he was about to say next, exhaled and went for it. "I have a confession to make. There's another, more selfish, reason I want you to move to a new department."

"Oh?" Lauren replied, intrigued.

"I don't want to be your boss anymore," Drew admitted, swallowing the lump in his throat but maintaining outward confidence.

Lauren looked taken aback. She took a minute before responding and hesitantly replied, "I'm sorry to hear that." All of her previous excitement evaporated, and she appeared to withdrawal.

Drew reached across the table to take her hand. She seemed confused but slowly moved her hand toward his. He wrapped his fingers around hers and looked her in the eye. "I don't want to be your boss anymore because I'd like to see you outside the office." *There, I said it. No going back now.*

Her face flushed − a reaction Drew found charming − and she squeezed his hand, as if trying to steady herself. She stared at him, speechless.

"Lauren?" Drew asked, his heart pounding, waiting for a response. *Oh shit. What if this was a really bad move?*

The waiter returned with the wine, giving Drew a brief reprieve as he let go of Lauren's hand. The waiter displayed the label, and Drew nodded. After pouring a taste, Drew gave his approval, and the waiter filled both glasses before asking if they had any questions about the menu.

"I think we need a few more minutes," Drew replied.

"Certainly, sir. Take your time," the waiter said and left them alone.

Drew turned back toward Lauren who was still sitting in silence. "Lauren?" he said nervously.

Lauren cleared her throat. "Um, see me outside the office, like, uh, like a date?" she finally asked, her voice soft and hesitant, embarrassed that she might be getting it wrong.

"Yes, Lauren. I'd like to take you out," he said committing to the invitation, hoping for the best.

Lauren fell silent again, as if weighing the decision of a lifetime. A prickly feeling crawled up the back of Drew's neck, and he glanced around hoping the waiter might return and ease the tension, but there was no sign of him. The silence continued to stretch, and Drew knew he had to do something to change the mood. He opened his mouth to say God knows what when Lauren finally replied, "I'd like that very much."

Drew collapsed inside with relief but didn't show it; he just looked at her affectionately, "Phew," he exhaled and swiped the back of his hand across his forehead for effect. "I didn't think you'd take so long to think about it."

Lauren hesitated for a moment, her fingers tapping nervously on the edge of her glass. "I'm just a little shocked, that's all."

"Shocked?" Drew leaned in slightly. "Why would you be shocked? I enjoy your company and want to spend more time with you."

Lauren glanced away, biting her bottom lip as she considered his words and what hers would be next. "Drew, I don't think you realize just how much of a big deal you are around the office. You're... well, *you*," she said with a soft laugh. "Any of the single women would jump at the chance to go out with you."

"And I don't think you realize how special you are," Drew said, watching her blush and divert her eyes from his. "None of the other women in the office hold a candle to you." When she finally looked back across the table at him, he reached for her hand again, and this time, she didn't hesitate to take it.

She paused for a moment contemplating their current situation, smiled and asked, "Are we on a date right now?"

"The first of many, I hope," he said, his gaze lingering on her.

The rest of the evening flowed effortlessly. With the tension lifted, they both relaxed, and conversation came easily. They talked about their backgrounds, hobbies, travel — where they'd been, where they wanted to go — books, what they were watching on

Netflix (Drew was relieved to learn she wasn't a fan of Bravo), and any other topic that came to mind. She even asked about his tattoos, making Drew wonder how she knew he had any. Maybe she'd been paying more attention to him than he realized.

After dessert, Drew asked if she'd like to come back to his place for a nightcap.

"Come back to your place after our first date? Scandalous!" Lauren teased.

"Well, we've known each other for a while, so maybe we can fast-forward a bit."

"Drew Davis, this is a side of you I haven't seen before," she said but didn't answer the question. Sensing she was considering it, Drew decided not to push.

When they reached the car, he turned to her. "Lauren, you'll have to tell me where we're going. And before you answer, I promise to be a perfect gentleman."

She hesitated for a moment. His eyes met hers and something unspoken passed between them. "Well, I suppose it would be rude to turn down a gentleman."

Lauren

Drew opens the door to his apartment, and I can't help but stare. The space is stunning, far beyond anything I expected, (not that I know what I think I was expecting). "Wow, your apartment is gorgeous," I say, my eyes taking in the sleek, modern furnishings.

"Thank you," Drew replies with a modest smile. "My mother's an interior designer. This was all her. But I'll admit, she does have impeccable taste."

"Does she dress you too?" I tease, looking him up and down.

He chuckles, shaking his head. "No, that's all me. I've always had a thing for clothes. I've been propositioned by gay men more than once, so I must be getting it right." He winks at me, enjoying the banter.

I laugh and smile back at him. "Nikki is always styling me. She has been since we were kids. She says I dress too prudish when left to my own devices."

"I get the impression the two of you rarely leave each other to your own devices," he says with a grin, clearly entertained by Nikki and my relationship.

"True enough," I reply amused at how well he's read us.

We slip off our coats, and Drew walks over to the bar, easy and comfortable in his own space. "What would you like for a nightcap?" he asks, glancing over his shoulder. "I make a mean Old Fashioned."

"Gentleman's choice."

"Okay, make yourself comfortable." He returns with the drinks and sits next to me on the couch putting his hand down on my thigh. I'm a little uncomfortable that he's touching me in a rather intimate way. This is just all so different and new. My thoughts only stay there for a second before I move on. "Drew, what if the News Department doesn't want me?"

"That'll never happen," he says patting my leg reassuringly. "They're smart and when they read your article, they'll want you on their team. Next week when we're back in the office, I'll set up the meeting for you and I'll go to HR to discuss office relationships with no reporting structure." He takes my hand and looks me in the eye. "I've already read the policy and had my sister review it. I don't think there'll be a problem, but we need to be up front from the beginning," he pauses, "assuming you want to go on another date with me."

I can't help but giggle. "It doesn't take an investigative reporter to figure out that you were pretty confident I would if you've already researched the policy."

"Well, you know," he says, a devilish grin forming on his lips. "I'm apparently thought of as quite a catch around the office, so I gambled. How'd I wager?"

I'm still trying to get used to this new, strange air between us – it's casual, somewhat electrified and playful – a huge shift from the professional relationship we had just a few days ago. "I think you hit the mark." My words come out softer than I intend and once again I feel the heat creeping up my neck.

Drew leans forward clearly happy with my response, but also recognizing my mild discomfort. He squeezes my hands and looks at me warmly. "Then, may I take you out on New Year's Eve?"

I hold his gaze for a moment appreciating how he's trying to make me feel at ease – and I am – the flush that was creeping toward my face retreats. "That would be lovely," I say with a relieved smile.

"Would you like to go to the fireworks on the waterfront?" he asks. "There are two shows. One at six, the other at midnight. We could either go to dinner first or the fireworks first, your choice."

I lean back slightly, amused. "Not bad for someone who didn't have a date until two minutes ago," I laugh.

He shrugs, unapologetic, a smile growing on his face knowing he's been caught in the act. "What can I say? You've been on my mind."

I consider the options for a moment... "I think I'd prefer the fireworks first. Then we'll have the rest of the night free to do whatever we want."

"Sounds perfect," he says, slapping his leg lightly with satisfaction. "I'll call around tomorrow for reservations. I'll make it work."

We continue chatting, the conversation again flowing easily. I'm still finding this change of events hard to believe but I'm enjoying it all the same. When our glasses are empty, he stands with a sigh, brushing a hand through his hair. "Guess I'd better take you home before I break my promise of being a gentleman."

I reach for my coat, but before I can slip it on, Drew gently takes my hands, turning me to face him. His eyes search mine, a flicker of determination beneath his easygoing air. "May I kiss you, Lauren?"

Before I can even form a reply, he leans in, and his lips meet mine, warm and unexpected. It's soft but certain, and for a heartbeat, this moment is all that matters.

When he pulls back, I try to regain my composure, rejoin the present. "Well, this day has certainly been full of surprises," I say awkwardly not knowing how to manage the flood of emotions I'm feeling.

Drew doesn't say a word. Instead, he pulls me back toward him, taking control of the situation, kissing me again, this time with a bit more urgency. My heart pounds in my chest as my lips respond to his and my mind races – I can barely believe the course of events this evening has taken – is this actually happening?

When I get home, I'm on Cloud Nine. Nikki is waiting up for me anxious for a full report, "Well?" she asks eagerly.

I try to contain my excitement knowing how broken up she is about Chris but I'm sure it's written all over my face.

"Lauren spill!" she demands.

"Well," I begin, "the evening was *way* more than I expected." Nikki is literally on the edge of her seat, and I feel a rush of pride in her genuineness amidst her own turmoil. "He told me the article was excellent, and he already sent it to the News Department – get this – he also recommended me for a transfer there!"

Nikki jumps to her feet and claps her hands. "Lauren, that's incredible! Congratulations! I know you've been hoping for that. This is huge!"

"I know, I know! If it all works out, it could be a game-changer for me professionally." I pause and inhale leading up to what's next. "But wait, that's not even the best part…"

"Oh my God, what?" Nikki throws her hand over her mouth in anticipation.

"Well, he… he told me he wants me transferred because he doesn't want to be my boss anymore." I pause for effect, letting the words sink in. "At first, I was kinda shocked, like what does that even mean? But then he said the reason is because he wants to pursue a relationship with me!" My voices pitches higher on the last sentence – I really am excited.

"What?! No way!" Nikki gasps excitedly. "I *told* you he was into you! So, what'd you do?"

"Well, you know me," I chuckle. "I was a little floored and didn't know how to go from talking business to talking... well, this," I say, gesturing with my hands. "But after a second, I told him I'd like that."

Nikki squeals, grabbing my hands and hopping up and down, then stops and shifts thinking it through, "Wait... What about office relationship policies? Is that gonna be a problem?"

"He already looked into it. Can you believe it?" Even I'm still a little shocked by that. "He's meeting with HR next week to make sure everything's kosher. I think he's serious, Nick."

"Jesus, Lauren, he's been thinking about this for a while. I told you he seems like a guy who finds a way to get what he wants. I'm so happy for you."

I laugh softly, a little giddy and then feel guilty knowing that Nikki's love life is at the opposite end of the spectrum right now. "Enough about me," I say, shifting the focus. "Any new developments with Chris?"

The excitement drains from her body with a heavy sigh. "No. He finally said he'd give me some space when I didn't answer any of his calls or texts, but we had plans for New Year's, and I know if I don't talk to him before then, he's just gonna show up at my place." She sounds deflated now. "And if I'm not home, he'll just come here. I have nowhere to hide. Everyone's home for the break."

I mull her predicament over for a moment. She's right; he knows there are only two places she'll be. "Well, Drew asked me out for New Year's, why don't you come out with us?"

Nikki considers the offer and then shakes her head. "I appreciate it, Lauren, but I don't want to be the third wheel – we've already done that once, and I'm not in the mood for a celebration anyway. Honestly, I'd rather just be alone."

"Okay, I get it," I say softly, but then offer another solution. "Wait... how about this? I could ask Drew if you can hide out at his place while we're out?"

"Are you comfortable doing that?" she asks, surprised but also intrigued by the notion.

"Yeah, I'm fine with it," I reply. "After you invited him to my house on Christmas Eve, it doesn't seem like much of a stretch."

Nikki laughs, a little of the weight lifting from her voice. "Alright, let me think on it, but that actually sounds like it could work."

Feeling like that's resolved, I move on. "Oh, and wait until you see his apartment. It's *amazing*. I mean honestly spectacular."

"You went to his apartment?" she says with surprise in her voice and shock on her face.

"Nothing tawdry, Nikki. He's a gentleman. But..." I pause, the memory still making my heart race, "he did kiss me."

Nikki raises an eyebrow, "And what was that like?" she asks with eager curiosity.

"A little earth-shattering, honestly," I admit, feeling my pulse quicken at the thought.

#

The next day after breakfast I call Drew and explain Nikki's circumstances. He offers up his place before I even have to ask. "Thank you so much Drew, that's a perfect solution."

"No worries, I'm happy to help. The two of you can have the guest room."

"Oh, we don't have to stay the night. She can just come home with me once we get in." Spending the night seems like a little much for a second date, but he suggests we bring our bags anyway. I know his intentions are in the right place – he's just trying to be helpful. Besides, I wouldn't put it past Chris to just camp out in front of Nikki's door until she gets home, so I leave that option open.

WEEK SIX

New Year's Eve, Week 6

Desperation

The last three days had been torture. Instead of exploring the city with Nikki and playing house together, Chris spent every hour pacing the floor and staring at his phone, waiting for any sign from her. He now had the pointless knowledge that it took exactly 42 steps to circle the living room. The silence in the house only made the noise in his head louder. *To hell with this*, he thought. *If she doesn't call by five o'clock, I'm going to her place.*

He had a few hours left to kill, so he picked up the guitar and kept practicing, trying to master the song he hoped would win her back. But patience wasn't his strong suit. By four thirty, Chris was already at Nikki's door, knocking relentlessly. No answer. *Thump, thump, thump.* "Nikki! Are you in there? Please, open the door!"

He kept at it for a few more minutes until the next-door neighbor poked his head out, "Dude, quiet down. I'm pretty sure she's not home."

"Did you see her leave?" Chris asked, not bothering to hide his desperation.

"No, but I haven't heard any sound from there all day," he said.

"Shit. I bet she's at Lauren's," he said not realizing the neighbor thought he was still talking to him.

"Whatever dude," he said, and he shut the door.

Getting around wasn't easy with the crutches, so Chris called an Uber and headed to Lauren's place. When she opened the door, she was dressed to go out. For a second, he forgot she wouldn't care to see him. "Wow, you look great," he said, though her expression told him she didn't care.

"What do you want, Chris?" she asked in a way that suggested she saw this coming.

"Is Nikki here?" he asked, the hope in his voice painfully obvious.

"No," Lauren answered flatly, "she's not."

"Do you know where she is? She's not at her place."

Lauren hesitated, then sighed. "Yes, but she asked me not to tell you if you came by."

"Lauren, please," Chris pleaded, leaning on his crutches for support. "I love her. You have to help me."

Lauren shook her head. "I love her too Chris and I have to help *her*. I'm sorry." She started to close the door, but Chris blocked it with one of the crutches.

"Wait — will you just give her a message for me?"

Lauren paused, considering. "Okay, that I can do."

"Can I use your phone?" Chris asked. "She'll open a message if it's from you."

With a reluctant sigh, Lauren turned to grab her phone. She handed it to him, and he airdropped her a video.

"Thank you, Lauren," Chris said, handing the phone back to her. "Happy —" But before he could finish, she shut the door. *New Year…*

Nikki

I found things to do all day that would keep me out of the apartment in case Chris just showed up – I ran errands, took a long walk through the park, even stopped by the library – the library on Christmas break... anything to fill the hours and distract my mind until it's time to meet Lauren at Drew's place. My overnight bag is packed, in case we decide to stay there tonight, which I think at this point is a given.

When I arrive, Lauren answers the door with a bright smile, her face glowing. "Hey, Nick. Come on in!" she says, stepping aside.

I stop short, taking her in. She's wearing a classic black sequin dress coupled with a leather jacket. A perfect mixture of casual elegance for New Year's Eve. "Wow, you look great. And I didn't even pick that out for you."

Drew appears behind her, grinning warmly. "Hi Nikki," he says with that easy-going charm. "Isn't she gorgeous?" His gaze shifts to Lauren with an affection that's so natural, it makes me blink. Just a few days ago they were fumbling all over each other. It's hard to believe how much easier Lauren is around him now. He called her *gorgeous* and she only turned a light shade of pink instead of bright red.

My mind makes the connection that just a few days ago I was falling in love, and a sadness sweeps over me. "Hi, Drew." I do my best to smile, but it feels like a mask, and I can hear the hesitation in my voice, "I hope this isn't weird for you?"

"Not at all, Nikki. I'm happy to help," Drew assures me. "The guest bedroom is down the hall if you want to put your bag in there. Make yourself at home."

"Okay, thanks." I nod and head toward the bedroom taking the rest of the apartment in along the way. Lauren wasn't kidding – this place is fantastic. The space is open, modern, with sleek lines and pops of color, and there's a view of the city skyline that makes me catch my breath. This is the kind of place people dream about. I set my bag on the bed, where I notice Lauren's already neatly stowed her things.

When I return to the living room, Drew is helping Lauren with her coat, his hands brushing against her back in a way that seems effortless but intimate, and *way* different from Christmas Eve. "Nikki, there's food in the fridge," he says with a casual wave toward the kitchen. "And the bar is fully stocked so, help yourself to anything."

Lauren looks at me with a sad smile. "Are you sure you don't want to come with us?"

"I'll be fine," I say, trying to sound cheerful, but knowing I'm not pulling it off. "I brought my sketch pad, so I'll just work on some designs... and cry in my wine."

Lauren's eyes soften, and she pulls me into a tight hug, reminding me that she's always there for me. But the second she turns back toward Drew her eyes sparkle with excitement again. He wraps his arm around hers, and they share a little giggle as they head toward the door.

I watch them go, my emotions at odds. The happiness I feel for her is tangling with my own sorrow leaving me just plain numb.

I pour myself a glass of wine and get to work. I'm sketching like crazy. One page after another as if in a mad frenzy. I tear the pages from the pad as I go letting the designs pour from my mind onto the paper and then onto the floor. My thoughts race away from Chris, turning to creativity with everything I've got.

Then, suddenly, the sound of fireworks interrupts my sketching mania. I stand, glass in hand, and walk over to the window, the city lights stretching out before me like a blanket of stars. As I watch the sky explode in vibrant colors, a flood of emotion hits me all at once. Tears well up in my eyes before I even realize it. The wineglass shakes slightly in my hand, and I have to set it down on the windowsill before it slips from my fingers entirely.

I've always enjoyed fireworks; they're beautiful. But tonight, they only remind me of what I've lost. And somehow, that's too much to bear. I should be in Chris's arms right now admiring this spectacular, feeling warm and excited about the year to come.

The tears spill over, rolling down my cheeks, and I let them fall, my heart aching finding no comfort in the beauty around me. The world outside keeps celebrating, but here I am – just standing, watching, alone and feeling like I'm stuck in a moment I can't escape.

My phone dings startling me out of my thoughts. It's a text from Lauren.

> Sorry I forgot to send this earlier. I
> was running late for Drew's.

There's a video attached so I click on it. Chris's face comes into view. He's sitting down with the guitar, and I can see he's still limping. I want to turn it off, but I can't look away. He starts strumming and then begins singing, "Jersey Girl," but starts with the chorus before beginning the first verse, so that "I'm in love with a Jersey girl" is up front. I'm mesmerized by what I am seeing. His voice sounds completely different than it did the other day. It's beautiful, but now it's sad and soulful. He keeps looking up at the camera as he sings, and the sadness in his eyes has me paralyzed. I don't even realize I'm sobbing until he finishes and simply approaches the camera wearing a broken expression and turns it off without saying a word.

I throw the phone on the couch as if it's burning my hand and cry into one of the pillows for wanting to be with him so desperately and knowing that I can't.

EPILOUGE

Spring Semester

Chris tried everything he could to get Nikki back spring semester, but she completely ghosted him, and when that girl puts her mind to something, she gets it done. He went to her apartment building and the doorman told him she asked that he not be let in. When the café reopened, he went there, and Lucy said she took another job but wouldn't tell him where. Chris pleaded with her, but she completely shut him out. John called his cousin to see if Amanda knew where Nikki was working, but neither of them would help – those girls were pissed! On the night Chris and Nikki had theater tickets, he waited out front like a lovesick puppy hoping she might show up with a friend, but she was too smart for that. He sent her flowers with an apology note and got no response. He walked aimlessly around Rittenhouse Square hoping to run into her walking Chester but never saw her. She blocked him from her social media accounts, and he gave up calling and texting her because she never once answered. Her stubbornness, which he used to love because it challenged him, was now aimed directly at him with all its might and he couldn't figure a way out of the crosshairs. He finally had to come to terms with the fact that she wasn't going to forgive him and that he had royally fucked things up.

Rocco must have given Tony up because he was arrested as an accomplice in the robberies and never came back to school. Chris and John never figured out how Tony could have copied Nikki's keys. They just changed the locks on their door, packed up Tony's stuff and left it at the frat house in case he ever returned.

In one final hail Mary attempt to see Nikki again, Chris went to Drexel's graduation ceremony, but his prayers weren't answered. He couldn't find her. The universe was working against him at every turn. He didn't even know what her plans were after graduation, so he had to accept that he might never see her again – the only girl he ever loved.

Three Years Later

Chris

I live in DC now. After losing Nikki I had to get out of Philly and took a job as a Corporate Risk Manager for Aramark. I'm back in town for a few days for meetings at our Philadelphia Headquarters. I'm early so I check into the hotel first and turn the TV on in my room. Well, I'll be damned. There's Lauren on the screen, "I'm Lauren Taylor Davis reporting live for Action News." Davis, wow, she must have gotten married. Seeing Lauren makes me ache for Nikki again. Even after all this time, the thought of her – of us, still stings.

My first meeting isn't until ten o'clock, so I decide to check out the continental breakfast in the hotel lobby. It's just the basics. I get a cup of coffee, grab a muffin to-go and head out to HQ. After a few blocks, I do a double take at a sign on a boutique: "Philly's Top Hen." There's a logo of a little yellow chick wearing chic sunglasses, red lipstick, and a sun hat. This has to be a nod to Nikki's sister. She was a Blue Hen and wrote 'Philly's Top 10.' I throw the muffin and coffee in a nearby trashcan and open the door to the boutique.

"Good morning. I'll be right with you," I hear her call from the back. A few minutes later Nikki appears, and my heart grabs in my chest. She is just as beautiful as ever and I actually feel dizzy at the sight of her. When she sees me, she stops dead in her tracks – frozen.

"Hello ma'am," I say trying to present the usual swagger she's accustomed to from me even though I'm nervous as shit, "I'm hoping you can help me pick out something for someone special. You see, a few years ago, I was a dumb kid who made a stupid mistake that hurt someone I loved. I lost her because of it, but I've found her now, and I'd like to try to make it up to her."

She's still just staring at me, her gaze steady and guarded. I take a tentative step toward her, but she raises a hand, the gesture firm, signaling me to stop. "Chris, what are you doing here?" she asks in a tone I can't read.

"I'm in town for a meeting and was walking by," I answer, forcing my words to sound casual. "I saw your sign and knew it had to be you." There's a pause, a weight in the air while she contemplates her response.

Just then the door opens, and a young woman walks in, breaking the tension. "Excuse me," Nikki says, quickly turning her attention to the customer. "May I help you?"

"Yes," the woman answers eagerly. "I'm looking for something unique to wear to a wedding, and I heard all your designs are originals."

"That's right," Nikki replies, her voice shifting into professional mode. "The dress section is in the back, and the pant suits are along this wall," she explains motioning to her right with a sway of her arm that looks smooth and perfected from practice. "Why don't you take a look, and I'll be with you in a minute."

"Okay, great," the woman says, offering a polite smile before walking toward the back of the store.

I watch Nikki for a moment, taking in what I just heard. "Nikki, are these all *your* designs?" I ask in amazement.

"Yes," she answers flatly, her professional pleasantries gone.

"This is incredible!" My eyes scan the room. There are racks upon racks of unique clothing for all occasions. It's beyond impressive. "I can't believe how much you've done."

"I've been busy," she says, completely devoid of emotion.

"You always were," I respond, forcing a chuckle to ease the tension while simultaneously racking my brain to find a way to turn this conversation in my favor. But before I have a chance, the young woman calls from the back of the store. "Miss?" Her voice is pleasant but insistent.

"Coming," Nikki replies, her attention already shifting. She gives me a quick nod. "Excuse me, Chris."

As she walks away to tend to her customer, I feel the minutes slip away with her. I wait patiently but I'm running out of time. I've got to make a move.

Nikki returns with a look of resolve and starts speaking before I have the chance. "Look, Chris, I don't think..." I don't like where this is headed so I cut her off before she can say what I don't want to hear, "Listen, Nikki, I'm going to be late for a meeting, but I have so much I want to say to you and so much I need to know. It's been three years, and everything's changed. I've changed. Will you please let me take you to dinner tonight?"

She flinches slightly at the question, as if the idea of spending time with me is something foreign to her. Her mouth opens, and I can already hear the refusal before she speaks, like it's a reflex for her now. "Chris," she starts, but I can't let her say it. I interrupt again. "Nikki, it's just a conversation. What's the harm?" I plead, my heart caught in my throat.

There's a pause, a beat where I can see the conflict in her eyes, but at least she's considering it. She starts to say something but stops. I hold my breath with anticipation and try to swallow my heart back to where it belongs. She sighs and starts again, "I guess there are a few things I'd like to understand."

I can hardly believe it. The tension I hadn't noticed in my shoulders releases with relief. I want to reach out, to grab her, pull her close, kiss her like I used to but know I can't. "Is your number still the same?" I ask trying to mask the excitement in my voice.

"Yes."

"What time do you close?"

"Six o'clock."

"I'll be back before then in case you decide not to answer your phone," I say with a grin trying to lighten the mood and recapture even just the tiniest bit of our once fierce connection.

She smiles that beautiful familiar smile, the one I've waited three long years to see again and the air between us seems to soften. I savor the moment while it lasts. Her hard exterior has cracked, just a little, but it's all I need – it's a chance. I remember all too well how stubborn and determined she can be, so this is far from a home run, but it's an opening. An opening full of possibilities – possibilities I'll use with everything I've got.

I leave for my meeting with a range of emotions sweeping over me, excitement – anticipation – fear – regret, but mostly hope – hope that maybe, just maybe, there might still be a chance for us, yes us – our us, *the* us... us.

Coming this Spring

from **Rebecca Gould Baeurle**,

the next piece in the Sisters Series...

Twelve Weeks of Love & Loss

Wednesday, Week 1

Chris

I show up at Nikki's boutique at five thirty knowing she'll still be there and won't have a way to avoid me. She's busy with a customer when I walk in. When she sees me, she doesn't actually roll her eyes, but her expression says the same thing. I smile at her and take a seat in one of the chairs in an area of the shop that appears to be a waiting room of sorts for people accompanying shoppers. I envision these chairs being occupied by mothers, best friends and sucked-in husbands or boyfriends (I'd kill to be in that category right now).

I pull out my phone and pretend to be busy with something but have one eye trained on Nikki the whole time. Whenever she catches my glance, I flash her another smile and relax more comfortably in the chair letting her know I have no intention of leaving or giving up. After about the third time we have one of these silent conversations communicated only through expression and body language, I see the corners of her mouth start to curl as she fights back a grin. Ok Chris. Keep it up. You've only got one shot at this.

Once she finishes with her last customer, she finally turns to me and says, "Well sir I don't suppose you're here to buy something for your mother or girlfriend?"

"Nikki, you know why I'm here. You told me this morning you'd have dinner with me tonight."

She leans against the counter, crossing her arms, her voice steady but distant. "Actually, I said there were a few things I'd like to better understand. You're the one who assumed I agreed to dinner. I've had all day to think about it Chris, and I'm not sure it's a good idea. We can just talk here." She flips the open sign to closed without looking at me.

I stand and walk closer, stopping at a comfortable distance. I know if I get any closer, she'll ask me to step back. "Nikki, I'll have this conversation anywhere you want, but it's dinner time, and wouldn't a glass of wine be just the thing right now? I promise I won't consider it a date."

She thinks about it for a minute and then shrugs half-heartedly, "Alright but only because I'm starving. I haven't eaten since breakfast and that was just an orange."

We step outside into the warm summer air, and she turns to lock the door. My car is parked out front, so I open the door for her. "You brought a car? There's a diner up the block."

"Nikki," I sigh, "are you going to push back on everything? Please get in."

She throws her bag over her shoulder and, after a brief hesitation, climbs into the car. It's only a five-minute drive to the restaurant, so I figure I better get a few pleasantries out of the way while I've got her confined. "Before we get down to more serious matters, can I ask you a little about the past three years?" I keep talking before she has a chance to answer – I have more nervous energy than I want to admit. "Your shop is amazing. I don't want to sound patronizing but I'm really proud of you."

She looks out the window for a moment, then sighs. "Well, after we broke up..."

"You mean after you iced me out of your life," I interrupt. "We never had a chance to break up."

"Okaaay... after I iced you out of my life," she repeats, dragging out the words, "I got really focused on my work. It was all I did. I didn't want to go out, didn't want to run into you. I just wanted to finish spring semester and move on. The breakup – sorry, the ice-out – was really tough on me, so I channeled all my energy into my designs. Enough to fill a small boutique."

"It's incredible how much you've done. Nikki, I want you to know how hard I tried, really tried, to see you that last semester. I did everything I could think of to run into you. In one last-ditch effort to find you before school ended, I even went to Drexel's graduation ceremony hoping to see you, but you literally vanished."

She glances at me, her expression softening just a fraction. "I spent a lot of time at Lauren's place and Drew's place that semester, knowing how persistent you are."

"Me? Persistent?" I let out a small laugh. "It was like you took a CIA course on professional ghosting or something. And who's Drew?" I ask pulling into a parking garage in Rittenhouse Square near The Love, trying not to sound a little bit panicked about the Drew question.

Nikki looks at me with an expression that is equally pissed off and sad. She knows what I'm doing. "Chris?!"

"I just know we both like this restaurant," I say and park the car. I get out and she still hasn't unlocked her seatbelt, so I know she's contemplating her options. I open her door and look down at her making strained eye contact.

She stares back at me for a minute before relenting and getting out. "You also know the food isn't the only reason we both like it," she says, almost as a warning. "It's where we had our first date, and you know it."

This is going to go one of two ways. She's either going to walk out of the garage and keep walking or follow me into the restaurant. I know I can't hold her hand, so the next move is truly hers. This was a bigger gamble than I thought. Starting down the ramp toward the street, I can feel her walking behind me. I slow my pace so she can catch up, but she slows hers as well. Damn it! She doesn't even want to walk next me.

She follows me when I turn right onto the sidewalk. Relief washes over me for a second until I realize I no longer know where she lives. She could very well be headed home. I go back to holding my breath while trying to act calm and confident. We reach the restaurant, and I open the door. She walks through and I exhale.

"Sheppard. Table for two," I say once we reach the hostess stand.

"You made a reservation?" She's wearing an expression of astonishment at what she clearly thinks is my audacity. Uh oh...

She turns to leave, but I grab her arm. "Nikki, please. Sometimes it's hard to get a table at the last minute."

The hostess is obviously confused by Nikki's reaction which thankfully makes her embarrassed. She yanks her arm away from me and stands stiffly beside me not wanting to make a scene.

"Right this way," the hostess says still bewildered as to why someone would be upset about making a reservation in advance.

We reach the table, and I restrain myself from pulling out her chair since I promised this wouldn't be a date and know I'm already on shaky ground.

"Chris, I know what you are up to," she says as she sits. "This is why I didn't think it was a good idea to come."

"I'm not up to anything," I lie. "I just want to clear the air and find out more about the past three years, and I'd rather do it over a nice meal."

"Fine," she says with a huff, but I know she doesn't trust me and I'm going to have to be careful.

"So, when we were pulling into the garage you were about to tell me who Drew is." I try to sound casual but am hoping against hope he's not her current boyfriend. That would mean a three-year relationship by now, but why else would she have been staying at his place frequently spring semester? Please no, please no.

Her expression shifts, loosening. "Drew's my brother-in-law. Lauren married him a year and a half ago. They started dating the week we broke up."

I try to contain my relief, but it still doesn't mean she's not with someone else. "Oh, nice. Do you like him? Are they happy?"

"He's a great guy, and he absolutely adores her. They're really happy together. When Drew was ready to propose, my dad was too sick and confused. Since my mom is gone, he asked me. I was really touched by that. He's thoughtful that way. We even went together to the care facility to try to explain it to my dad, but I'm not sure how much really got through," she says, a mix of acceptance and sorrow in her voice.

"How's your dad now?" I ask gently.

"He passed away last year," she sighs. "Honestly, it was a blessing when it finally happened. Alzheimer's is a cruel disease that affects everyone in its orbit."

"I'm sorry Nick. I know it was tough for a long time," I say, my eyes meeting hers. "I saw Lauren on TV this morning in my hotel room reporting for Action News. That's a huge step up from writing 'Philly's Top 10' for *The Inquirer*."

"Well, the investigative piece she wrote about date rape drugs on college campuses..." she pauses, "you know, the one that drove an iron wedge between us, really got her noticed. After Amanda finished her internship with Lauren, she took over 'Philly's Top 10' and Lauren poured herself into investigative reporting. Drew has a senior position at the paper and really helped Lauren get noticed by other media outlets."

Hoping to keep the conversation casual for a bit longer, I pivot from the news story that destroyed us, "Speaking of Amanda, your friends were an impenetrable wall of steel during the ice-out. They wouldn't give me an inch."

She smiles, clearly proud of their loyalty. "Where are you living now?"

"I'm in DC," I reply. "I couldn't stay in Philly after losing you and I didn't know if you planned on staying either, so I didn't see the point. I took a job with Aramark. Our headquarters are here in Philly. I'm in town for meetings."

Nikki suddenly catches herself becoming too open to casual conversation. Her expression turns more serious. "Okay, let's stop pretending we're trying to get to know one another and figure out what we're going to order so we can get on with the real conversation."

I open my menu and make one final attempt at an explanation knowing she wants to get down to it now. "I get that you're surprised by all this – by me – us being here tonight, but I honestly care about how you are. More than you know," I throw in at the end and then feel a little desperate.

A waiter approaches the table. "Can I interest you in anything else besides water?" he asks politely as he fills our glasses.

I glance over at Nikki. "I'm going to drink wine, but if you are too, I'll order a bottle."

"Are you going to have red or white?" she asks, closing her menu and putting it down in her lap.

"Whatever you want I'll share," I say with a smile.

She doesn't return my smile and answers directly. "Okay. Chardonnay then."

I turn back to the waiter, "May I see a wine list please?"

"Of course, sir. I'll be right back with that," the waiter responds with a nod before walking off.

Nikki is clearly done with the pleasantries and jumps right in. "So, Chris, what is it that you wanted to say?"

I'm not really prepared for her forwardness, but also am not sure why, she's still Nikki after all – the woman I fell in love with – straight forward, self-assured, not intimidated, and of course, demanding.

I sit up straight in my seat, exhale and begin. "First and foremost, I never meant to hurt you. I hope you know that." I notice a brief nod and think maybe she's going to hear me out. "I started falling in love with you the first day we met, which ironically was the same day I met the drug dealer. A week later I cut ties with him and his operation, and as I told you at the time, I never sold anything to anyone. I realized Rocco was dangerous and didn't want you near any of it. I know now I should've forced Tony out then too, but honestly, I was falling in love with you so hard that it took over everything else. I wasn't focused on Tony; I was focused on us and only us. I guess it clouded my judgement, what little of that I had at the time." She's looking at me intently and I can't read her expression. I'm telling her the truth and trying to make her understand that I know I was wrong but can't tell if she's buying any of this or thinks I'm full of shit. Damn she's good.

I take a deep breath and continue. "Nikki, I was a stupid self-indulgent college kid who pretty much had the world by the tail until you turned it upside down. I realize now how much more responsibility you had in your life at the time being a full-time student, working two jobs and helping with your dad's care. You never would've made haphazard or reckless decisions without thinking about the consequences. I'd never suffered real consequences before. You taught me that lesson in the harshest possible way." I pause for a brief moment to collect my thoughts... "Nikki, you were my judge, jury and executioner. I just want you to know that I learned from it, and I've changed."

The waiter returns to the table with the wine list. I peruse it briefly and turn to Nikki, "Is the Cakebread okay?"

"Yes. That's lovely," she says to the waiter, not to me.

He smiles at her, "Very well then," and walks away.

I ignore being brushed off just then and put the wine list back on the table. When I look up at her again, her penetrating green eyes are burning a hole right through me. "Tell me how you've changed Chris."

Talk about being in the hotseat, Christ… "Well, I have a real job now and I take it very seriously. It's the top priority in my life next to my parents. I'm more respectful of them and appreciative of all they've done for me. I don't take any of that for granted anymore." I stop and think for a moment. "And I guess I try harder now to put the feelings of others above my own, not be so selfish."

"How do you do that?" she asks and sits back in her chair looking at me skeptically.

"I don't know," I shrug. "Like when I'm dating and know it's not going anywhere, I break it off instead of taking advantage of the situation like I once would've."

"Well gee, that's big of you Chris," she says, heavy on the cynicism.

"Nikki, you know what I mean. Guys are pretty motivated by certain things, and I don't put my own desires or needs above someone else's feelings anymore."

The waiter returns to the table with the wine and tells us about the specials. I thank him and let him know we'll need a few more minutes to decide.

I raise my glass, "To second chances."

Nikki raises hers, "To honesty."

I don't like the sound of that, but I don't push back — I know I'm in no position to. We clink our glasses, and each take a sip. There's an awkward silence after the uncomfortable toast and I'm suddenly aware of the hum of casual dinner chatter in the air around us and wish we were part of it. She seems to sense something similar, and we both open our menus again and pretend this is a normal evening.

Once Nikki closes her menu and places it back on the table, I work up the nerve to ask, "So, are you seeing anyone?"

"Chris, you know you don't have the right to ask me that," she says, her voice firm and unyielding.

"I know Nikki," I reply, my tone a little more pleading than I intend. "But I also can't spend the rest of the night thinking up creative ways of finding out the answer to the question and I *have* to know."

"You don't *have* to know Chris; you just want to know." Her eyes narrow slightly. "I could very well ask you the same thing."

"And I'm happy to answer. The truth is you ruined me when it comes to dating. I compare every woman to you and the beginning of any relationship to the one we had. I either wind up breaking it off by the second or third date or she'll beat me to it knowing that I'm half-assing it. I even found your doppelganger in DC. She had porcelain skin just like yours and beautiful auburn hair, but she wasn't you. I wanted her fierce green eyes to look at me the way yours used to, and her full lips to speak to me the way yours used to, but they didn't because she wasn't you. She broke it off on our third date because she thought I was weird. And I couldn't blame her. If you looked up "weird" in the dictionary at the time, the definition probably would have simply read: Chris Sheppard. I was trying to mold her into my dream girl; the one and only Nikki Taylor."

Nikki is squirming a little uncomfortably in her seat, but I can't stop. I pause for a split second and then gamble – this might be my only chance; I have to put it all out there. "Babe, I've never loved a woman before or after you."

Her eyes begin to well up and I think my words may have been worth the risk. The waiter returns before Nikki has a chance to say anything. He asks her what she'd like but she defers to me to go first, clearly needing the extra few seconds to pull herself together.

After we place our orders, she inhales a deep breath and says, "Chris, I was devastated by our break-up, but I also realized the earth was not going to stop rotating around the sun and that I'd have to move on. So, yes, I'm dating."

"Anything serious?" I ask knowing I'm over-stepping but not being able to control myself.

"You're really pushing it."

"I know. I'm sorry," I lie again. "I can't help myself around you." Even though she didn't answer the question, I got what I was looking for. If she wanted to close the door completely, she could have answered 'yes' whether it was true or not.

Getting back to the matter at hand she asks, "Do you have anything else you'd like to say?"

"Yes," I answer, swallow and go for it – my voice firm and confident now, "I'd like to know if I've served my sentence and can be let back into your life on parole?"

She actually laughs at that and now I'm hopeful. "Let's just get through tonight and see how it goes. This is a lot to process."

"Okay, fair enough. Is there anything else you'd like to ask me?" I offer trying to clear the air to her satisfaction.

She leans forward slightly, curiosity in her eyes. "I suppose I'm curious whatever happened to your roommates?"

"Tony was arrested as the accomplice in the burglaries," I sigh, the memory of all of it still stings. "To this day, I don't know how he copied the keys to your dog-walking homes. Please tell me you know I never would've knowingly put you in danger. I would've killed him first."

"I believe you Chris," she says in earnest. "Did he go to jail?"

"I don't know. I never spoke to him again. He didn't come back to school, so I assume that was the reason. I don't know if he was charged for selling drugs too, but probably because I'm sure Rocco gave him up to lighten his own sentence. John and I just packed up Tony's stuff, dropped it off at the frat house and changed the locks on our door."

"And what about John?" she asks with an easier way about her.

I'm hoping her slight change in demeanor means she's not holding John and me in the same category as Tony, and luckily, I have 'growth' news to report about John. "Believe it or not, he moved to New York after graduation to be with Michelle. They live together now."

"Wow! Good for them," she says with genuine surprise before turning right back to the thing that ruined us. "Does Michelle know what happened?"

"I don't think so. Why would John tell her?" I sigh knowing she'll disapprove, then try to rationalize it. "He didn't have anything to do with it, but he didn't stop it either. He saw what happened to us because of that. He grew up a lot just watching me suffer. I think it's the reason he moved to New York — he couldn't risk losing Michelle after seeing what I went through loosing you."

The food arrives and the waiter refills both our wine glasses. "Can I get you anything else?" he asks.

"I think we're all set," I reply. "Thank you."

"Enjoy," he says with a little bow, clicking his heels before walking away. We both begin eating, the conversation falling quiet for a few moments. Then Nikki asks, "You said you're more respectful of your parents now. I know I was only with you for a weekend with them, but I didn't notice you being disrespectful. What did you mean?"

"Probably a poor choice of words. What I meant was, I appreciate them more. I took them for granted before. Hell, I took everything for granted before you, but not anymore. They've always been great to me, and I've had a great life because of them. I hate to admit it, but as an only child, I think I was just... well, kinda spoiled."

"You think??" Nikki says, smiling and stifling a laugh that almost makes her choke on her food.

Okay, now we're getting somewhere. I lean in with a teasing grin. "What? You thought I was spoiled?"

"Um, yeah! Ya brat," she says, emphasizing the 'yeah' and 'brat' in full Jersey-girl style.

Okay this is the girl I recognize. The girl I still love. "You never told me that," I say with a laugh.

"Well, I thought it was just assumed. Jesus, the charmed never realize they're charmed." She shakes her head, but I still see the humor in her eyes. I know I'm making progress.

"I realize now that my life was charmed, but I took it all for granted until I met you. You made me think about the future and what would be next for us. I was full of hope and anticipation." I pause to find the right words. "I don't want to be over dramatic, but I've had a long time to think about this, and you actually changed me – made me a better person. I know you still need convincing of that, but loving you was the first time I cared about someone else more than myself. You know I would have done anything to protect you the night of the burglary. Anything."

Her eyes well up again and she blots them with her napkin. I just had the old Nikki back, why did I take the conversation in this direction? I really can't think straight around her. I want her to know how I feel, but that could've waited. Fuck.

She breathes in a huge breath and lets it out with a sigh. "It took forever for me to get over you and sitting here now listening to you say these things is really difficult." She wipes her eyes, puts her napkin back in her lap and continues, "I want to believe you're telling me the truth but trusting you is what broke my heart the last time. You didn't deserve my trust then and you're going to have to earn it now." She sniffles and bows her head, "And you promised this wouldn't be a date, damn it."

"I would've said those things to you in your shop. Being in a restaurant makes no difference." I reach across the table and lift her chin to face me. "And for the record, I'm *still* not over you. The minute I saw your beautiful face this morning, my insides did flips. No one has ever had that effect on me."

"Chris," she sighs, "I don't know what to say. It took me a long time to move on. And I told you I just started seeing someone."

Okay, the "just" in that statement is encouraging and she hadn't previously mentioned it. "I don't care if you are dating someone. You know I'm competitive and will happily take on the challenge. I just want the opportunity to prove to you that I understand why you were so upset with me back then and that I've changed because of it."

She's looking at me thoughtfully and suddenly I'm afraid of what her next reaction will be, so I jump in ahead of her. "Nick, I'm only in town for three days; can I take you out again tomorrow? I know I've had three years to think about what I'd say to you given the chance but seeing you unexpectedly this morning threw me for a loop, and I feel like there's more we need to say," I blurt out in one hurried run-on sentence.

"A flustered Chris Sheppard. Well, this is something new." Her easy smile returns, and she looks at me under thick lashes knowing she has the upper hand.

"It's what you do to me Nick. You didn't answer the question." I hold my breath.

"I have plans tomorrow, but Friday would be fine."

"Okay, Friday it is." I try to sound casual while high fiving myself in my head.

We finish our meals, and the bill arrives; I reach for it to pay, and she puts her hand down on top of mine. "No Chris. Remember this isn't a date. I'm splitting it with you." Fine. Stand on ceremony, but she just agreed to see me again on Friday and whether she likes it or not, that's officially a date!

We step outside, and I start toward the parking garage, but Nikki lingers by the entrance of the restaurant. She pulls out her phone and begins tapping on the screen.

I stop and twist my head over my shoulder, "What are you doing, Nick?" I call to her, "I'll drive you home."

She doesn't look up from her phone for a minute while she finishes typing. "I just ordered an Uber. Don't be offended, but I don't want you to know where I live. I've been through that before."

I tilt my head, a little hurt. "Jesus, Nikki. I'm not a stalker!"

Her eyes turn playful as she meets my gaze. "Um, you kinda are," she teases. "And I already agreed to see you on Friday night, so take the win."

Christ she's tough. I have two choices. I can either leave for the parking garage and follow her Uber to find out where she lives or wait with her on the street until the Uber arrives, which is the gentlemanly thing to do. Of course, I pick the chivalrous route because I'm in full blown winning her back mode now.

The Uber arrives and she gets in, not ever letting me get close enough to try to kiss her. "Goodnight Chris. I'll see you Friday."

"Okay. I'll pick you up at your shop. Am I allowed to make a reservation somewhere or is that going to set you off again?" I ask with a grin.

She doesn't answer but tilts her head and offers a wry smile before pulling the door shut.

Nikki

Did Chris God damned Sheppard really just walk through that door this morning and back into my life? After all the time it took me to get over him and he shows up again now that I just started seeing Rich. I'm going to have to hear him out because he knows where to find me, but maybe dinner isn't the best idea. And why does he still have to be so freaking gorgeous? He could've put on a few pounds or lost some of that beautiful wavy brown hair, but no, hot as ever. And those huge brown eyes still make me want to melt. It isn't fair.

Dun, dun, dun, dun, dun... breaks my train of thought. The Law-and-Order theme song is Rich's ring tone. It dawns on me that I haven't programmed a ring tone in my phone since I was dating Chris. What's that all about?

I answer. "Hi Rich. What's up?"

"Hey love." He calls me love but we're not at the point in our relationship where we're *in* love or have ever told one another that. We haven't been intimate. I'm not ready for that yet and he's been patient. He's a nice guy and I enjoy spending time with him but that's it for now. "Can I take you out after work tonight?" he asks.

"I can't tonight. I have a lot to catch up on. I'm behind on my designs." And there it is, the first lie I've ever told him and of course it's because of Chris Sheppard.

"Okay. How about tomorrow night?"

"Sure. I should be in better shape by then."

I'm busy all day with customers but can't keep my mind off Chris and if any of what he has to say will change my opinion of him now. It has been three years, I tell myself. I've changed plenty in that time, maybe he has too.

Chris walks through the door at five thirty knowing my boutique is open 'til six and I'll still be here. He smiles smugly and takes a seat by the dressing rooms. I'm still tending to shoppers but every time I glance over at him, he's staring at me confidently and positioning himself in the chair in a way that lets me know he's planning on waiting as long as it takes. Looks like he hasn't changed much, cocky as ever. When I finish for the day, he talks me into dinner which I assumed meant grabbing a burger. Instead, he takes me to the restaurant where we had our first date. It's infuriating how overt he is. Suddenly, I'm on a date I didn't intend on having. And I don't like feeling tricked! I should know better than to let my guard down around him.

I want to be mad but it's hard when he's being so sweet and pouring his heart out to me. He's trying to convince me that he has grown up and changed and I want to believe him, but I guess the only way I'll know for sure is by spending more time with him. Is that even a good idea?

I agree to see him on Friday and immediately feel guilty about Rich. I told Chris I was seeing someone, but Rich has no idea about the tidal wave that just washed over me today. He and I have never discussed being exclusive, but I know we both are and now I feel like I'm cheating. God damn you, Chris Sheppard!

Twelve Weeks of Love & Loss

BY REBECCA GOULD BAEURLE

Coming Spring 2026!

Acknowledgements

First and foremost, to my besties and family who endured reading my "shitty first draft" and tried their best to offer constructive feedback on what was quite obviously a piece of crap, you know who you are, and I love you for your support. To my test readers, all the Allie's, Samantha, Randi, Taylor, Renee, Charolette, Jonnie, Tanya, Joan and Erin, I thank you for making time for me in your busy lives and offering your valued opinions. A huge thanks goes to my childhood friend V.C. Chickering who is an accomplished author, singer, songwriter, performer, artist and all-around badass. She willingly shared her own experiences and shined a light on a path forward for me. And to another high school friend, Steve Patrick, who is a huge cheerleader of all the people in his life – even those going back forty years – for remaining interested in my work and connecting me with my editors and publisher. Speaking of whom, many thanks to editors Lyle and Heather Smith and publisher Zolly House Press for bringing it all together, transforming manuscript to novel and giving life to the ideas in my head. And lastly, to my husband, who never once questioned why I spent days at the kitchen counter in my yoga pants tapping away at my computer. He offered silent support and the occasional raised eyebrow smirk as he lovingly indulged my whims - and I love him back for it. Okay, enough, enough, I hope you enjoyed...

About the Author

Rebecca Gould Beaurle has spent a lifetime helping others chase their missions—now she's chasing one of her own. After a successful career in the nonprofit world (think education, healthcare, disability inclusion, and community magic-making), she's traded grant proposals for plot twists.

Originally from a small town in North Jersey, Rebecca earned her degree in Communications and English from the University of Delaware and never stopped writing. She lives just outside Philadelphia—close enough to cheer for the Eagles loudly—and has been known to disappear to the Delaware beaches with a good book and a better cocktail.

Six Weeks of Love and Larceny is her debut novel, though her storytelling chops were finely tuned over decades of hilarious family group texts and sisterly banter. She's been married to her college sweetheart, Mike, for 36 years, has two grown children who still keep her on her toes, and yes—she really does have a sister she adores.

www.ingramcontent.com/pod-product-compliance
Lightning Source LLC
Chambersburg PA
CBHW060815120726
47909CB00006B/1930